Praise for Under

"*Under the Blue Skies* is escapism at its best, an Amish romance to cherish. I fell in love with Lovina, Thomas, and Emily, and I could feel God's thumbprint on this lovely novel."

BETH WISEMAN, BESTSELLING AUTHOR FOR
HARPERCOLLINS CHRISTIAN PUBLISHING

"*Under the Blue Skies* features protagonist Lovina Graber, a truly endearing character! She keeps this Amish story fast-paced, while hero Matthew Smucker has enough flaws to make the story realistic—and unpredictable. Add a delightful five-year-old orphan, and this charming novel absolutely sparkles as it sheds light on family dysfunction, hope, and healing. Bravo to co-authors Tricia Goyer and Elly Gilbert!"

LESLIE GOULD, #1 BESTSELLING AND
AWARD-WINNING AUTHOR

"I truly enjoyed every minute of this book. I found Lovina so endearing. Emily, the niece to Thomas, is precocious but a sweetheart. She just needed a place to be loved, accepted, and safe. Thomas is prickly but he grew on me. I found myself cheering for him and respecting how he viewed Lovina as beautiful and capable."

PARKLAND MOM, GOODREADS

Under the Blue Skies

BIG SKY AMISH || BOOK 3

TRICIA GOYER

ELLY GILBERT

sunrise
PUBLISHING

Alberta, Canada

Amish Bachelor Cabins

WEST KOOTENAI

Graber's Christmas Tree Farm

Lovina Graber's House

Annie's Place

Kraft and Grocery

Volunteer Fire Department

Logworks

Ike Sommers' Cabin

Auction Barn

Amish School

Summit Community Church

Lake Kootenai USA

Elder Martin's House

Abe Sommers' House

Reuben Milner's House

Horseshoe Cove

Tooley Lake

Dodge Creek

Bridge

Ben and Mariannas House

*This book is dedicated to those who
never let me give up.
This harvest is yours, too.*

"Let us not become weary in doing good, for at the proper time we will reap a harvest if we do not give up."

Galatians 6:9 NIV

Chapter One

MONDAY, JULY 24

Asteady torrent of rain wet Lovina Graber's eyelashes and fell like tears as she hobbled to the waiting SUV caked with mud and grime. While she loved the smell of rain in Montana, she wished it would have lightened up until she was safely in the car. With her uneven gait she struggled on the slick ground. *Slowly. Just a few more steps.*

One foot slid, and Lovina released the tote bag she'd been holding as she reached for the side of the car to catch herself.

"*Ach*, no!" The contents of her bag spilled all over the wet pavement. As gingerly as possible, she bent over to scoop up the assorted books, craft supplies, and papers, including a large manilla envelope, that had tumbled out.

Her *Englisch* driver, Wyatt, an older fellow who looked every bit the stereotypical Montana mountain man, hurriedly approached as she stuffed her bag with damp skeins of yarn and rain-slicked magazines. "Let me help you with that, Miss Graber," he offered, his deep, gruff voice and scraggly gray beard concealing his kind nature.

She clutched the envelope to her chest, then peeked inside her bag to inventory the contents and forced a wide smile in appreciation of his offer of help. "*Danke* anyway, Wyatt. I think I've got everything now."

Wyatt mopped his brow on the arm of his tattered flannel shirt before opening the beat-up SUV's back passenger door and offering a hand. She accepted and awkwardly situated herself in the seat. While buckling herself in, she noticed an Amish man she didn't recognize sitting in the front passenger seat. Immediately her cheeks heated as she realized he'd just witnessed her near fall, but she quickly pushed the thoughts away. *Not that it matters none anyway.*

The Amish man looked older than most of the new bachelors coming to the area, and the sharp cut of his jaw made him appear handsome. Her heartbeat quickened.

Lovina pulled in a breath and released it just as quickly, reminding herself of the truth she knew. No matter how many bachelors came into West Kootenai, it was useless to get her hopes up. Even if she caught a bachelor glancing her way, one rarely gave her a second look. Although it had pained her for years, Lovina had worked hard to move past it. She could live a happy life without becoming a wife and mother . . . couldn't she?

"Why, hello there!" Lovina chirped a welcome to the passenger. When he didn't turn to acknowledge her or even grunt a reply to her greeting, Lovina fidgeted with her *kapp*, tucking damp, brown curls back inside. Perhaps he didn't hear her.

"Miss Graber, I hope you weren't waiting out here too long." Wyatt's apologetic gaze peered at her in the rearview mirror as he adjusted it and pulled out into traffic. "Mr. Smucker's train ran a little later than expected. Then an accident in front of the depot backed up traffic. I sure hated to have you waiting here in the rain, but I couldn't call you since you don't have a cell phone."

As Wyatt prattled on, Lovina assessed the tight-lipped Mr. Smucker. Dressed Plain and clean shaven, she figured him to be an Amish bachelor near her age, mid-twenties. Beneath his hat, he kept his hair short, but the glimpse she caught when Wyatt adjusted the rearview mirror revealed that his eyebrows were a dark, sandy blond and his eyes greenish-blue, much like the color of Lake Koocanusa on a sunny day.

Feeling heat rise in her cheeks, she ducked her eyes before he noticed her staring and pretended to smooth out an imaginary wrinkle on her apron. "Not to worry about being late, Wyatt. I chatted with Mrs. Robinson, the librarian, while I waited." Hopefully her cheerful voice belied the exhaustion radiating through every muscle in her body even as she rubbed her aching leg. "I helped her straighten up the magazine display, and I found a new cooking magazine to bring home."

"I should have known you'd find a way to keep busy. Now, where are my manners? I haven't properly introduced the two of you yet, have I? Lovina Graber, please meet Mr. Thomas Smucker, formerly of— I don't believe I caught where you lived before, Mr. Smucker." Wyatt had a crafty way of eliciting conversation from even the most tight-lipped.

Thomas Smucker didn't take the bait. The three sat in uncomfortable silence for a few too many seconds before his clipped response came. "Back east."

Wyatt chuckled, persistent as ever. "Most Amish people are from the east. Whereabouts did you grow up?"

Mr. Smucker appeared to have figured out Wyatt's game and threw the driver a bone. "Belleville, Pennsylvania," he replied tersely.

"Ah," Wyatt replied. "I don't think I know anyone from there. Is it a pretty small community?"

Mr. Smucker squirmed in his seat and grunted in the affirmative. Lovina almost pitied her riding companion. He obviously didn't wish to share much, but she had to wonder why. Did he have something to hide? She made a mental note to flip through past issues of the Amish newspaper, *The Budget*, to check for any mention of Smuckers in that area.

"Mr. Smucker's moving in at the bachelor camp. Gonna work up at the Log Works doing—what was it again, Mr. Smucker?"

The unsociable fellow drew in a deep breath before he responded. "Maintenance. I might try some woodworking on the side."

Was Lovina mistaken or did she note some pep in his voice when he mentioned woodworking?

Unable to resist chatting for another moment, Lovina inserted herself into the conversation. "It's nice to meet you, Mr. Smucker. I'm Lovina Graber. My family owns a Christmas tree farm a little ways down the hill from the Log Works. Welcome to Montana." Lovina chattered pleasantly, though the stranger didn't return her enthusiasm. She continued, hoping to engage him. "West Kootenai is a lovely little community. The guys up at the cabins sure do have a good time together, playing horseshoes and cards, hunting and fishing. There's never a dull moment."

Mr. Smucker's stony silence contrasted harshly with Lovina's bubbly and sociable nature, making the ride more unnerving than it ought to be. Wyatt drove down the quaint main street lined with old-fashioned wooden buildings. Tourists walked from store to store with smiles despite the rain, their good spirits mocking the tension in the van.

Even the usually oblivious Wyatt seemed to notice and redirected the conversation, putting Lovina at ease. "Tell me about the recipes in that new magazine. I'd be glad to taste test them for you."

"I haven't had a chance to give it a good going over, but there was a divine-looking bacon-wrapped meatloaf. Are you up for that?" she teased the older *Englisch* man in return, grateful for the change in subject.

"I think I could make the sacrifice, but I doubt you could improve upon your own meatloaf recipe." Wyatt patted his round belly and chuckled.

Silence descended on them again, but with less unease this time. Lovina pulled the magazine from her bag and leafed through it, shifting her attention to the glossy pages full of mouth-watering soup, stew, cake, and pie recipes, all perfect for the upcoming fall.

Visiting the library in Whitefish when she had her monthly physical therapy appointment afforded her one of her greatest pleasures in life. Mrs. Robinson knew Lovina loved cooking and crafting, so she saved the copies of magazines that were going out of circulation for Lovina to take home. In return, Lovina brought the librarian a homemade treat to enjoy.

This afternoon, however, she found it hard to focus on the recipes, her brain abuzz with questions about the mysterious, silent man in the front seat and her hip and leg muscles screaming with every pothole Wyatt hit. Well, that and the contents of the envelope she had picked up at the library.

She shifted in her seat, attempting to reduce her discomfort, but it was no help. Lovina concentrated on relaxing her jaws, then her shoulders, then her arms and fingers, and so on, down to her toes, like her physical therapist had shown her. She worked hard at PT today and would be sore tomorrow, especially with the late July rain pummeling down all day. She rolled her head from side to side, breathing deeply.

Physical exertion aside, her therapy days in Whitefish felt almost like a brief vacation for Lovina. It was the one day each month she set aside for herself. No cooking or baking, no sewing or babysitting, no visiting shut-ins—just a luxurious visit to the library, some window shopping in the Whitefish stores, a cafe lunch she didn't prepare, served on dishes she didn't have to wash, and physical therapy.

"Shew-ee!" Wyatt exclaimed. "It sure is pouring out here. I can hardly see the road in front of me." He seemed focused on driving, and Mr. Smucker hadn't so much as made a peep in nearly half an hour.

Lovina continued leafing through the magazine in silence, occasionally sneaking a look at the stranger in the passenger seat. What was his story?

His silence prompted a flood of questions. Most newcomers

had dozens of queries about the area, yet he remained mute. Bachelors were plentiful in West Kootenai, but they generally traveled together and were in their late teens—a good bit younger than Mr. Smucker.

She tilted her head in curiosity. Most Amish men married young. Of course, who was she to judge? At twenty-five and single, most Amish would call her an *aldi maed*. Still, his presence in the van gave her imagination lots of fodder.

The van curved up the tree-lined, single-lane highway north. In the distance, the Rocky Mountains jutted into the sky in shades of green and gray shrouded in the rainy fog. The highway sign claimed Canada was straight ahead, but Lovina knew they'd veer off and head west, up into the mountains, before getting to the border.

After a few more miles of silence, Wyatt tried again. "Do you have kinfolk around here, Mr. Smucker? You're a long way from home all on your lonesome."

Lovina cringed. Sometimes Wyatt had no boundaries.

The air in the van grew thick with tension when Thomas Smucker didn't respond. Finally, he offered, "No, Wyatt. It's only me. My folks died, and I was"—he hesitated for a moment—"the only child. Our dairy business was more than I could handle on my own, so I sold it and headed to Montana for a fresh start."

"*Es dutt mer.*" Lovina whispered her sympathies, almost involuntarily, at the mention of his parents.

"*Danke.*" Mr. Smucker turned around and nodded. His eyes definitely were that deep-lake greenish-blue and much kinder than she had imagined earlier. Now that his face was a bit more relaxed, she spotted a pair of dimples and a shy half smile.

Lovina's hand flew to her left cheek. She pretended to brush away stray hair, but she really wanted to prevent Mr. Smucker from noticing the zigzagged line that ran diagonally down it. Though smoothed by the passing of time, the scar still drew the kind of attention Lovina hated—that pitying condescension she knew too well.

What if Mr. Smucker thought she was flirting with him? She hastily broke eye contact, signaling an end to further conversation. Lovina busied herself with pulling out another magazine from her bag.

Bliss-filled faces of doting mothers and angelic children stared at Lovina from the pages. The children held their mothers' hands and clung to their skirts, casting admiring looks of love at them. The kind of look Lovina longed to have directed at her but knew never would be. Tears pricked her eyes when she realized she had taken a parenting magazine from Mrs. Robinson's stack.

Lovina scoffed at her foolish response. She would pass the magazine along to one of her *schwesters*. Three out of four of them were blessed with children, and while Lovina was thankful for her nieces and nephews, sometimes jealousy reared its ugly head. Lovina prayed to overcome that someday, but she had to admit, whenever she rocked one of them to sleep and felt their little warm bodies nestled next to hers, it stung.

She stuffed the magazine back in her tote and closed her eyes, crossing her arms on her chest. Mothers were indeed the luckiest women in the world. Long ago she'd given up hope of ever being loved like that. Instead of having a husband and family to dote on, she filled the void that was left by staying busy and helping others. It kept her hands occupied and her heart full—or at least pretty close.

The rest of the ride passed slowly in uncomfortable silence, but finally, Wyatt's SUV reached West Kootenai.

The small community tucked into the mountains of Montana near the Canadian border was home to Amish and *Englisch* alike. It wasn't a town really, just a few businesses and houses scattered along dirt roads. It was a *gut* community, where neighbor cared for neighbor. Lovina couldn't imagine living anyplace different, especially back east where hundreds of Amish made up a community. *Helping the few dozen Amish families here keeps me busy enough.*

"Mr. Smucker, if you don't mind, I'll drop Miss Graber off

first, since she's only a few houses down from the store here. If you need anything, pop in and let Annie help you out. I'll take you up the hill to the bachelor camp next."

Thomas barely glanced over. "I don't need anything from the store tonight, but please, go ahead to Miss Graber's house."

Within minutes, Wyatt pulled his SUV in front of her family's comfortable log home, situated in front of a hillside full of evergreens. Lovina cringed. As ready as she was to get home and change into dry clothes, she dreaded getting out of the van in front of Mr. Smucker.

She couldn't quite explain why it bothered her so much. First, she'd tried to hide the scar, and now she didn't want him to see her walk. She'd walked with a limp her whole life—her right leg considerably shorter than her left—but it was simply part of who she was. Despite years of physical therapy and attempts at specially built shoes, she had convinced herself she wasn't embarrassed by it a long time ago, especially since everyone in West Kootenai was fully aware of it.

Still, she loathed the attention her limp and scar drew. New people always had questions and pitying looks. She might as well get it over with.

Wyatt parked in their driveway, and Lovina gathered her bags. The older *Englisch* man opened the door and offered her a hand. Lovina thanked him, straightened her back, and shuffled with as much grace as she could muster into the house, praying that Mr. Smucker wasn't looking.

Chapter Two

MONDAY, JULY 24

Right now, all Thomas Smucker wanted was a nice, warm bed. Well, maybe a quick, hot shower too. Grime covered every inch of his body. A two-day train ride from Pittsburgh to Whitefish would do that to a man.

Instead, he had to make polite conversation with strangers.

And yes, one of those strangers might have the prettiest brown eyes he'd ever seen on a woman, but Thomas wasn't here for love.

He was here to work. To find peace. To escape.

But first . . . sleep.

Just not yet. He sighed.

As Wyatt helped Miss Graber out of the van, Thomas stole a long look at the energetic, nearly elfin woman. The headlights of the van illuminated her slight five-foot frame. Like him, she had to be in her mid-twenties. Frizzy spirals of brown hair dared to escape from her *kapp*. The dark expressive eyes he'd noticed earlier remained lowered, and her jaw clenched tightly, as if she concentrated on each movement.

And along the left side of her face ran a puffy, purplish scar.

She trudged toward the house, and he noticed a limp. Initially, he believed she was having trouble balancing her bags while keeping her long dress from dragging in the mud, but the farther away she walked, the more obvious the limp became. He couldn't help but wonder if the limp and the scar were connected.

Thomas broke his gaze when Wyatt got in, slammed the driver's side door closed, and backed out of the Grabers' driveway.

"Now, Mr. Smucker, we'll get you to the bachelor camp and settled for the night. I'm sure you're ready for a good rest!"

Thomas nodded. While most Amish men wanted a wife and *kinner*, all he wanted was to live in a place where no one had any expectations of him. He craved peace and quiet, time in nature, and most of all, privacy. Between Wyatt's never-ending questions and being scrutinized by Miss Graber, he had spent the last hour and a half feeling like cattle at an auction. Nothing exhausted him more than dodging nosy questions and avoiding aimless chatter.

Thomas tried to stifle a yawn, and the driver laughed. "That Miss Graber sure is a sweet lady. I've been driving her to and from Whitefish for over a year, and she never fails to bring me some homemade pie or other goodies. And she's sharp. Every trip has included a visit to the library. She writes for that Amish newspaper too. Yessir, she's a dandy young lady. I can't figure out why one of those Amish bachelors hasn't snatched her right up yet."

Thomas thought he might know why. For one thing, she talked far too much. She wrote for that gossip rag, *The Budget*. And a well-read Amish woman? He could almost hear his father's stern voice parroting the words of King Solomon. *"'Be not wise in thine own eyes: fear the LORD, and depart from evil.'"*

As a little boy, Thomas had loved to read from the limited books his schoolteacher kept on the shelves. His *Englisch* friends had The Hardy Boys mysteries he enjoyed. However, Thomas learned the hard way that *Dat* only allowed the Bible—in German, of course, though somehow *Dat* could quote the taboo

King James Version—and *Martyrs Mirror* in his home. Book learning made a man prideful and arrogant.

As for women, his father believed educated women lacked humility, which led to disobedience. And he prized obedience over all virtues. *Mem* read very little beyond an occasional copy of *The Budget* she borrowed from their neighbor. *Mem* never seemed prideful or disobedient—she simply enjoyed hearing the comings and goings of Plain people near and far. What was wrong with that? Thomas had always wondered, but never dared question *Dat*'s opinions. That would have been foolish.

Wyatt continued his chatter. "Sure do hate that she has that limp and that scar. It must hurt something fierce, but she never complains. Why, she hardly lets me help her in and out of the SUV. She's one tough cookie."

While Thomas was quite curious about Miss Graber's condition, he didn't want to be impolite and ask too many questions. Despite the scar, Miss Graber had a kind face and, of course, those intense, thick-lashed eyes. Besides, Thomas would hate for Wyatt to discuss his business with other people. The only thing Thomas hated more than idle gossip was a liar. *Dat* had a proverb for that too. *A wicked doer giveth heed to false lips; and a liar giveth ear to a naughty tongue.*

At the thought of his father's words, Thomas shook his head. His father had died three years ago. Not a day went by that Thomas wasn't haunted by his memory. Today, though, as he started his new life, his father's voice was the last one he wanted to hear.

Wyatt turned the SUV onto an even more narrow and rutted side road. West Kootenai was more remote than Thomas had imagined when he initiated his move out west. He loved the town's location in northwestern Montana, near the Canadian border. It boasted a small Amish community, job opportunities at the Log Works, and plenty of hunting, fishing, and hiking. He didn't know a single soul in the area. Best of all, no one knew him either.

Just the way he liked it.

"Not much farther now, Mr. Smucker." Wyatt pointed to a rise. "You'll see the cabins when we top this little hill."

Excitement for his future bubbled up inside Thomas. The view opened up to a clearing with a smattering of cabins. Thomas took in the sight, his eyes wide with shock. The rain had stopped, and young men gathered outside, some pitching horseshoes in a muddy pit and others talking and laughing. Several sat in dilapidated rocking chairs on the rustic front porches. Animal pelts hung on the sides of the cabins and on the clotheslines. It looked less like a bachelor camp and more like a junkyard.

His spirits fell. The camp's reality was a far cry from what he had envisioned when he decided to move here. He was at least six years older than most of the fellows in the camp. They looked like *kinner* to him. And they acted like it too.

Thomas swallowed hard as Wyatt pulled the SUV to a stop. He came here for a fresh start. He must put his expectations and preconceptions to rest and enjoy the new life he came to build. Thomas willed himself to relax as he opened the passenger door and walked to the trunk to gather his belongings.

A young man with alarmingly red hair came bounding toward him. "You must be Thomas. *Willkumme.* Ike Sommers told us to expect you. My name is Charlie Hostetler. I'll show you to your bunk."

Thomas slipped cash to Wyatt and thanked him for the ride, then followed Charlie into the cabin, bracing himself.

Inside, he encountered even more disorder than he had witnessed outside. He stepped over shoes, piles of clothes, plates with crumbs, and piles of rubbish as he followed the young man up the stairs and to the bedroom on the left.

"It's a bit of a wreck." Charlie grinned sheepishly. "This is the first time most of us have ever lived without our *mems* or *schwesters* to tell us to clean up."

"*Ja, vell . . .* " Thomas had never lived on his own either, not until *Mem* passed. Even still, he knew how to keep a tidy house. *Dat* wouldn't have tolerated this filth and chaos.

"Here's your bunk." Charlie gestured to the one empty bed. Three other beds sat in the room, sheets and blankets sloppily piled atop them. "We've already had dinner tonight, but you can probably scare up some leftovers in the kitchen. Guys take turns fixing meals, but most of us prefer to get our meals down at the store. You can't beat the cooking or the price." Charlie paused for a breath, leaving Thomas to wonder if everyone in West Kootenai talked with such exuberance.

The spirited young man continued. "You'll be working at the Log Works, right? We usually meet out front and walk down together. My room is across the hall. Let me know if you need anything else and make yourself at home." With a smile and a hearty pat on Thomas's shoulder, Charlie turned on his heel and left the room.

Thomas blinked a few times as he took in his surroundings.

As exhausted as he was, he couldn't allow himself the luxury of crashing into bed in a messy room. Thomas craved order and needed to put things in their places. An empty dresser drawer held enough space for his clothes. He made his bed neatly, like *Mem* had taught him. Thomas lined the stray shoes up against the wall and pushed the pile of dirty clothes into a corner. After a moment of searching, he found a broom in the hall closet and swept the floor of his room and down the hallway.

One leg of the nightstand next to his bed wobbled when he placed his wallet on it. Thomas quickly inspected it and determined that a new dowel and a dab of wood glue would fix it up. He dug in his toolbox to find what he needed. He made the repair, then dusted the top of the table before putting his wallet and an oil lamp back in place.

There. That was better.

Thomas knew he would eventually adjust to his new life—he must shift his thinking. Living in the bunkhouse would require flexibility, which was a struggle for him. He left Belleville so that he could live a different life than the one that loomed over him, and so far, West Kootenai had delivered on that promise. When he thought about spending the next fifty years running the dairy farm under the scrutiny of Belleville's hard-nosed bishop, he shuddered. Life in West Kootenai would be a grand adventure.

He just had to open himself up to accept it.

Chapter Three

TUESDAY, AUGUST 15

Thomas patted his belly with satisfaction and signaled the waitress that he was ready for the check.

Charlie had been right when he touted the excellent food at West Kootenai Kraft and Grocery. In the weeks since arriving, Thomas had taken almost every meal at the store. He appreciated the time alone to enjoy his meals, trusting that the cooks prepared the food with safety and care—in sharp contrast to the slop mustered up by the guys at the bachelor cabin. He winced at the memory of the bear meat surprise they'd offered to share. Thomas never liked surprises, but that one was especially distasteful.

Red-checked curtains framed breathtaking views of the mountains already capped with snow, even though the calendar still showed that it was late summer. The store, the cornerstone of all social activity in West Kootenai, bustled with activity. Even on an ordinary Tuesday at four in the afternoon, a steady flow of customers moved through this place. Early diners filled nearly all the heavy wooden tables. Several women—both Amish and

Englisch—busily shopped in the small grocery section. Friendly chatter swirled all around him.

As he savored the last bite of today's dessert special—butterscotch pie—Thomas felt a hand clamp on his shoulder. To his right stood Ike Sommers, one of the few friends Thomas had made in the weeks since his arrival. Friendly but not probing. Thomas didn't mind exchanging pleasantries with Ike.

"Looks like you enjoyed your meal," Ike teased, nodding at the empty plate in front of Thomas. A good fifteen to twenty years older than most of the other guys, Ike was good humored, balanced out by his wisdom and patience, making him an ideal mentor to the bachelors in town.

"What's not to love about butterscotch pie?" Thomas returned.

Ike shrugged and grinned. "I heard you saved the day this morning at the Log Works." He sat down across from Thomas.

Thomas felt heat rise in his cheeks. He hated getting even a little attention. "*Ach*, it was not a big deal."

Ike wouldn't drop the subject. "That's not what I heard. You noticed that the hydraulic lift was jamming and you fixed it. Without the lift, they couldn't have moved the load of lumber scheduled to arrive today. Without you, they would have had to call a mechanic to come from Whitefish. You saved them several days of wasted productivity and kept a lot of guys from going without pay."

Jenny, the *Englisch* waitress, arrived with Thomas's check. She was always friendly, but respectful and appropriate too, not the behavior Thomas had expected of an *Englischer*. His father had always cautioned him against trusting the *Englisch*, but things in West Kootenai were different than back in Belleville. Amish and *Englisch* lived in harmony here, and no one thought it was strange—yet another opportunity for Thomas to grow.

Jenny tucked a strand of light brown hair behind her ear and placed the green ticket before him. "Here's your check, Mr. Smucker, and a coffee to go. How was the pie today?"

Before Thomas could answer, Ike snatched the check away from him.

"My treat today, Jenny. This guy deserves it. And bring me a turkey sandwich to go, please."

Thomas protested, but Ike shot him a determined glance. "I insist. It blesses me to get to bless you this way. It's all part of being in community together. Don't steal my blessing, Thomas."

Thomas considered his new friend's words, then tucked his cash back into his wallet. "*Danke*, Ike. I'm a slow learner, I guess."

He took a sip of his *kaffe*, letting the hot liquid warm his belly. Letting others care for him wasn't easy—it went against everything his *dat* and *mem* had taught him.

Just as Thomas stood to go, cup in hand, the front door swung open. A small girl, no older than five or six, burst in with gusto.

An exasperated woman dressed in a business suit hurried to follow and caught the heel of her shoe on the threshold. With the desperate flailing of her arms, she squealed and then caught herself on the doorframe.

Without a look back, the girl picked up speed and barreled forward. Before Thomas could sidestep her, the girl crashed right into him, sending his to-go cup flying.

Steaming black liquid splattered everywhere—on Thomas's shirt, on the floor, and on the little girl's shoes.

"Emily Grace! Slow down!" the woman called as she wobbled forward, her tall heels skidding through the spilled liquid. Then spotting Thomas's crumpled cup and spilled *kaffe*, she approached him with a look of worry. "Are you all right? I don't know how she's ever going to be tamed." The frazzled middle-aged woman offered an exasperated sigh as she eyed the mess.

"*Ja*, I'm *gut*. But is she?" Thomas peered down at the girl sitting with her back pressed against the front counter, her arms wrapped around her legs. The tips of her scuffed pink light-up sneakers sat inches from the puddle of *kaffe*. "Did any of the coffee get on you?"

Avoiding the puddle, Thomas knelt beside her. He usually steered clear of *kinner*, but something about this little girl drew him to her.

Large tears welled up in the girl's greenish-blue eyes, yet not a sound emerged from her lips. She sniffled and shook her head but refused to meet his gaze.

A stirring of compassion caused emotion to swell his chest. Or was it something more? The freckles that smattered her nose and cheeks seemed oddly familiar, as did the sandy blonde hair that had pulled free from her ponytail and framed her face.

With a gasp, Jenny rushed from the kitchen with a handful of towels. "Here, Mr. Smucker. Let me help you get this cleaned up." Jenny quickly and skillfully cleaned up the spilled liquid on the floor and handed Thomas a dry towel to soak up the coffee on his shirt.

"Smucker? You wouldn't happen to be Thomas Smucker, would you?" asked the well-dressed woman.

"I am." Thomas stood and eyed her curiously. Of all the places for someone to know his name, especially an *Englischer* like her.

"Oh, isn't this a happy accident? I wondered if we would ever find you, and we literally bumped right into you."

Thomas's brow furrowed. He swallowed and shook his head, looking from the woman to the girl and back, his confusion growing. She was looking for him? What on earth for? He had never seen this woman before.

Clearly intrigued by the conversation, Jenny surveyed the now-spotless floor and collected the dirty towels but didn't move.

"I don't think you have the right Thomas Smucker." His words echoed in the room.

Looking back to the restaurant, all the conversation had died away and all eyes were trained on him, the woman, and the little girl.

"No, I know you're the one. I'm positive." The woman's voice rose. Whispers and murmurs came from around the room.

Thomas's chin dipped down. Heat rose to his ears, and he was certain they were turning red. His gut told him that this situation was about to become fodder for West Kootenai's gossip mill, yet he knew arguing would not help.

Thomas stepped forward. He offered a tense smile and motioned to the door. "Well, you've found me. Would you care to step outside to discuss, uh, whatever it is you've come to see me about?"

The little girl jumped to her feet and stomped her foot. "Pleeease, Ms. Williams! I'm so hungry, and I need to go to the bathroom! Do you want me to pee my pants?"

Thomas winced and his eyebrows shot up. No Amish child would be so whiny and demanding. Where he came from, children obeyed without question. He cringed, imagining how his father would have reacted if he were here.

Ms. Williams, as the girl had called her, moved past Thomas. She took a deep breath and lowered herself before the girl, careful to keep her skirt from touching the still-damp floor. "Okay, Emily. We've talked about the appropriate way to ask for something you need. I'm sure we can find you a bathroom and we'll grab a snack, but you'll have to use your manners." Her voice was soft, yet still held a scolding edge. "Mr. Smucker and I have some things to discuss. How about you ask that nice lady to show you the restroom?" Ms. Williams gestured toward Jenny, who still stood watching events unfold.

Jenny reached out her hand, and the girl reluctantly took it. "Sure thing. Right this way." She cheerfully led the little girl toward the bathroom, glancing over her shoulder a few times as if not wanting to miss anything important.

Ms. Williams scanned the busy dining area . . . "Is there somewhere we can sit for a moment, Mr. Smucker?"

Ike hopped up from his seat and offered it to Ms. Williams, exchanging a worried glance with Thomas. "I'll wait for my order at the counter. We'll talk later, Thomas."

Thomas nodded and sat back in the booth, assessing the

situation as best he could. Now that Emily wasn't present, the woman's expression had grown grim. He swallowed hard and prepared himself for whatever it was she had to say.

"Who are you and why have you been looking for me?" He decided directness was the best move in this situation. He wiped his hands on a napkin then folded it in a perfect square and placed it on the table before him.

"I'm Virginia Williams. I'm a social worker with the state of Montana." She fished a business card out of her pocket. "I'm afraid I have some bad news to share with you. There's no easy way to tell you this. Your sister, Anna Ruth, died in a car accident in June. Lawyers and social workers have been trying to find you since then."

Thomas's chest constricted and tears blurred his eyes. "Anna Ruth?" Emotion caught in his throat, and he attempted to swallow it away.

Though Thomas hadn't spoken to his *schwester* in twelve years, he thought of her every day. Every day since the day she left their family home after a nasty blowup with *Dat*. In his mind, Anna Ruth would always look the way she did that day—stubborn, sassy, and seventeen years old. She couldn't be gone.

"Anna's gone?" Thomas's voice trembled, sounding so foreign in his ears.

"I'm afraid so. She and her husband were returning home to Cincinnati from a conference in Cleveland. A big rig blew a tire on the interstate and knocked their car into oncoming traffic." The woman's eyes softened as she offered him a grim smile. "I'm sorry for your loss."

A heavy weight of regret settled on Thomas's chest. *Her husband.* He hadn't even known his *schwester* had gotten married. He'd missed years of her life, ones he'd never be able to make up for.

Ms. Williams paused, which gave Thomas a moment to process the news.

Thomas nodded for her to continue, still not trusting himself to speak.

"I know this has to be a terrible shock. As I said, it has taken a bit of work to find you. She left instructions in her will that you were to care for Emily, but she gave your address as Belleville, Pennsylvania."

The no-nonsense social worker sighed. "Ohio authorities contacted Pennsylvania child welfare services who looked for you in Belleville, but you had moved, and no one wanted to tell them where you were. Someone finally let it slip that you'd come to Montana, and the Pennsylvania social workers transferred her case to me. Anyway, we've found you now, and that's what really matters. Emily needs you. She has been staying with a friend of your sister's who was certified for foster care, but the will explicitly stated that Emily was to live with you in the event that anything happened to her and her husband."

"Emily? The little girl with you? She's my . . ." His voice trembled as he tried to find the right words.

"She's your niece."

Chapter Four

TUESDAY, AUGUST 15

F rom her corner booth at the Kraft and Grocery, Lovina couldn't hear the conversation between Mr. Smucker and the *Englisch* woman. But something serious was going on. Even her white-and-gray Shih Tzu, Gus, still had his ears perked up after the commotion with the *Englisch* girl.

Not wanting to eavesdrop visibly, Lovina kept her eyes focused on the stack of papers in front of her. She'd only stopped in to rest for a moment after delivering ginger chews to her friend Susanna Milner Baker, who was expecting her first baby soon. And to enjoy a scone while she finished her weekly column for *The Budget*, which she needed to get in the mail today for next week's edition.

She did one last proofread of the article and put it in an envelope. After a quick look around to make sure no one was watching her, she pulled out a second sheet of paper. Excitement and nervousness churned in her belly as she scanned that for errors too.

Dear Western Wildflower,

A new family moved in down the road from us recently. Their community had different rules and expectations, so they are having a hard time adapting to life here. How can I help them?

Sincerely,

A Helpful Neighbor

Dear Helpful Neighbor,

First, lift this family in your prayers daily. Second, make sure they know you are friendly. Being new and different can make a person feel lonely. Having a friend you can count on makes a big difference! Finally, invite them to your home for supper. This will help them see that, despite different rules, both of you serve the same God and seek to glorify Him.

Sincerely,

The Western Wildflower

In Whitefish a few weeks back, the librarian had given her an envelope addressed to her in care of the library. It had been a request from the publishers of *The Budget* to answer some letters they'd received asking for advice on personal matters. Because Lovina's regular column was so well liked, the publishers thought she would be a great choice to write the responses. She'd agreed, but on the condition of anonymity. Even though West Kootenai was more progressive than some Amish communities, Lovina wasn't sure the elders would take kindly to a single woman dispensing advice. Besides, she doubted that anyone would want advice from someone like her.

In a few short weeks, the column had become quite

popular, which took Lovina by surprise. She folded the letter and shoved it into the envelope with her regular column and sealed it, breathing a sigh of relief. Lovina needed to talk with *Mem* and *Dat* about the extra writing she had taken on, but she didn't know how to bring it up. Right now, only Susanna knew that Lovina was the Western Wildflower, and Lovina hoped to keep it that way until she could figure out how to tell her family.

She looked over again at Mr. Smucker and the woman. They were still talking, and Lovina's overactive imagination dreamed up numerous possibilities. Maybe Mr. Smucker came to West Kootenai and left a wife and child behind? Actually, it would make more sense if the lady was his secret *Englisch* girlfriend, and the girl was their love child. Perhaps that was why he was so tight-lipped that night when Wyatt asked him about his past.

Lovina's fingers drummed on the stack of papers, and her cheeks burned with shame. It just wasn't right of her to dream up such outlandish scenarios, putting Mr. Smucker in a negative light. She'd seen him at church services and in the store from time to time, but they had never spoken since that first day on the ride home from Whitefish.

Lovina had no reason to assume this was anything inappropriate. Maybe the woman, who looked too old to be Mr. Smucker's girlfriend, had met the handsome bachelor on the train and her little girl had wanted to return a book he'd loaned her. *Ja*, that sounded plausible. Then again, the look in the woman's eyes seemed far too serious for that.

Lovina packed her bag to leave. She had snooped long enough, and *Mem* expected her home already. Gus needed to stretch his legs too. She stood, and as the two of them reached Mr. Smucker's table, Jenny returned with the girl, who eyed Gus with curiosity.

Lovina smiled at the little girl. Her tear-streaked, freckled cheeks and mussed pigtails stirred something within her. She longed to draw the child into her arms and comfort her, but how strange that would seem to the girl. Instead, she tried a different tactic.

"Would you like to pet Gus?" Lovina whispered, offering a warm smile.

The girl's eyes grew wide, but she didn't speak. She looked up through her dark brown lashes at the *Englisch* lady. The tense conversation at the table halted abruptly, and the woman turned her attention to the youngster.

"You want to pet the dog? I suppose that's fine, Emily. But stay where I can see you."

"Thank you, Ms. Williams!" The girl's face lit up with joy, and Lovina moved out of the way, with the girl following. When they reached the bulletin board near the door, Lovina stopped. She leaned to pet Gus's head, beaming at the girl. "This is Gus the wonderdog and my name is Lovina. What's your name?"

"I'm Emily Grace Spencer. Why is he a wonderdog?" Emily's voice grew bolder with each word.

"Well, I call him a wonderdog because he's wonderful. But I guess the thing about him that makes him really special is that he only has one eye that works. He doesn't let that bother him, though. He's really smart and knows lots of tricks! Want to see one?"

Emily Grace giggled. "Of course!"

Lovina's heart swelled with compassion, and she couldn't stop a smile. Whatever Mr. Smucker and the serious *Englisch* lady were discussing no doubt had something to do with the tears Emily had shed earlier.

"Gus, sit!" Lovina commanded. Gus obeyed.

"Now, give me five!" He stuck his little white paw out and placed it in Lovina's hand.

"He is smart!" Emily marveled. "Can I try?"

"Sure," Lovina agreed with a grin. "Be gentle with him."

"Sit, Gus!" Emily instructed. Gus eyed the little girl, then looked at Lovina for approval. She nodded, and Gus sat.

"Give me five!" He stuck his paw out to her. "Good boy!"

Emily placed her hand on his furry head and gave him a good scratch. He reveled in the attention.

Lovina reached into her pocket and handed Emily a dog treat. "Give this to him."

Gus gobbled up the treat Emily offered, then licked her hand. Giggles emerged and the sadness from the girl's face turned to joy.

Then, as if remembering the real purpose for their visit, Emily dropped her arms limply to her sides and looked over at the table where the odd couple still sat talking.

As if sensing the girl's gaze, the *Englisch* woman looked up and gestured for Emily to come over. Emily's smile faded, then she trudged toward the woman and Mr. Smucker.

Lovina stood back and read the bulletin board. It seemed the Troyer family was looking for household help, and the Martins had a buggy frame for sale. As usual, Lovina made mental notes about ideas for upcoming articles. Then she trained her eyes back on Emily Grace, whose whole posture changed as she approached the table.

The *Englisch* lady took Emily Grace's hand. Emily scooted into the booth next to her. "You know how we talked about coming to Montana to meet your uncle on the plane ride here? Well, this is Thomas Smucker, your mother's brother."

Lovina held her breath like she'd just gotten to the really good place in a book. She exhaled with relief. He was the little girl's *oncle*. That made more sense. But Emily Grace was *Englisch*, so was this lady Mr. Smucker's *schwester*? She kept listening.

"It's nice to meet you, sir." Emily's voice had a rehearsed, almost robotic quality.

"Nice to meet you too." Thomas Smucker's voice didn't sound much more natural.

The lady looked at Emily. "Remember how we talked about you staying with your Uncle Thomas for a while? Because that's what your mother wanted for you?"

Emily nodded. The woman had introduced Thomas Smucker as the little girl's *oncle*. Yet where was this girl's mother? And what would lead up to this precious little girl being dropped off on her bachelor *oncle*? There had to be more to the story.

All the color had drained from Thomas's face, and his gaze was vacant. However, the pieces began to fall into place. Thomas Smucker, the mysterious bachelor from back east, had gotten himself an unexpected pint-sized houseguest. That would go over great at the bachelor cabin.

Lovina chewed on her thumbnail as she mulled over the situation. From her regular trips to deliver birthday cakes to the bachelor cabin compound, she knew it was hardly suitable for habitation by the young men who lived there, never mind a little girl. What would Mr. Smucker do? He appeared too shaken to make any decisions. And poor Emily. She looked like a little lost puppy. One more disappointment or rejection could crush her.

Lovina's heart thudded faster and faster. A voice within her prompted her to act, and she knew exactly what she had to do. She was a helper, and God knew these folks needed her. He placed her here, at the store, at this very moment for a reason.

"Excuse me, Mr. Smucker?" Her voice came out higher-pitched and squeakier than she intended, but the possibility of helping Mr. Smucker with his niece filled Lovina with energy.

He sat unmoving in the booth, eyes fixed straight ahead at nothing in particular. Did he even hear her?

"Mr. Smucker?" She tried again, softer this time. "I'm Lovina Graber. We rode back from Whitefish together a few weeks back."

"*Ja, ja.* Sorry. Now isn't a good time, Miss Graber."

"I know, but, ah, Mr. Smucker? I want to help you." Lovina tried to keep her voice even, but her words came out all in a rush. She scanned the faces at the table. The social worker watched Emily, and Emily gazed up at Lovina. Thomas sat with his jaw clenched tight and his eyes fixed on the table.

"Help me?" Thomas shook his head, as though waking himself from a bad dream. He turned to Lovina, blinking as if to bring her into focus.

"*Ja. Vell,* I couldn't help overhearing your conversation. It sounds like you might need a place to stay if Emily is going to be visiting with you for a while."

"Oh, *ja*! I hadn't thought about that." Thomas snapped back into reality, his eyes wide. The social worker crossed her arms over her chest and gave him a disapproving look.

"My family has a cabin that would fit you and Emily. Our tenants moved out last month, so it is vacant. I'm sure my *dat* would be glad to have the two of you stay there."

"Oh, please, please, Uncle Thomas!" Emily chimed. A slow smile spread across her face, almost reaching her eyes. "Lovina and Gus are my friends! If we stay in their cabin, I can visit them."

Gus gave a short bark and settled himself at Emily's feet, affirming the little girl's claim. Emily slipped out of the booth and onto the floor and lavished him with soft strokes.

Ms. Williams looked from Emily to Lovina and finally to Thomas. "If your living conditions aren't suitable, then I'm afraid I can't leave Emily with you. She'll have to go to a foster family or a group home. As it stands right now, you only have temporary provisional custody until I can make a thorough examination."

Thomas nodded. "Well, in that case . . . Miss Graber, if you are sure it isn't an imposition, we will take you up on that. At least until I have time to think this situation through. This is all such a shock."

"Of course, Mr. Smucker. It's what neighbors do."

Emily reached up and took Lovina's hand, squeezing it gently. Lovina thought her heart might explode with joy. While she would never know the blessing of holding her own *kinner*, God had placed one in her life who needed her just the same.

Chapter Five

Numb. That's the only word Thomas could find to describe his current state.

In the last thirty minutes, he had lost his *sister* and gained a *niesse*. And apparently, committed to moving into a cabin on the property of that talkative little woman he'd ridden into town with.

That butterscotch pie now soured in his mouth. He needed time to process these events, but a moment of quiet wasn't likely to come soon. The little girl—Emily—shuffled along behind him as they followed the *Englisch* woman to her car.

"Before I go, I'll need to take a look at the place Emily will be staying. There are some minimum requirements that must be met. She will need her own room with a window, indoor plumbing, those sorts of things. Can you all ride with me so I don't get lost up here?"

"Certainly, Ms. Williams. The cabin should do nicely. It has one bedroom and a sleeping sofa in the living room," Lovina responded when Thomas's mouth remained clamped shut.

On the short drive to the Graber home, the social worker

explained the next steps in the guardianship process and rattled off a list of things Thomas needed to do before her next visit. Both he and Emily would need to see a therapist for an evaluation; he'd need a physical exam and a background check. There were financial records to gather, and he would need to consult an attorney. Since Emily was Thomas's niece, her placement with him wasn't considered foster care. Instead, it fell under Montana's Kinship Caregiver program, which made the process a bit easier, according to Ms. Williams.

Thomas's head swam with the details. Lovina Graber listened intently and asked lots of questions. Thomas hoped she would remember the particulars because he was certain he wouldn't.

The West Kootenai Christmas Tree Farm sign indicated they had arrived at Lovina's home. Spruces, firs, and pines lined the hillside as far as the eye could see, and their intoxicating scent filled the air.

"Here we are, Emily Grace," Lovina announced as they pulled in the driveway. "This house is where Gus and I live with my *mem* and *dat*. You and your *oncle* Thomas will stay over there." Lovina pointed toward a well-worn path that ran beside the house. "Do you see all those trees on the hill? What do those look like?"

"Christmas trees?" she returned, her eyes wide.

"That's right! We grow Christmas trees here. Can you smell them?" Emily closed her eyes and inhaled deeply, grinning. Lovina continued, "Now, let me show you to the cabin."

She led Thomas, Emily, and the social worker past the barn on their way to a small but sturdy cabin.

Emily's wide eyes took in the sights, and she wrinkled her nose at the scents of a barnyard. Clearly, his *schwester* had raised a city girl, which didn't surprise him. Anna Ruth had always longed to live a fancy life and had never been content in the small town of Belleville.

Inside the cabin, Thomas was relieved to find a furnished living area, kitchenette, bathroom, and single bedroom. Just enough room for the two of them. While the cabin could use a dusting, it was far cleaner than the bachelor camp.

Lovina showed Ms. Williams around the cabin, leaving Thomas and Emily alone in the living area.

"Where can I plug in my tablet, Uncle Thomas?" Emily's voice broke through his thoughts.

He looked up to see Emily holding some electronic gadget in her hand. Her pink sparkly suitcase lay open at her feet, clothes spilling out in a jumble. A brown-haired doll stuck out of the pile, looking almost as bedraggled as Emily herself.

"We don't have electricity. Amish people are Plain people. We live simply. You will need to get used to that," Thomas replied, his words sounding much harsher than he had intended.

Emily's lip quivered, but she set her jaw and nodded. "Ms. Williams told me, but I forgot."

What a tough little girl. Thomas thought of all she had experienced in the last few weeks—losing both parents, then being uprooted from her temporary home and shipped across the country to live with her uncle, a total stranger, in a world that was so different from everything she had ever known.

Thomas was ashamed of the pangs of homesickness he had felt when he first came to West Kootenai. Compared to Emily's journey, his had been a breeze. He was here by his own choice to begin a new life. She had been ripped from her home and placed in a strange new world. He would do well to keep this in mind.

Lovina and Ms. Williams emerged from the small bedroom. The social worker handed Thomas a thick packet of paperwork. "This cabin will do nicely for the two of you as long as Mr. Smucker doesn't mind sleeping on the couch."

"No problem," Thomas croaked.

"Well then. You should find everything you need in this folder. Emily's health records, the legal paperwork granting you temporary custody, checklists to guide you through the process ahead—it's all in here." She tapped the folder, then lowered her voice to almost a whisper. "Also, there is a copy of your sister's will, along with a letter she wrote to you."

He nodded. A letter from Anna Ruth. He couldn't handle that today.

"I think we've covered everything. Here is my card if you need to contact me at any point before my next visit. I know the Amish don't have telephones, but is there a number where I can reach you in an emergency?" Ms. Williams raised her eyebrow at Thomas.

Thomas closed his eyes and sighed. There was a phone shanty at the bachelor cabin, but he was leaving there today and he didn't know where another one was located. Perhaps he could give her the Log Works number, but he didn't know it off the top of his head.

Lovina interjected, "Why don't I give you the number for the store? Annie is always glad to take messages and pass them along."

Though sometimes she talked a bit too much, Lovina Graber had a knack for knowing what to say and when to say it. He'd met Annie, the store owner a few times, and Annie had told him the same thing herself. Why hadn't he thought of that? Then again, when had he asked Lovina for advice?

Thomas couldn't decide if he was more in awe of Lovina's capabilities or irritated by her constant meddling. He reserved judgment until he could see how this new living situation would play out.

The social worker scheduled a visit for September 8 and bid them goodbye. She drove away, leaving the three of them standing in the cabin. They surveyed the load of boxes and bags that Ms. Williams had left with them. This little girl sure did have a lot of stuff.

"Mr. Smucker?" Lovina Graber interrupted his swirling thoughts. "I'll run over to my house and speak to my parents about this arrangement. I'm sure it will be no trouble. Let me know if you need anything. See you later, Emily."

"Bye, Miss Lovina! Bye, Gus," called Emily as she bent down to pet the little furball.

Thomas had to hand it to the woman. She knew how to distract his niece. Lovina Graber's intervention had been nothing short of miraculous. He would be in the woman's debt.

He nodded a solemn goodbye, marveling at the woman's generosity and noticing for the first time the kindness in her dark brown eyes. As much as he liked the idea that this would be "no trouble," Thomas was certain he was in for more trouble than he'd ever experienced.

He began opening the suitcases and boxes Emily brought with her. He cleared his throat, then tried to make conversation with his niece. "So, Emily. You lived in Ohio before?"

She nodded, tracing an imaginary circle on the floor with the toe of her pink light-up tennis shoe. She chewed on her trembling bottom lip without looking at Thomas.

"I know this is hard for you, Emily. It's hard for me too. We will figure out what to do, okay? Trust me?" A lump rose in his own throat.

"I can do hard things. I can do *all* things through Christ because He makes me strong," Emily said, meeting Thomas's eyes. A missing top tooth caused her to lisp just a bit.

Thomas cocked his head in surprise at hearing her quote Scripture. When Anna Ruth left home, he assumed she left behind religion as well, not that he had given it much thought. *Dat* had made it pretty clear that Anna Ruth was dead to them and banished any talk of her, although Thomas often caught *Mem* with a faraway look in her eyes, obviously remembering the daughter she loved so well.

Dat and *Mem*. What would they think of all this?

Mem would welcome this little girl with open arms, as long as *Dat* wasn't looking. On the other hand, *Dat* would have denied having a daughter, if he had even spoken to Ms. Williams at all. He wasn't a fan of *Englischers* anyway, but there was no way he would have taken this outspoken little girl into his home.

Thomas took a deep breath to clear his head. There was no use in thinking about what *Mem* or *Dat* would have done. He was on his own now, and he had little choice but to take care of Emily Grace, at least until he could figure out a better option for her. Besides, it was the right thing to do to honor Anna Ruth.

Thomas squatted down to meet Emily at eye level and offered her what he hoped was a reassuring smile. "I'll tell you what, Emily. You can take some things to your bedroom. Put things where you would like. I'll bring the boxes in a minute."

Emily retreated to her room, and Thomas sank down onto the sofa, burying his head in his hands and uttering a desperate silent prayer. *Oh, God, what am I to do? This little girl needs so much more than I can give her. Direct my paths. Help me know how to move forward.*

Thomas had decided a while back that he didn't want to have a family of his own. His *Dat* hadn't been the best paternal figure. So often in Amish families, fathers were like his own—legalistic, harsh, and distant. Thomas didn't want to subject a child to that. Never mind the fact that to become a father would require him to become a husband first. He knew that was something he didn't want. Again, *Dat* was the closest example of a husband he had known, and even Thomas knew that *Mem* had spent her entire married life in fear of *Dat*'s moodiness and judgment.

He shook his head. *Ne*, he wasn't meant to be a family man. He had an obligation to take care of Emily, but he wondered if she wouldn't be better off with a father and mother who could give her a stable, loving family.

One like Anna Ruth had provided.

Again, the grief of losing his sister washed over Thomas. Even though she had been gone from his life for twelve years, knowing now that he would never see her again made the sorrow even more intense. All those wasted years they'd spent apart. If only he had stood up to *Dat* or gone after Anna Ruth when she left. But he had been a young boy, and *Dat* . . . *Ne*, opposing him then was unthinkable.

"Uncle Thomas?" Would he ever get used to that name? "I need my baby dolls. They are in that box."

Thomas picked up the box Emily Grace pointed to and followed her into the bedroom. He used his pocketknife to cut the tape then began pulling the dolls out one by one, laying them across the bed.

"No, no, Uncle. Not like that! Molly needs to be beside Kit, not Kirsten!" The little girl corrected Thomas's errors and fussed with the dolls. She whispered to them as she placed them in the right spots, giving hugs and kisses as she went along.

Thomas smiled. Plain dolls were different than *Englisch* ones. Amish didn't give their dolls faces, and of course, they were homemade. Still, he remembered being very young and seeing Anna Ruth mother her rag doll in this same way. Watching Emily was like being transported back in time twenty years.

There were still a couple of boxes left to unpack. Thomas opened them and consulted Emily as to where to put those items. Soon, the room looked like a little girl lived there. Emily's *Englisch* toys and clothes contrasted with the simple furnishings of the cabin. Emily would stand out just as severely if she stayed with him in West Kootenai. He was going to need some help with her clothes and hair if she was going to fit in at all.

"What time is supper, Uncle Thomas? My belly is grumbly!" Emily announced.

Supper. He hadn't thought about picking up some food when they were at the store. He berated himself for not being better prepared.

"I don't have anything to eat, Emily." He looked at his niece, noting the exasperation in her eyes.

"Well, duh! I bet Miss Lovina does!"

And with that, Emily ran out the door of the little cabin and made a beeline straight toward the Graber house.

Chapter Six

TUESDAY, AUGUST 15

The whole way home from the store, Lovina rehearsed her explanation for the sudden appearance of Thomas and Emily. *Mem* and *Dat* had grown quite accustomed to accommodating her projects. She knew *Mem* and *Dat* would support her offer of lodging and help, but she didn't want them— or anyone else—to get the wrong idea about her motives. Sure, Thomas was a handsome, single Amish man, but that's not why she stepped up to help him. *Mem* would understand, Lovina hoped.

After leaving Thomas and Emily at the cabin, Lovina entered her house breathlessly, crumpling into a chair at the kitchen table with Gus collapsing at her feet. Her mother stood at the sink, washing the leftover lunch dishes as well as those she had used to prepare dinner. The scent of meatloaf wafted from the oven and made Lovina's mouth water.

"Where on earth have you been, Lovina? I expected you home an hour ago! And did I hear a car pull in?" *Mem* wiped her soapy hands off on her apron and sank into the chair across from Lovina.

"I had to go to the store to mail my column, and you'll never believe what happened while I was there." Lovina launched into telling the story of the afternoon's shocking events.

Her mother nodded along as Lovina relayed the details. Storytelling was one of Lovina's gifts, and this was such a wonderful story! *Oncle* and *niesse*, estranged for years, brought together through tragic circumstances.

"And you told them they could stay in the cabin?" *Mem* chuckled.

"Oh, *Mem*! It has been vacant for weeks since Mr. Fisher moved out. And you will adore Emily! She's so sweet and wonderful with Gus. Besides, Mr. Smucker couldn't take her up to stay in the bachelor cabins. Can you imagine?"

"It's not a problem. I'm sure your father will agree as well. But I thought you'd decided to commit to fewer projects, especially since you've taken on writing for *The Budget*. I don't want to see you stretch yourself too thin."

She did have a lot on her plate right now, between writing for *The Budget*, helping *Mem* and *Dat* around the house and at the tree farm, working in her garden, sewing and crocheting, and making her visits around the community. Not to mention, harvest season was in full swing and she would be canning vegetables and making jams and jellies soon. Christmas tree season would kick into high gear in November. And of course, there was her advice column, which she still couldn't bring herself to tell *Mem* about. However, when it came to inviting Mr. Smucker and Emily to stay in the cabin, she couldn't stop herself.

"I know, *Mem*. I don't know how to explain it to you other than to tell you it was a God nudge."

When Lovina and her sisters were little girls, *Mem* had always told them when they didn't know what to do in a situation, they should ask God for help and then wait for a "nudge" from Him to move. It was *Mem*'s way of teaching them to obey the Holy Spirit, and it had served Lovina well. Her intervention today was nothing short of divinely inspired.

"Well, when God nudges, we need to move. Whatever He has planned for us will be good. Now, we just need to get out of the way and let Him do it." *Mem*'s gentle laughter filled the room.

"Do you need help getting anything ready for supper?" Lovina felt guilty for lingering at the store longer than she'd intended. Though *Mem* was more than competent to prepare dinner single-handedly, Lovina loved to help. They shared some of their best times in the kitchen. But if she was perfectly honest, she was also bursting to write down today's events in her journal while they were fresh in her mind.

"*Ach*, no. All that's left to do is mash the potatoes, and I'll do that when your *dat* comes in from the barn so they don't get cold. You've got a few minutes to rest if you'd like. I can tell that your hip is troubling you. I'll call you when it's dinnertime."

Relieved, Lovina headed upstairs to her bedroom. While her leg did ache, she relished a few minutes to unwind from the excitement of the afternoon, and she wanted to write. That was the best way she knew to process things. When she couldn't find the words to speak, Lovina wrote.

Beyond a hobby, it was her outlet for the thoughts she kept bottled up so tightly. Sometimes, it was even a means of worship. Now that she wrote for *The Budget*, she also thought of it as another of her ministries.

Lovina scribbled down the details of the afternoon in her journal as quickly as she could. Then she went back with a highlighter and identified parts that she'd want to include in her next column. She already had a couple of sentences running around in her mind. *Mr. Thomas Smucker, formerly of Belleville, Pennsylvania, welcomed his niece, Miss Emily Grace Spencer, formerly of Cincinnati, Ohio. Emily will be staying with Mr. Smucker as guests of the Graber family.*

Did that sound too proud? Her *dat* had pointed out that, in the past, sometimes her columns told more about the good deeds she did than the people she helped, so she tried hard to avoid that.

She didn't mention that she'd volunteered to give them a place to stay, so it passed that test.

Was it too gossipy? She'd left out the whole dead sister story and didn't tell about the huge scene in the store. Plenty of locals had witnessed that, and out-of-towners didn't need to know.

Satisfied she had captured enough of the story to make it worth sharing, she flipped to the back of her journal where she kept a prayer log. She closed her eyes and after a moment of silence, began to write.

> *Oh, Lord. Mr. Smucker's whole world has turned upside down today. And Emily Grace—she's so full of sadness for such a little girl. God, if I can carry some of their burdens, show me how. You nudged me to invite them to stay here. I trust that You'll keep nudging me when they need me. In Your Son's name, amen.*

A knocking on the front door startled Lovina, and her eyes opened. She scrambled to get up from her chair and tuck her journal away before lumbering back down the stairs. Before she could even descend the steps, though, she heard a commotion and knew who her visitors were.

"Come here, Gus! You are a good boy! Yes you are!" Emily's enthusiastic praise for Gus brought joy to Lovina's ears.

As Lovina ambled down the stairs, she imagined that Gus was lavishing his typical enthusiastic kisses on the little girl. Before she reached the foyer where *Mem* stood greeting the pair, she heard Thomas's sharp words scolding Emily to leave the dog alone.

"I hope you two found everything you needed in the cabin." Lovina forced herself to sound upbeat, interrupting Thomas as he needlessly rebuked the little girl. He seemed taken aback by her cheerful interjection.

"Oh, it's fine, and I do appreciate you inviting us to stay until we can get our situation figured out. I hate to ask for anything else since you've already been so generous, but Emily is hungry, and I didn't think to pick up any food before we left the store. And I need to go up to the bachelor cabin and pick up my belongings too. I hate to impose upon you anymore, but could she stay for supper while I take care of some business?" Thomas swallowed.

Mem answered quickly. "It is no trouble at all. We have plenty of food, and I can't wait to get to know Miss Emily. I've heard so much about you already."

The little girl eyed *Mem* suspiciously. "Are you Miss Lovina's mother?"

"Why, *ja*, I am. You can call me Mrs. Graber or Mrs. Rose, whichever you like best."

Emily's eyes crinkled into a smile. "I like Mrs. Rose. What are you having for supper? I'm starving!"

Mem laughed at the little girl's bluntness. "Me too. We have to wait for Mr. Henry to finish his work before we can eat, but I could use your help in the kitchen. Are you a good cook?"

Emily giggled. "I just turned five! I don't know how to cook."

"Would you like to learn? I need someone to help me put butter in the potatoes while I mash them. Can you do that?"

Emily nodded and followed *Mem* into the kitchen.

"I think they are going to get along fine and dandy." Lovina grinned.

Thomas sobered quickly. "I do hate to ask you and your family for so much, Miss Graber. I promise I will repay this kindness." He removed his hat, smoothed his sandy blond hair back, then turned the hat over in his hands. The hard edge he had held when she first met him, and even earlier today, had melted. Right now, he appeared vulnerable, tenderhearted even.

Compassion overwhelmed her. A breath caught in Lovina's throat, and she struggled to eek out words. "It is no trouble at all. And please, call me Lovina."

"Lovina," he repeated, letting her name hang in the air

between them. "Only if you call me Thomas. I appreciate this. It shouldn't take me long to get my things from the camp and pick up a few snacks at the store. I guess she will need something for breakfast and lunch tomorrow too. Tomorrow . . . Oh no!" His shoulders slumped.

"What's wrong?" Lovina asked.

"I have to go to work tomorrow. She can't go to the Log Works with me. It's too dangerous for her. I need to let my boss know I won't be coming in tomorrow, or at least until I find a better place for her during the day." Thomas rubbed his forehead and replaced the hat on his head.

"She can stay with us." The words escaped Lovina's mouth before the thought fully formed in her brain. In fact, Lovina felt a bit like a ventriloquist's dummy. Her lips were moving and making sounds, but those words came from somewhere else.

"I can't ask you to do that on top of everything else," he replied, but Lovina put her hand up to stop him.

"I won't take no for an answer." She fixed her eyes on him. "Emily needs some stability in her life, and I can provide that during the day. *Mem* will love having a little one around. We'll help her learn more about the Plain life. We can take one more thing off your plate. Please let us."

Thomas squirmed under Lovina's stare. He released a deep breath and nodded. "Fine, fine. But I will repay you for this."

He smiled rather solemnly, revealing the dimples she'd noticed the first night they met. Lovina's heart gave a little jump, which she promptly ignored.

Lovina sent him on his way to the bachelor cabin to retrieve his belongings. She headed to the kitchen to help *Mem* finish dinner and found Emily sitting at the table, completely engrossed in her task of buttering and mashing potatoes.

"Look, Miss Lovina, I'm cooking!" Emily flashed a gap-toothed smile at Lovina.

She looked so out of place in this Plain kitchen. *Mem* had wrapped an apron around her, covering her princess T-shirt and tattered denim jeans, but her uncovered scraggly hair hung midway down her back, so unlike Lovina's and *Mem*'s neatly covered buns.

Lovina settled into the chair next to the girl, warmth filling her chest at the sight. "I see that. Do you like mashed potatoes?"

"I love them. And these will be the best-est because I made them." Emily jutted out her chin.

Mem smiled from the stove where she stirred a cooker full of peas. Lovina joined her.

"I told Thomas that Emily could stay here while he's at work. I hope that's okay."

"My dear girl, this is not something you need permission to do. Remember that 'God nudge' you had? That's all the permission you need. We'll support you along the way. I suspect that the Lord has placed these people in your life for a purpose. Now you just need to follow Him and see how He works it all out."

Lovina thanked God for her supportive family. She really did need to tell them about her advice column—keeping that secret weighed heavy on her heart.

She opened a cabinet and pulled out five dinner plates to place on the table. As she fell into the familiar routine of setting the table, she fought against the swell of doubts forming in her mind. She was a helper—God had made it plain that she wasn't meant to be a wife or mother, but she could always serve others with a generous heart.

Years ago, she'd made a begrudging peace with that plan for her to remain single, though it still stung sometimes. It didn't mean she couldn't be a friend to someone in need, just like she was to everyone she met. She just needed to remember not to grow too attached to Emily, or to Thomas for that matter. Yes, helping Thomas and Emily get acquainted with one another was her first priority.

Her second, maybe the more difficult one, was to guard her heart.

Chapter Seven

Thomas shuffled around the Log Works like a sleepwalker. Just like he had the last two days. Each night, he'd tossed and turned on the cabin's living room sofa, too much on his mind to sleep soundly. He would have loved to pray, but words escaped him. When he did manage to doze off, dreams of the past plagued him, along with worries about his future. Anna Ruth was dead. Her daughter, his responsibility.

This couldn't be real.

The raucous laughter from the bachelors he was working with, combined with a lack of sleep, made his head throb. He envied the carefree lives of the other guys—what he had envisioned for himself when he moved here. Now, such a life would be out of his reach.

Should he try to find a better home for Emily? That shouldn't be too hard—anything would be better than having to live with him. He wandered into the break room and flopped into a chair, his head in his hands, as he tried to reclaim a steady breathing rhythm.

A voice in the hallway called his name. Ike Sommers? Ike was just the person he needed to see. He raced into the hallway hoping to catch Ike before he left.

"Ike, can I talk to you for a moment?"

"*Ach*, sure thing. In fact, I came here to see you."

"You saw all that mess in the store the other day. What am I going to do?" Thomas led Ike back into the break room and sat down at a table.

Ike shifted his weight from one boot to the other as he filled a Styrofoam cup with stale *kaffe*. "Slow down. I saw what happened but I'm still pretty confused. You'd better start from the beginning and tell me everything."

Thomas took a deep breath before launching into his account of Tuesday afternoon's events. Ike joined him at the table. His eyes grew wider with each additional detail Thomas revealed. When Thomas got to the part of the story about moving into the Grabers' cabin with Emily Grace, Ike's hand reached up to cover his mouth, as if trying to stifle a laugh.

"Son, that is some mess you are in, but it sounds like the Lord provided just what you needed. He sent Lovina Graber to help. She's the most kind-hearted and efficient person I know. She'll make sure Emily is well cared for, and she'll help you with all the custody details too. You are in good hands."

Thomas considered Ike's words for a moment. He'd been so overwhelmed that he hadn't stopped to consider how well God had provided for him and Emily Grace. He certainly hadn't taken a moment to show the Lord some gratitude. Thomas ought to be ashamed of himself.

But at the moment, a bigger dilemma consumed his thoughts.

"Ike, I don't know what I'm going to do. I am not cut out to be a *dat*. I can't raise a little girl. Where do I go from here?" Thomas eeked out the words as he ground his teeth together.

Ike put his hand on Thomas's shoulder. "Well, let's look at your options. You've got a place to stay and people who will help you with your niece, so you don't have to make any quick decisions. It comes down to two things—you keep her and raise her, or you find someone else who will."

Ike dispensed logical, godly wisdom through plain talk, but hearing the choices put so bluntly cut through Thomas's gut. Neither option sounded possible, but Ike was right—those were his choices.

Thomas rose and paced the concrete floor. The silence hung heavy between the two men, as Thomas weighed the different sides of his situation. Maybe Ike could help him figure out what to do, but he sure hated to bother anyone else with his problems. Already he'd inconvenienced the Grabers more than he would have liked.

"So, what are you thinking, Thomas?" Ike cut straight to the point.

Thomas sighed deeply. "I think Emily needs a real home. She needs to feel safe, and she needs someone who can raise her right. I can keep her safe. I can feed her and provide for her, but I just don't know that I can give her the kind of life Anna Ruth would have wanted."

"Why is that? You said your *schwester* wrote instructions for Emily to live with you. She knew you would be a *gut* man. Sure, learning to raise a little girl will take some effort, but you're a hard worker. What makes you think you wouldn't make a good *dat*?"

Ike's straightforward question cut through Thomas like a hot knife through butter. Thomas could think of at least twenty reasons right off the top of his head, but he wasn't sure how much he wanted Ike to know about his past. He decided to keep his answer brief—and vague.

Thomas cleared his throat. "I never had much of a role model growing up. As you can see, my *schwester* left the Amish and that was because of the way my *dat* raised her. I wouldn't want to pass that on to her little girl."

Ike's eyebrows furrowed. "But she picked you, right? She wanted you to be the one to raise her daughter if anything happened to her."

"I still don't understand that. Why me? She wrote me a letter, but I haven't had time to read it yet." Thomas rubbed where the tension had settled in his forehead.

"Perhaps that's what you need to find out—read the letter and pray on it. Take your time and don't make any decisions before you've really listened to what God has to say."

Thomas nodded, but without conviction. "Another thing that worries me is that she's an *Englisch* child. She won't fit in here. She doesn't know our ways. Anna Ruth left the Amish world behind. I can't imagine she would want Emily to be raised Plain."

Again, Ike simply nodded, giving Thomas time to collect his thoughts.

"But I believe the Amish ways are right. If I had a daughter, that's how I would raise her. Not that I planned on having *kinner* . . ." Thomas trailed off, then cut his eyes to Ike. "Aren't you going to jump in here, Ike?"

Ike shot Thomas a sheepish grin. "Sounded like you were working it out on your own, my friend."

"I could use your input. If you were in this position, how would you handle it?"

"Like I said, I'd give it a little time," Ike responded thoughtfully. "All of this is new to you. It's new to Emily too. It might be wise to take things slow. Don't make any decisions right away. Be a safe place for Emily now, and seek the Lord's will in this situation. Whatever you decide to do, I will support you. I'll be praying about it too. Look at it this way—you have a duty to your family, and you will have to decide the best way to fulfill that." Ike grimaced as he swallowed the dregs of coffee in the cup he'd been nursing.

Duty. That word set off alarm bells in Thomas's head.

His *dat* had always emphasized that a *gut* Amish man honored his responsibilities to provide for his family. For now, that looked like Thomas taking care of Emily himself—at least until the Lord showed him another way.

Thomas folded his hands and took a deep breath. "I will seek the Lord's will in this. That's *gut* advice, Ike. You are right. It may be too soon to make a decision, but I can't help but feel completely unqualified to be a *dat*. I just don't know how to raise a child, especially an *Englisch* girl. However, I know that it is my duty to care for her right now."

"If this doesn't work out for you to keep Emily, where would she go?"

Thomas winced. "The social worker said the state would take her into foster care or place her in a group home." That wasn't what he wanted for his niece. That definitely wasn't what Anna Ruth would have wanted either.

Thomas bit the inside of his cheek, pondering an idea that had occurred to him during one of his bouts of insomnia last night. "Do you suppose we could find a *gut* Plain family to raise her? I'd like to have her nearby and be part of her life. That is, if things don't work out for me to keep her." Just hearing himself say the words sent a pang through his heart.

Ike rubbed his chin. "*Ja*, I'll pray on that too, Thomas. Maybe the Lord will point us to the right family. In the meantime, enjoy getting to know your niece. Let the Grabers help you. Pray for strength and guidance from God. That's all anyone can do right now." He rose from the table and nodded goodbye to Thomas.

Thomas sat a few more moments, weighing Ike's advice.

Ike was right. He didn't have to make a decision about the future today. All he had to do was his duty—love Emily and make her feel safe. He had been raised to be obedient to what the Bible commanded, and somewhere in his mind he could recall a verse about caring for the orphans. That's what he would do until the Lord showed him otherwise.

Chapter Eight

FRIDAY, AUGUST 18

T he clock above the sink in the Grabers' kitchen showed half past four. Lovina finished cleaning the kitchen countertops and wiped her hands on the dish towel before folding it and placing it on the side of the sink. She turned the burner on the gas stove down so that the stew could simmer until dinner time, and she preheated the oven for the biscuits she and Emily had rolled and cut. The rich aroma of the stew wafted through the kitchen.

She stretched and twisted her back to release the tension she held, then glanced down at the little girl beside her. *Mem* and *Dat* had joined them for lunch but had since returned to the tree farm to finish up some work, so it was just the two of them in the house now.

"Emily, you did a *wunderbar* job drying the dishes. I appreciate your help. Now that we have that chore taken care of, let's see if *Mem* left any cookies in the jar that we can have for dessert."

The little girl's face lit up.

Lovina stretched to reach the cookie jar atop the refrigerator, nearly stumbling as she pulled it down.

"Miss Lovina, what happened to your face?" Emily's question was blunt, but her voice held a tender edge to it.

Her hand instinctively covered the puckered magenta blotch that marred the left side of her face. Lovina swallowed hard before answering. As much as she tried to pretend the scar didn't bother her, deep in her heart, shame still kept its grip. "When I was not much older than you, my twin sister had a little accident with the fire, and I got burned."

"Oh, no! My mommy always said not to get close to fire." Emily's eyes were wide with concern for Lovina. She scrunched her nose up. "Did you stop, drop, and roll? That's what we learned at preschool."

"That's exactly right! You are a smart girl. I did stop, drop, and roll and that kept me from getting any other burns on my body." Lovina rubbed at the blotch on her cheek as she finished the story.

"What about your leg?" Emily probed. "Did that happen in the fire too?"

Lovina had fielded many questions about her leg over the years. She hated drawing attention to her shortcomings. It brought back terrible memories of her school days, when other *kinner* always liked to point out her differences and all the things she couldn't do. Somehow, though, Emily's earnest innocence compelled her to share more than she normally might.

"No, I was born like this. I have one short leg."

Emily scanned Lovina from head to toe, as though trying to figure out what to make of that new information. Finally, a worried look crossed her face. "I thought it was bad that I had two short legs. I can't imagine just having one!"

Lovina grinned, glad for the levity in the conversation. "I didn't mean that I just have one leg. I meant that one of my legs is shorter than the other." Lovina hitched up the bottom of her dress to prove that she had two fully intact legs.

Emily looked relieved. "How did it get that way?"

"We aren't sure. At first, when I was a *boppli*, it wasn't as noticeable but once I began toddling around, *Mem* could tell that I struggled. I started seeing a doctor and a physical therapist. I wear a special shoe that is supposed to help even out my leg length, but I still limp."

She gestured to Emily to take a seat at the table then plopped down across from the girl.

Emily took a cookie and munched on it. "Does it hurt?"

"My back and hips ache when I walk a lot. Other than that, I'm used to it." And she was used to the pain, the pitying glances, the shame she felt for being different.

"My mommy said that God made us all different, with special gifts," Emily proclaimed, then fell silent. Her bottom lip began to quiver and her eyes welled up with tears.

"Oh, sweet girl. You miss your mommy so much, don't you?" Lovina wrapped her arms around the child. Gus, who had been curled up under the kitchen table asleep after feasting on scraps Emily had fed him, woke with a start and nuzzled into the embrace as well.

Emily sniffled. "I know that she and Daddy are in heaven, and I can see them again, but I wish they were here now. I miss them. I miss my house and my friends too." The floodgates opened again.

As Lovina held Emily, her heart broke for the little girl's many losses.

Her mind drifted back to Thomas Smucker. He'd told her he was an only child, which maybe wasn't technically a lie—as his *schwester* had been as good as dead to his family when she left the Amish. He had grieved her once before and now would grieve her again. Briefly, Lovina wondered what would have prompted Anna Ruth to leave her Amish ways, but she shook that aside and instead allowed a swell of compassion for Emily and Thomas to overtake her thoughts.

After Emily had seemed to run out of tears, Lovina patted her on the knee. "I have an idea. Let's get your face washed and then, how about I braid your hair for you?"

Emily nodded. "Is your hair braided under that hat thing?"

Lovina smiled. "This is called a *kapp*."

She carefully removed the head covering to show Emily that her hair was in a bun, then quickly pinned it back in place.

"Why do you wear it? Doesn't it get hot and itchy?"

"Sometimes," Lovina admitted with a shrug. "I've always worn one, so I am used to it. The Bible says for women to cover their heads when we pray, which we are also to do without ceasing, and the Amish take that very seriously."

"Is that why you wear funny clothes too?" Emily's inquisitive nature and blunt vocabulary might have annoyed some people, but Lovina found her intelligent and endearing.

"We call our style of dress and our way of living Plain," Lovina explained, walking to the sink to wet a washcloth for Emily to use on her face. "Different Amish churches have slightly different ideas about exactly how we should dress, but all of us agree that our clothes should be modest and practical and they should set us apart from the rest of the world."

Lovina returned to the table and pulled a brush out of her tote bag. She parted Emily's hair to make even braids on each side of the girl's head.

"Do you think I'll have to wear dresses like yours now that I'm living here?"

Lovina paused, unsure of how to answer. If Emily lived with Thomas, she would follow Amish traditions. However, it wasn't Lovina's place to make the rules for Emily. "That's something for your *Oncle* Thomas to decide. I bet we can order some pretty fabric to make your dresses." She deftly laced the three strands of hair on the right side of Emily's head into a tight braid and secured it with a rubber band.

Emily's eyes lit up with excitement. "Can we make matching dresses for my dolls too?"

"I'm sure we can. Now, your hair looks very *gut*. I think your *oncle* will be pleased. Let's go to the other room. There's a red book on the shelf there. It is full of good stories if you would like to hear one."

Emily and Lovina pushed their chairs in and moved into the living room, where Emily found the book. The two settled in on the well-worn couch. Gus followed them, making himself at home on the sofa too.

Before long, the back door screeched open. *Mem* and *Dat* returned from their afternoon chores. She could hear them washing up in the kitchen.

Dat joined them in the living room and sat in the wooden rocker across from them. "Those braids look right pretty on you, Miss Emily. Reminds me of how Lovina used to fix her *schwesters'* hair when they were girls."

"What's a shew-es-ter?" Emily tried to imitate *Dat's* use of the Pennsylvania Dutch term, her faint lisp making her mispronunciation even cuter.

Lovina giggled. "It means sister."

"You have more sisters? Lucky you!" Emily exclaimed.

"I have a twin, Josie, who I told you about, and three other *schwesters*. Most of them are married now." Lovina held up her hand and counted off a finger for each sister. "The oldest is Amanda. She's twenty-seven and lives in Michigan. Josie lives in Kentucky. Melanie is twenty-three and she lives in Indiana. And Geneva is nineteen, and she's gone to help Melanie because Melanie just had a baby boy!"

Emily's eyes widened in awe. "Wow! Five girls make a big family."

"Sure does!" *Dat* agreed, a twinkle in his eyes. "Why, sometimes, I would spend the whole day in the barn just to get a moment of quiet."

"Now, Henry Graber, you know those girls were a blessing from the Lord!" *Mem* entered the room with a giggle. She swatted *Dat* with a rolled-up copy of *The Budget* before handing the newspaper to

Lovina. "I just finished reading this week's copy. There were some good recipes in Maudie's column, as usual, and a hilarious story about a husband and wife trying to catch a mouse, except the wife pepper-sprayed the husband in the eyes when she aimed for the mouse."

"Pepper spray?" *Dat* wheezed with laughter. "Why on earth would someone try to catch a mouse with pepper spray?"

Mem shrugged. "You'll have to read it and see, won't you? Be sure to read Lovina's column too. She wrote a nice story about the Milners and their *Englisch* guest."

Lovina suppressed a smile and tucked the newspaper in beside her, her cheeks burning. She ducked her head at her mother's praise. *Pride goeth before destruction, and a haughty spirit before a fall*, she reminded herself.

"Oh, and that Western Wildflower wrote another advice column," *Mem* said. "This time there was a letter asking for remedies for morning sickness. The answer was peppermint tea and ginger chews. Sounded like something Lovina would say."

Lovina's heart dropped to her stomach. They published another advice column this week.

She stared at the floor, avoiding eye contact with *Mem*. Did she suspect that Lovina was the Western Wildflower? How would she react if she found out the truth?

"Maybe this Western Wildflower can advise folks not to use pepper spray to catch a mouse," *Dat* responded, still catching his breath after his laughing spell.

Lovina managed a nervous laugh, but the burden of her secret filled her with anxiety. Maybe it was time to tell her parents the truth about the Western Wildflower.

"*Mem* and *Dat*, I, uh—"

A knock sounded on the front door and Thomas entered the room. He removed his hat but fidgeted with it as he shifted from side to side, as if he were unsure of how to take up space in the room.

"Ahem." He cleared his throat, but that didn't stifle the

gruffness in his voice. "Hello, everyone. I appreciate you taking care of Emily again. Emily, did you behave for Miss Graber?"

Lovina's eyes shifted to Emily, who was lying on the floor coloring. Lovina spoke up, proud to give an excellent report. "As always, she was a perfect little lady."

Thomas breathed a sigh of relief. Lovina noticed the dark circles under his eyes. Stress plagued all of his features.

"Yes, indeed!" *Dat* proclaimed. "Why, we've had a lovely time with Emily. She's been a big help—rolling out biscuit dough and washing dishes." He rubbed his round stomach in delight.

Emily beamed with pride at *Dat*'s words. How desperately the little girl needed to feel wanted and loved. All the loss and upheaval Emily had endured must have devastated her sense of security. She needed to experience normal life again.

Suddenly, Lovina's heart swelled in her chest, and she knew exactly why God had put her in the pathway of this man and his *niesse*.

The task the Lord required of her wouldn't be easy. She'd have to put her own preconceptions and feelings aside, but she was used to that by now. She was a helper, and this situation required her best effort, for Thomas's sake and Emily's too.

Lovina needed to help Thomas find a wife.

Chapter Nine

The letter Thomas had tucked into his back pocket weighed heavily on his mind. He had put off reading it since Emily had arrived last Tuesday, but over a week had passed and he had run out of excuses.

For Thomas, the last week and a half had been about survival. He and Emily still didn't know each other well enough for their routines to become natural. The small cabin seemed to close in on the two of them as they did a delicate dance, wary of one another and never sure of how close was too close to get to each other.

Emily had begged to stay with Lovina this morning, which freed Thomas to spend the day on his own.

He couldn't say he blamed Emily. Spending time with Lovina was like being wrapped in a warm blanket on a cold winter's night. Her kindness and thoughtfulness soothed both Thomas and Emily, and her beautiful, brown eyes held compassion and understanding.

Still, the tension he'd carried in his body had built up, and he needed a good hike to let it go.

The late summer air held a slight chill, promising cooler

weather coming soon. He breathed in the fresh, clean pine scent that permeated everything near the West Kootenai Christmas Tree Farm and followed the trail Henry Graber had pointed out to him this morning.

With each step, he felt his burdens lightening.

He focused on the beauty surrounding him—the lush evergreens, the worn dirt under his feet, and the stunning blue sky that peeked through the trees. In all the chaos of the past weeks, Thomas realized he'd neglected to be grateful for the gifts the Lord had given him.

The rhythm of his footfalls became a silent prayer—*thank You, thank You, thank You.* He climbed higher and higher until he finally reached an overlook where he could view the mountains and expansive blue sky in all its glory.

He sat down on a rock to admire the view and pulled a handkerchief from his pocket to wipe away the beads of sweat that had popped up despite the cooler morning temperatures.

He took a long draw from his water bottle. Gazing out over the trees below and the sky above, he marveled at God's artistry.

Despite the sudden turn his life had taken, he was glad he'd come to Montana.

After resting for a moment, Thomas reached into his back pocket and withdrew the envelope the social worker had given him containing the letter from his sister. These were the first words he had heard from her in twelve years, and they would also be the last. A breath caught in his chest.

Why did Anna Ruth choose me to raise Emily?

There was only one way to find out.

Thomas slid his finger under the flap and loosened the glue. He unfolded the letter, written in Anna Ruth's neat script.

Dear Thomas,

If you are reading this letter, I have gone on to heaven and have left Emily in your care. I know you have a million questions and I'll try to answer those as well as I can.

One of the hardest things I ever had to do was to leave you behind when I left Belleville. I knew I was leaving you to endure the abuse Dat had heaped on me for seventeen years, and for that, I am truly sorry. I always meant to come back for you once I settled somewhere. I wrote letters to you, but you never responded, so I figured Dat had kept those from you.

Please forgive me for leaving you there.

You've probably wondered how I managed to get away. If you remember, I had been babysitting for the Troyer family and giving most of my money to Dat as he demanded. Sometimes I also worked for an Englisch family, the Bradburys, who Dat didn't know about. They paid better than the Troyers, and they had a computer I used to plan my escape.

Once I had saved up enough money and had everything in place, I left the first chance I had.

Dat and I had fought about something—it's funny that I don't even remember what now—and I just bolted out of there. I'm sorry I didn't say goodbye, but I'll never be sorry for leaving.

The Englisch world always held a certain mystery to me. Dat made it seem so forbidden and dark. As a seventeen-year-old girl who knew so little, leaving the familiarity of the Amish world terrified me, but I knew that life in Belleville with Dat would crush my soul.

When I left, I found love and acceptance and healing.

I went to the Englisch family I babysat for and they helped me get to Pittsburgh. From there, I took a bus to Cincinnati, where the Bradburys had relatives who would help me get a fresh start. It was far enough away that Dat wouldn't find me there, if he bothered to look for me at all, but also not so far that I couldn't get back to Belleville if I changed my mind.

When I arrived in Cincinnati, I was angry. I rejected the Amish teachings I had grown up with and made a new life for myself. I earned my GED, started community college, and got a job. God began to soften my heart and heal my anger and I found an Englisch church where I met a wonderful man. Gabe Spencer and I married shortly after my twenty-second birthday. A few years later, we had Emily Grace.

You are probably still wondering why I want you to care for Emily in the event that something happens to both Gabe and me.

Gabe has no living family to speak of and we want Emily to know her only uncle. Though I rejected the Amish life, I don't disagree with everything the church stands for. As I've grown in my faith, I appreciate the simplicity and devotion that Plain people exhibit. I just couldn't stay in Belleville where I had to face Dat's judgment every day.

Thomas, your heart is kind. You are not like our father. You love nature and stories, and so does Emily.

While I hope that you will never need to see this letter and I will be able to raise Emily, if I am not, I can't imagine anyone who would make a better father for her.

Raise her in the church, Thomas, but when she is old enough to choose, support whatever decision she makes. I know it is possible to live outside the Amish church and still have a life that honors God. I also know there are good, kind people within the church. I want you to support her in whatever life she chooses.

I hope you can forgive me for disappearing from your life all those years ago. Please know that I wanted to see you, but I knew Dat wouldn't allow it, and I thought I could protect you from his wrath by staying as far away as I could.

I love you, brother. I always have. I am entrusting you with my greatest treasure because I know you are the right person to care for her.

Remind her every day that her daddy and I loved her. Raise her to be thoughtful and compassionate, creative and kind. Show her how God's love shines through into even the darkest spaces.

Love,

Anna Ruth

After reading it several times, Thomas turned the letter over and over in his hands. Anna Ruth had written it less than a year ago. Not long after *Mem* had passed away. How Thomas wished that *Mem* could have known Emily, that she could be here now with him as he tried to care for his niece.

Thomas had never allowed himself to dwell on Anna Ruth's leaving. *Dat* would never permit them to discuss it, so Thomas had just stuffed all the questions and sorrow deep inside. But now, reading this letter, it all came surging back.

Life at the Smucker home had been turbulent.

Dat's constant demands for perfection created tension for everyone, but somehow, it grated like sandpaper on Anna Ruth. *Mem* and Thomas strove to keep the peace, but they could do little to intervene when *Dat* and Anna Ruth tangled. The older she got, the more severe his criticism became and the wider her rebellious streak grew.

How could she possibly trust Thomas to care for her daughter when he was to blame for her leaving in the first place?

He folded the letter up, stuck it in his pocket, and made his way back down the hill to the Graber home.

Chapter Ten

"I win again!" Emily squealed, startling Gus, who dozed at her feet.

"Are you sure you aren't cheating? I thought I had a great memory, but I can't beat you," Lovina returned with a smile.

Lovina and Emily made a great team. All morning long, the two worked together to prepare sandwiches, cookies, and a fruit salad to take for tomorrow's after-church lunch. They tidied the kitchen, swept and dusted the living room, and still had time to play Emily's favorite memory matching game before Thomas returned from his hike.

"I can help you, Lovie. It's not a hard game. You just have to put the pictures on the cards into your brain." Emily held one of the small cards against her forehead, closing her eyes tightly as if she could absorb the image through her skull.

Lovina marveled at the intelligence of the little girl sitting across from her. She hadn't started school yet back home in Cincinnati, but she already knew her alphabet and numbers and could read and write many words.

She could have started school with the Amish children, but Thomas thought that might be a bit overwhelming, so he allowed her to stay home with Lovina. When she did start next fall, she would be leaps and bounds ahead of the other scholars.

"Let's get this game cleaned up and then we can work on some sewing and mending. Have you ever sewn before?" Lovina hated asking Emily questions about her past but sometimes she had to be direct to get the information she needed.

Emily shook her head. Her greenish-blue eyes, so much like Thomas's, lit up. "Are we making doll clothes?"

"Not today," Lovina replied. "Today we're just going to fix some buttons that have come off and things like that. I'll tell you what, though. Tonight, I will show you how to crochet and you can make a doll blanket."

While Emily put the game away, Lovina retrieved her sewing basket. The two met back in the living room and settled in on the couch. Lovina showed Emily how to thread a needle and gave her a scrap piece of fabric to practice her stitches on.

After a few minutes, Lovina looked up to realize that Emily had dozed off. Lovina removed the sewing square from her small hands and covered Emily with a blanket.

Lovina gazed down at Emily, her heart melting with each rise and fall of the little girl's chest. How life had changed for this child in such a short time. Lovina lamented every loss Emily had suffered, wishing she could take the little girl's pain away with a simple hug. All she could do, however, was love Emily and help her heal.

The sound of the back door opening and closing signaled that Thomas had returned from his hike.

Lovina moved into the kitchen to warn him that Emily was napping. She found him at the sink washing his hands and staring out the window.

"Emily is asleep, Thomas," Lovina whispered. "Do you want a snack or a drink?"

Thomas shook his head but didn't speak.

Thick silence filled the room as Thomas stood stiffly with his hands shoved into his pockets, shoulders pulled up next to his ears, and his jaw set in place. His green-blue eyes had gone dark and narrow.

Lovina was usually good at sensing what others needed from her, but she had never seen Thomas look so burdened.

"Have a seat here and I'll make you a cup of tea," she offered. She figured the warm liquid might thaw the hardness that had overtaken Thomas's posture.

Thomas wordlessly removed his jacket and slid into a seat at the Grabers' dining table. Lovina bustled about the kitchen preparing the tea, but she kept watch on Thomas out of the corner of her eye.

"This is one of my special blends." Lovina brought the teapot and cups over to the table and sat down across from him. "I grow raspberries and dry the leaves, then mix them with some hibiscus and dandelion petals. It will need to steep a couple more minutes. Let me know what you think."

"You make your own tea?" Thomas smiled at Lovina. "Why am I surprised? You can do anything."

Lovina felt her cheeks grow hot at his words. "Believe me, there are a lot of things I can't do. Making tea blends came about out of necessity. Annie doesn't stock anything except plain old black tea, and I like to experiment with the herbs in my garden. I found a book at the library that showed how to dry flowers and herbs and make delicious healing teas, and I was hooked."

"Healing?" Thomas raised his eyebrows, uncertainty evident in his tone. "What do you mean?"

"Well, plants and herbs have different healing properties. Peppermint, of course, soothes an upset tummy, and lavender treats insomnia. I make different blends that treat different symptoms. This one is my Feel Better blend. It works when you don't know exactly what is wrong but you know you need a little something."

Thomas smiled and nodded at the teapot. "And you knew I needed that?"

"I could tell something was bothering you." Lovina rose to pour the tea. "It's already a little sweet, just from the hibiscus, but if you need more sugar, I will get some."

He lifted the cup and inhaled deeply before taking a sip. His eyes widened.

"I don't know if this will heal anything, but I'll admit that it is good tea." He took another sip and sighed appreciatively. "Do you sell this?"

Lovina shook her head. "*Ach*, no. I just make it to share with family and friends."

Thomas gave her a confused look but continued drinking. The two didn't speak again for a few moments, but the tension from earlier had faded.

Lovina sipped her tea, her mind wandering.

She could almost picture pouring tea for Thomas and tucking Emily in for a nap—but in their own home, as a family. She could feel her cheeks flaring again and hoped Thomas didn't notice. She needed to get her mind on something else. "I have to tell you how much I enjoy Emily. She's so smart and funny and a good little helper. Thank you for letting me spend time with her."

"You've got that backwards. I should be thanking you. I'll never be able to repay you for everything you've done to help her. To help me." His voice wavered. His green-blue eyes held such appreciation, such respect for her that it caused her to blush yet again.

"Thomas, it has been a blessing to me to be able to help you both. You don't need to worry about repaying me. It's a joy to spend my days with Emily."

He stared down at the table, embarrassed. "I have a hard time accepting help, I suppose."

"I can understand that. Sometimes it's hard for me too. I've spent so much time trying to prove that I'm capable and independent, in spite of my . . . " She gestured to her face, forcing a laugh. "People think a little scar and a limp make me helpless."

"I don't think that anyone who has spent two minutes with you would think you are helpless." As he spoke, a gentle smile spread across Thomas's face.

"Th-th-thank you," Lovina stammered, processing Thomas's compliment.

She swirled the tea around in her cup. Her scar always deepened its red when she blushed, so she figured it must be glowing like a fiery coal now. He must think her a fool.

"I mean it, Lovina." His usually gruff voice was gentler, yet still husky. He reached across the table and took her hand. "You always know what to do, especially with Emily. You are so good with her. I'm surprised you don't have a family of your own."

A thrill of electricity ran up her arm. She reflexively pulled her hand back. "Oh, no. That's not what the Lord has planned for me."

"I have a hard time believing that. You would make a great mother, Lovina."

"That's kind of you to say, Thomas, but I'm afraid that ship has sailed. A young man courted me once, long ago, and that ended badly. I'm quite happy just being a helper." She swallowed the last bit of her tea and along with it, her secret longing, then stood and collected the cups from the table.

She desperately needed to change the subject. "Did you enjoy the trail you hiked today?"

He uttered an affirmative, but his eyes had lost their sparkle.

She hesitated before pressing him for more details. "You were gone a while. I started to wonder if you had taken a wrong turn."

"No wrong turns. I just needed some time to think. I had a letter from my sister that I hadn't read yet." His solemn voice strained against the words.

"From Emily's mother?" Lovina returned to the table to sit across from him.

"*Ja*. It was part of her will. It explained why she wanted Emily to stay with me, even though we've been out of touch for so long."

She could almost see the weight on his shoulders. How could she help him bear this burden? "No wonder you were gone so long. I'm sure that was a lot to take in."

"It answered a lot of questions for me. I still don't know that she made the right choice, but I'm going to do my best to honor her memory."

"You are doing a fine job. Emily needs time, consistency, and most of all, patience. Keep giving her those things and don't stop praying for her. Everything will work out—just wait and see."

Thomas gave her a skeptical look. "If you say so, Lovina. I just don't see myself as a patient man."

"Nonsense. I've seen you whittling on the back porch at night. That takes a ton of patience. I've been meaning to ask—what have you been whittling?"

"Just some birds." He shrugged. "They work up pretty quickly."

"That's great. I know many Amish think that having hobbies is a frivolous waste of time, but I think having a creative outlet is pretty important. I garden, of course, and sew and crochet, plus I'm a scribe for *The Budget*."

Thomas raised his eyebrows. "That *Englisch* driver, Wyatt, mentioned that. *The Budget* always seemed awfully gossipy to me."

"*Ach*, no, it isn't gossip at all. It's just another way to help people stay connected. Think about my *mem* and *dat*, for example. They can read about the communities where my sisters live and then when they write letters, they have more things to discuss. It helps close the distance between us."

He shrugged. "I guess that's one way to think about it, but—"

"Uncle Thomas!" Emily burst into the kitchen and threw her arms around him. "I'm so glad you're back."

Thomas listened attentively while Emily recounted the details of her time with Lovina. "Sounds like you two had a busy morning. What do you say we get out of Lovina's hair and let her get on with her day? We'll see her at dinner time."

Emily stuck her lower lip out. "I wanna stay!"

Lovina watched as Thomas balled his fists at his side. She didn't want to override his authority with his niece, but she did want to show him how to compromise when he could.

"Tell you what, Emily. I promised to show you how to crochet tonight. How about you go back to the cabin with your *oncle* and play a while, while I get all your materials together. You can come over later and help me fix supper if your *oncle* says you can."

Emily nodded reluctantly and gave Lovina a hug. Thomas gave Lovina a grateful smile as they left. Lovina waved, then watched the pair walk back to the cabin. Thomas's tall stiff posture contrasted with Emily's tiny frame bouncing across the yard. They were an odd pair, indeed, but somehow, Lovina thought they fit together just right.

Chapter Eleven

SUNDAY, AUGUST 27

"I want to wear my princess dress!"

Emily's voice reached an octave that Thomas figured could shatter glass. Just when he thought he had things in hand, she reached a new level of stubbornness and tested Thomas's patience in fresh ways.

And he failed every test.

"Absolutely not. Now get your Sunday dress on or we will be late!" The exasperation in his voice gave it a harder edge than he would like, but he simply lacked the right words to respond to her temper tantrums.

Today was the first church Sunday in the community since Emily's arrival and Thomas's nerves were already frayed.

Just last night, as he tucked her into bed, Emily pushed Thomas's buttons by trying to trick him into allowing her to stay up later. She asked for four drinks of water, three stories, two rounds of nighttime prayers, and a different blanket. At first, he played along, but the more demands she made, the less patient he became until he blew up and she burst into tears.

"As long as you live with me, you will follow my rules. Go to bed!" he had shouted at her before slamming the bedroom door, sounding just like his father. Her muffled sobs continued for an hour or more until she finally cried herself to sleep.

He knew what his *dat* would have done.

Charles Smucker firmly believed—and practiced—the old adage "Spare the rod and spoil the child." From an early age, Thomas had worked hard at being obedient, helping him avoid many of the beatings *Dat* had dished out to headstrong Anna Ruth. Even now, all these years later, he could picture his father's calloused hands grabbing Anna Ruth's arm and dragging her to the woodshed for what *Dat* called "discipline." His sister's screams pierced his eardrums then, and his heart now.

Anna Ruth had written in her letter that he wasn't like their father, but in moments like these, he definitely didn't believe her. And he sure didn't want to make the same mistakes with Emily that *Dat* had made with Anna Ruth.

Thomas took a few deep breaths to calm himself. He studied Emily for a moment. Strands of sandy blonde hair hung in her green-blue eyes. Freckles dotted her nose. She held her chin high, jaw clenched, and eyes narrowed. She planted her feet and crossed her arms on her chest. The slight cock of her head issued a challenge to him. Sometimes, her stubbornness, so like Anna Ruth's, was almost endearing, but not right now. His patience had evaporated, and he did not know how to get his *niesse* to cooperate.

Lovina Graber knew. She could convince Emily to do anything.

Lovina never raised her voice or lost her patience. Those two had found a rhythm to their days together that left Thomas mystified, and if he told the truth, feeling more and more like an outsider. Lovina, with her gentle smile and soothing voice, always knew what to do. And Thomas seldom did, affirming that he'd been right when he told Ike Sommers that he wasn't meant to be a father.

He could call social services and turn his *niesse* over. That was the easy thing to do. They would find her a qualified foster home and he wouldn't have to worry about her anymore.

However, growing up on his family's dairy farm, he'd learned that the easy thing was rarely the right thing. And this situation was no different.

No, giving up on Emily would not please the Lord or honor Anna Ruth's memory. She needed a loving home with parents who knew what they were doing.

The more he prayed for guidance, the more certain he was of the answer. He would catch Ike today and see if he knew a family in the area that could raise Emily. That way, he could still be in her life, and she would get the stability she needed.

For now, though, he needed Emily to put her plain dress on.

How would Lovina approach this?

Thomas thought through the miracles she had worked in the last several days. Instead of telling Emily what to do, Lovina always started with a choice. He couldn't fail any harder than he already had, so he gave it a shot.

"Which dress would you like to wear today? The purple one or the yellow one?" His voice sounded pleasant, but artificial. He hoped Emily wouldn't notice.

His frustration grew when he glanced around the cabin that looked like a toy store had exploded. The rest of Emily's belongings had arrived from Ohio and now dolls, clothes, art supplies, and books covered every available inch of the cabin.

"I want the pink princess one!"

So much for that strategy. He couldn't trick Emily.

Without the strength or the time to continue fighting this losing battle, he needed to call in backup.

Lovina.

Thomas marched out of Emily's bedroom, through the living area, and right to the Grabers' back door.

Lovina must have seen Thomas coming as she opened the door on his first knock.

"Need help?" she asked before he could even open his mouth to ask.

Nodding, Thomas let out a deep breath he had been holding since he left Emily in the cabin. The instant calm that Lovina provided washed over him.

For such a tiny, delicate woman, she possessed immense strength, which Thomas had come to rely on. "How did you know?"

"I could hear her. She's got a set of lungs on her, *ja*?" Lovina smiled, her kind brown eyes beaming with a warmth that drew him in and made him feel like everything would be all right.

Being in her presence calmed his fears about caring for Emily, but he felt an odd, unexpected hammering of his heart when she tilted her head to the side and gazed up at him.

"*Ach*. That she does. I'm sure you are busy getting ready for church yourself, but if you could help me convince Emily to wear an appropriate dress, I would certainly appreciate it." That and the hundred other things she had done since Emily arrived.

Lovina dusted her hands on her apron. "I'm ready for church, and I was just packing up some things to take for lunch."

Thomas's hand flew to his forehead. "Lunch! I didn't even think about that."

In Amish communities, families took turns hosting church at their home and the community brought lunch to share afterwards. The guys from the bachelor cabin usually chipped in to buy a few pies from the store as their contribution. Thomas hadn't even given lunch a thought this week.

"Oh, don't you worry about it for a second. *Mem* and I packed enough for the three of us as well as you and Emily, and probably four or five other families too." Lovina's brown eyes sparkled when she spoke.

Thomas noticed several dark spirals of hair escaping her *kapp*. Her tousled look belied her efficiency, but he found the contrast made her even more charming. He fought the sudden urge to reach out and tuck an unruly curl behind her ear.

She followed him out the door and toward the cabin, her uneven gait causing her to stay several paces behind him.

"This won't put you behind schedule, will it?" Thomas hadn't considered how his many impositions might have affected her routines. He stood at the door of the cabin, waiting for her to catch up to him.

Lovina limped along awkwardly, finally reaching the door. "Certainly not. Helping Emily is the highlight of my day. You have no idea what a blessing that *kinder* is to me."

Thomas hoped Lovina was being honest with him and not just trying to make him feel less guilty for all the favors he could never return. Somehow, he believed her.

The two entered the cabin to find Emily sitting on the floor, still wearing her nightclothes. Thomas looked at Lovina, silently pleading with her to work her magic on Emily.

Lovina smiled in return.

"Lovie! Where's Gus?" The little girl stood and threw her arms around Lovina.

Thomas smiled at the amazingly accurate nickname his niece had given their neighbor. She was the most loving person he had ever known.

"Good morning, Emily! Gus had a big breakfast, and he's taking a nap. We missed having you along to do our chores this morning. The chickens missed you too. I hear you are going with your *oncle* Thomas to church services this morning. The service itself can be long, but after it is over, you and the other *kinner* will have so much fun. They play games and eat cookies, and I happen to have packed some of your favorite oatmeal raisin cookies just for you. Now we need to get you ready."

Emily pouted. "I want to wear my princess dress, but Uncle Thomas won't let me."

"Do you know why he won't let you?"

Emily shook her head and turned her teary eyes to the floor.

"All the other *kinner* will wear Plain clothes. Your *oncle* wants you to feel like you belong here. He wants to help you fit in and make friends. What would Plain *kinner* think of a girl dressed like a princess?"

Emily raised her eyes to Lovina's. "They would think I'm a weirdo."

Lovina grinned and took Emily's hand. "And no one wants to feel like a weirdo. *Oncle* Thomas was trying to help you, not be mean. Does that make sense?"

Emily sniffled but nodded her head. She and Lovina retreated to the bedroom to get Emily dressed. Thomas could hear their giggles through the door.

He marveled at how easily Lovina brought Emily around to see his point of view. He could count on one hand the number of times Emily had smiled at him in the last week and a half.

Temper tantrums and tears were in abundance, though.

Lovina communicated naturally and effortlessly with Emily, while he seemed to speak an entirely different language.

Minutes later, the two emerged from the bedroom. Lovina had dressed Emily in a dark purple dress the two had made earlier in the week and neatly braided her hair. Emily hadn't quite adjusted to wearing a *kapp* yet, so Thomas was glad Lovina didn't insist on one. The dress was an acceptable compromise.

"Emily Grace, you thank Miss Graber for helping you get ready and we'll let her finish getting ready for church," Thomas directed.

"Thank you, Lovie. Do you want to walk with us to church?"

Lovina smiled at Emily. "I have a better idea. Since church is going to be all the way over at Brother Martin's house and we have so much we need to bring with us, we're going to take the buggy. Why don't you and your *oncle* ride with us?"

"Can we, Uncle Thomas?" Emily bounced on her toes, hands clasped in front of her.

Thomas stiffened. His initial impulse was to say no, to refuse yet more help from Lovina Graber and her family. However, Emily's pleading eyes reached deep into his soul. One glance in Lovina's direction and his heartbeat picked up the pace.

She was right—again. An Amish church service lasted several hours and would be an endurance test for the little girl. A three-mile walk to the Martin home would exhaust her before the service even started. She would be in a better mood if they rode with the Grabers.

And, to tell the truth, so would he.

Chapter Twelve

Emily shifted in Lovina's lap as Brother Martin continued his lengthy sermon. Lovina envied the *kinner*. No one batted an eye when they dozed off during the three-hour service, but if Lovina's head began to bob, Brother Martin would notice and call her in front of the congregation to repent. Lovina blinked rapidly several times to keep her eyes open. She'd lost track of the point of Brother Martin's sermon.

He began as he usually did, with an admonition to the congregation to remain humble and Plain, to avoid things of the world, and to stay separate from the *Englisch*. Lovina was glad Emily didn't understand much of the Pennsylvania Dutch the preacher spoke. She would hate for the little girl to think he was warning people to avoid her.

Somewhere along the way, Brother Martin had ventured into one of Lovina's least favorite of his sermon topics—warning them about the dangers of remaining single too long, which usually led Lovina to feel as though he directed his words at her. Today, though, she opted to conduct a mental inventory of all the single

Amish women in the room and consider who might make a suitable match for Thomas.

"It is not good for man to be alone," boomed the preacher, and Lovina stifled a yawn. Her eyes skimmed the *kapp*-covered heads in front of her.

Married, married, married, engaged. Single women were few and far between in West Kootenai. The annual influx of bachelors created an additional demand on the already short supply. Of the unmarried women in the room, only a few weren't courting anyone.

Well, a few, not counting Lovina.

Brother Martin signaled to the congregation to move from their seats onto their knees for the final prayer.

Lovina prodded Emily awake and whispered instructions to her. The two bowed with the other women in their row and Lovina closed her eyes, silently thanking God that the long service was finally winding to a close.

Following the benediction, a few announcements, and a lengthy closing hymn, the service concluded. The women began setting up the lunch while the men turned the benches into tables. Emily trailed after Lovina, occasionally casting envious glances at the *kinner* playing in the front yard.

"Emily, would you like me to introduce you to those girls? I'm sure they would love to play with you," Lovina offered.

Emily shrugged, her bottom lip quivering just enough for Lovina to notice. "I want to play with them, but I don't think they like me. They look at me funny."

"It's just because they don't know you yet." Lovina took Emily's hand in hers as they walked toward the *kinner*, Susanna's little sisters.

She understood the little girl's hesitation. Between her limp and her scar, Lovina often drew odd looks from people, even those who knew her already. Being different could be so isolating. Lovina fought that feeling everyday herself and didn't want Emily to have to face it.

"Girls." Lovina's cheerful voice interrupted the *kinner* playing. She spoke in *Englisch* to them, rather than the Pennsylvania Dutch that most *kinner* spoke before they went to school. The Milner girls all spoke *Englisch* from a young age because they'd had so many *Englischers* in and out of their home.

Their eyes turned toward Lovina and Emily and they quieted. "This is Emily Grace Spencer. She is new in town and new to our Amish ways. Could you help her meet some new friends and show her the game you were just playing?"

A trio of girls—a set of twins with brown hair and brown eyes and a smaller blonde girl—smiled at Emily and Lovina.

One of the twins stepped forward. *"Ja!* My name is Sarah Jane Milner, and these are my *schwester*s, Dorie and Marigold. Come play tag with us."

Emily's eyes lit up. Lovina nodded her approval and Emily scampered off with the other girls. Finding friends for Emily proved to be an easy task.

Now, if only finding a wife for Thomas could be so simple.

She scanned the crowd as she made her way back to the food table and her gaze settled on a pair of young women standing off to the side exchanging whispers and giggling as Lovina came nearer. Dorcas Martin and Frannie Yoder. They were both unattached single women, but neither one of them would make a good wife for Thomas or *mem* for Emily.

Dorcas and Frannie had been a couple of years behind Lovina's youngest sister, Geneva, in school. Despite being the daughter of one of the elders, usually a desirable catch in an Amish community, Dorcas never had any suitors court her more than once or twice. Perhaps young men found her father, Jonathan Martin, intimidating, or maybe it was the mean streak Dorcas didn't try too hard to hide. Frannie Yoder stayed in Dorcas's shadow most of the time, often imitating her friend's unkind behavior. They both seemed to be on the road to being an old maid, much like Lovina.

Lovina sighed, trying to push away the sullenness that Frannie and Dorcas projected. She attempted a courteous smile when she crossed in front of the two, but neither returned it.

Lovina's smile grew when she spotted Susanna, one hand rubbing her lower back. Susanna slipped out from behind the table and made a straight line toward her friend.

"Wonder what bee those two have in their bonnets today?" Susanna asked, tipping her head toward Dorcas and Frannie.

"Who knows? The sky is probably too blue to suit them." Lovina didn't want to talk about those two. "How are you feeling today?"

Susanna rested her hand on the swell of her belly and gave Lovina a smile. "Almost normal. Those ginger chews have been a life saver."

"I'm so glad. I can't wait until this *boppli* gets here. I've been crocheting the most beautiful little layette set for her . . . or him, I suppose." Lovina hoped she hadn't stuck her foot in her mouth.

"*Mem* thinks it will be a girl too. Which reminds me, *Mem* wanted me to let you know that we have plenty of dresses that Emily could wear. The twins have grown out of them and Marigold can only wear half of them," Susanna offered.

"That's so kind, Susanna, and it will help Thomas so much. Now, if I could just find him a good woman to marry, that would solve all his problems."

Susanna's eyes went wide, and her jaw dropped. "He's looking for a wife?"

"Not exactly." Perhaps it wasn't such a good idea to blurt out her plan, but Susanna was one of her dearest friends and if anyone could help her, it was Susanna. "I mean, he hasn't mentioned it, but aren't all Amish bachelors looking for a wife? I figured that's why he came here. Besides, Emily needs a *mem*." Her voice softened at the use of the term. A *mem*—something she would never be.

"Oh, Lovina. You are such a problem solver. Has it occurred to you to talk to him about his plans before you set a date for a wedding to an unsuspecting Amish girl?" Susanna's gentle voice probed.

Lovina paused for a moment.

No, she hadn't consulted Thomas at all. Perhaps he had already enlisted Ike in helping him find a wife, or maybe he had a sweetheart back home who would be joining him here in the spring. A longing filled her soul when she pictured Thomas with a sweetheart.

"I've done it again, haven't I? Put the cart before the horse, as they say." Lovina rubbed her temples and sighed. "Well, thankfully, I've been too busy helping him with Emily to actually do anything about matchmaking. Still, Emily needs a *mem* and Thomas needs a wife. Who do you know that isn't courting anyone, besides Dorcas and Frannie?" Lovina shuddered at the thought of either of them marrying Thomas. Neither was good enough for him.

"Are you serious, Lovina?" Susanna eyed her suspiciously.

"You don't think either of them would be a good match for Thomas, do you?" Lovina crinkled her nose and examined the two from afar.

Thomas needed someone who could balance his gruffness with nurturing, someone who was creative and patient with Emily, and someone who had a kind heart that could help him overcome his past. Dorcas and Frannie were entirely too self-centered and mean-spirited for him.

Susanna chuckled and shook her head. "Of course not! I was thinking of someone a little closer to home."

Lovina let her eyes roam over the women busily setting out lunch, supervising children, and chatting together in small groups. Who had she overlooked? "Do you mean Eve Peachy? She's courting one of those Swartz boys that came out here this spring."

"Lovina Graber, you are a wonder! I'm talking about *you*, silly."

Lovina flinched at the flicker of fear that welled up in her when Susanna mentioned marriage.

She looked at her friend, unable to speak or even think for a moment. Susanna knew that Lovina's place was at home with *Mem* and *Dat*. She owed them so much for taking such good care of her throughout her many hospital stays, doctor visits, and physical therapy sessions. It was the least she could do to make sure that all their needs were taken care of. With no brothers to take over the farm and almost all her sisters living out of state, it was up to her to take over the tree farm one day.

She would never forget that day near the end of eighth grade when she overheard her teacher, Miss Glick, in a whispered conversation with Mrs. Martin. Tears still threatened when she recalled Miss Glick's words. *"That poor family, with no sons to carry on the family name. But I suppose they'll always have Lovina to take care of them. After all, no one will want to marry her, considering all her issues."*

And then a few years later she thought, just maybe, Miss Glick was wrong. Dan Herschberger courted her very briefly and she thought he might want to marry her, but she was wrong about that too.

"Don't start that again, Susanna. You know where I stand on marriage. It's not for me." She'd hoped for a different outcome before and it crushed her spirit. She couldn't go through that again.

"Why not you? Didn't you listen to Brother Martin's sermon this morning? It isn't good for man—or woman, in your case—to be alone. I know you think you owe it to your parents to take care of them, and I know how badly it hurt you when Dan broke up with you, but this is different."

Lovina cringed at the mention of Dan Herschberger's name. "I did listen to the sermon, but I missed one of the announcements. Who did they say was hosting the quilting bee next month?"

"You know as well as I do that it will be at the Shetlers' home. You helped plan it." Susanna rolled her eyes. "I'm not going to drop this, Lovina. Don't you think that, just maybe, the Lord put you in Thomas's and Emily's lives for a reason?"

Clearly Susanna's hormones were interfering with her thinking.

Lovina tried again to change the subject. "Of course He did. I'm there to help them, just like I help everyone. By the way, what did you think of the advice column this week?"

"You know as well as I do that it was *wunderbar*. And you know that you can't distract me that easily. If I didn't love you so much, I'd call you a *dummkopf*. Lovina Graber, you are too stubborn for your own good. Why can't you see what everyone else sees?"

Lovina couldn't respond. Her heart beat like a drum in her ears.

What was it that everyone else saw when they looked at her and Thomas? Surely, they didn't see an ugly old maid offering to help a handsome bachelor just so she could get him to marry her. She hoped people in West Kootenai knew her heart better than that.

Before Susanna could continue, Lovina's mother called to her from across the yard. "I've got to go help *Mem*. I'm sure I'll see you before we leave today, and if not, I'll definitely stop by Tuesday with some more ginger chews." She patted Susanna's arm and turned to walk away, feeling the heat rise in her cheeks.

Susanna meant well, Lovina reminded herself. But every so often, her friend tried to persuade Lovina to change her attitude toward marriage. And every time, Lovina would gently remind her that Lovina had a different purpose in life, and they would move on to a new topic.

This time, it felt different.

Instead of some theoretical man Lovina might marry, Susanna was talking about Thomas, someone Lovina actually cared for.

And this time, Susanna didn't seem so ready to drop the subject. Lovina's discomfort set off alarm bells in her head.

A tiny part of Lovina hoped that this time, Susanna might actually be right.

Chapter Thirteen

WEDNESDAY, AUGUST 30

Lovina whisked milk into a pan, thinning out sausage gravy to just the right consistency. She dipped her pinky into the pan to taste test—a little more pepper and it would be perfect. The aroma of buttermilk biscuits baking in the oven wafted up, causing her stomach to grumble.

She crossed the kitchen to open the back door and call to Thomas and Emily that breakfast was ready, but that wasn't necessary. They were standing there waiting on the doorstep when she flung the door open.

"Oooh!" she gasped, wiping her flour-coated hands on her apron. The surprise of finding him standing at the door mixed with the fire she felt in her belly every time she looked at him. His green-blue eyes, those slight dimples when he smiled, and his strong, broad shoulders took her breath away. "I was coming out to let you know that breakfast is almost ready. I wasn't expecting you to be standing here."

Emily burst through the door and took what had become her seat at the table. "We could smell the sausage and the apples, and we were too hungry to wait."

"Remember your manners, Emily," Thomas scolded the little girl. He shook his head and took the seat next to her.

Lovina could feel Thomas's eyes follow her as she filled platters at the stove and carried them to the table. Knowing he was watching her made her even more self-conscious about her limp than usual. She ducked her head to avoid eye contact.

Dat sat across from Thomas and chuckled. "Now, now, Thomas. Everyone gets excited when Lovina makes her cinnamon apples for breakfast. That smell makes our mouths water and our bellies do flip-flops. Ain't so, Emily?" Lovina's *dat*—balding and slightly chubby—winked in the little girl's direction.

In the weeks that Emily and Thomas had been living in the cabin, the entire Graber family had fallen in love with the little girl. While she was a bit more boisterous than a typical Amish *kinder*, her precocious nature made her charming and impossible not to like. She had *Dat* and *Mem* wrapped around her little finger.

Lovina pulled the sheet of biscuits out of the oven and placed them on a platter. At the breakfast table amid the laughter and smiles, Thomas's stony silence stood out like a sore thumb.

First, he had snapped at Emily for being impolite and now he sat with his arms crossed and his jaw set. She wondered what caused his foul mood. She knew he had a lot on his mind, especially after he read his sister's letter on Saturday. Perhaps the grief was just greater today.

Or maybe he had suffered insomnia like Lovina had last night. Her conversation with Susanna had played over in her head and she wrestled with the implications of her friend's suggestion.

What if God *had* put Thomas and Emily in Lovina's life to show that more was possible than she had ever hoped to dream?

She yawned and shook her head to clear the confusing thoughts.

Mem handed her a bowl of gravy to take to the table. When everyone had settled in their spots, *Dat* and Thomas removed their hats, and they all bowed their heads for a moment of silent prayer before digging into the biscuits and gravy and cooked apples Lovina had prepared. The sounds of forks scraping plates and occasional murmurs of "mmm" took the place of the merriment of a few moments prior.

Perplexed by his behavior, Lovina watched as Thomas pushed his food around on his plate, every so often shoving a forkful into his mouth. She hoped he wasn't coming down with a stomach bug. "Is your breakfast okay, Thomas?"

"Hmm?" Thomas glanced up her, his forehead wrinkled. "Oh, I'm just a little distracted this morning. The food is good, as always. *Danke.*" With a forced-looking smile, he made a point of chewing a hearty bite of biscuits and gravy and swallowing.

Lovina struggled to maintain eye contact with Thomas.

"Why not you?" Susanna's words haunted her.

Worse, what if others really did judge her willingness to help Thomas and Emily as a ploy to catch herself a husband? Heat crept up her neck and filled her cheeks as though everyone at the table could hear her thoughts.

They finished breakfast, and Lovina and Emily began clearing the table as everyone else rose from the table to start the day.

"Bye, Mrs. Rose. Bye, Mr. Henry. See you at lunch time!" Emily waved and blew kisses at Lovina's parents. "Uncle Thomas, I'll bet Lovie has your lunch pail ready."

"I do, indeed. It's over on the hutch." Lovina nodded toward the pail. "I hope I'm packing enough for you." She pinched her eyes shut. Did she sound like she was flirting with him? She hoped not.

"The lunches are just right. I appreciate all your help, Lovina. I don't know how I'll ever repay you." His voice strained at the words.

"As I've already told you, there's no need to worry about that. It's what we do for one another in this community." She tried to keep the emotion out of her words. As the heat rose in her cheeks again, Lovina pulled a stepstool to the sink and kept her face turned away from Thomas. Emily climbed up and filled the sink with hot soapy water and began washing the dishes. Lovina busied herself tidying the kitchen.

"I wasn't raised to accept charity. Sometimes it overwhelms me just how kind you and your family have been to us," Thomas explained, his voice almost a whisper.

Overwhelmed. Lovina understood that feeling. The biscuits and gravy sat like stones in her stomach. She hoped Thomas hadn't picked up on her more-than-friendly feelings for him. She especially didn't want him to think she had ulterior motives for her kindness.

"Uncle Thomas, quit being such a grump," Emily interjected.

Lovina bit back a grin at Emily's spot-on commentary. "Perhaps your *oncle* is just tired this morning, Emily. Let's give him a little grace."

Thomas snatched up his lunch pail. "It's time for this grump to get to work. Emily, make sure you are on your best behavior for Lovina today. I'll see you at supper." His eyes briefly met Lovina's as he crossed the room, his gaze softer now than it was before. "Thank you for the lunch—and everything else."

The back door slammed behind him. Lovina absent-mindedly dried a plate and put it in the cabinet. Had she detected a note of tenderness in his voice just now? Or was she doing what she did best—overthinking a simple situation?

"I wish he wasn't so grouchy all the time," Emily said.

"I don't think he meant to be grouchy this morning, Em. He has a lot on his mind," Lovina explained. But sometimes he did have a sharp tone, especially toward Emily. He'd told Lovina that he didn't feel like a patient man, and she could tell this was something he wanted to change.

From the moment they'd met, Lovina had pegged Thomas as a hermit. He moved into the bachelor cabin in July and she'd seen very little of him between their ride from Whitefish until the day of Emily's arrival. The other bachelors interacted with the community more frequently, but perhaps that was because so many of them were looking for girls to court.

Clearly that wasn't on Thomas Smucker's mind.

Emily and Lovina finished the dishes in a silence interrupted only by Emily's humming of a tune unfamiliar to Lovina.

"What do we have planned for today?" asked Lovina, who wanted to switch gears in her head—away from Thomas and his mind-boggling behavior and onto more practical matters. "Today is Wednesday," Lovina said, answering her own question. "And on Wednesdays we sweep and dust the house and I plan my meals for the next week. I thought we might try to fit in time to make some crafts today, if that's something you'd like to help with. What else can we do?"

Emily's eyes lit up at the mention of crafts. "I think crafts sound just perfect. Maybe we could also read some stories."

Lovina grinned. "I think that can be arranged. Since we're in the kitchen, let's start by planning the meals and getting them organized." She pulled a notebook out of a drawer, grabbed a couple of cookbooks, and led Emily to the table.

"I liked the puh-sketti pie you made last week. Can we have that again?" Emily licked her lips at the mention of the dish.

"We will have that in two weeks. I need some special cheese for that, and I'll have to make sure Annie can get it. Next week, I'm thinking we'll have some beans to pick from the garden, so we'll want to eat those. I can make a green bean casserole one night, and maybe some green beans with cheese sauce another night. And we might have some fresh brussels sprouts, too, so we can roast those."

Emily scrunched her nose up. "What's a brussels sprout?"

"They look like tiny green cabbages. I like to roast them with mushrooms and garlic or cook them with caramelized onions and cream. They are very good for you."

"Maybe I can just have leftover green beans that day," Emily said.

"We'll see. My *mem* had a five-bite rule when I was a little girl. I had to try five bites of a new food before I was allowed to say I didn't like it. Some things I did learn to enjoy, but other things I didn't. Like celery—I still don't like it cooked in things like soups." Lovina shivered at the thought. "It squeaks when you chew it."

Emily giggled. "I like celery with peanut butter and raisins on it. My mommy called it ants on a log." At the mention of her mother, Emily's smile faded. Her eyes grew misty and her bottom lip trembled. She looked down at the table.

"Oh, Emily. I know you miss her so much. Tell you what. I'll fix some ants on a log for a snack this afternoon and I bet that I'll like celery that way. What else did your mommy cook that you liked? We can try to make some of those things, and you can tell us about her at dinner. That will help you remember the happy times and help us know what a good momma she was to you."

"*Oncle* Thomas doesn't like to talk about her," Emily replied, sniffling.

"I'm sure that's not true. It's just hard for him." Lovina thought back to Thomas's distracted mood this morning. Not only was he adjusting to taking care of a little girl, he was grieving a loss and had no way to process it. No wonder he was so irritable. Lovina offered up a quick silent prayer on his behalf.

Lord, hold Thomas close to You. Give him someone to talk to so he doesn't bear his grief alone. Help him be softer towards Emily and show me how to support them both.

"I don't think he likes having me here," Emily continued.

Lovina's heart ached for the little girl. "What makes you think that?"

"He's just always so mad. I'm too messy or too loud or I have bad manners. I try to be good, Lovie, but I never do it right." Tears flowed down Emily's freckled cheeks.

Lovina pulled the little girl into her lap. She wrapped her arms around Emily and let her cry until her tears ran out. Emily blamed herself for Thomas's anger, and that broke Lovina's heart. Emily was nothing more than an innocent child—she didn't ask to be uprooted from her happy life, relocated to rural Montana to live in a tiny cabin with an uncle she'd never met, and stuck in an

Amish community where nothing was like the life she knew before.

The longer Emily cried, the more angry Lovina grew.

How could Thomas be so impatient with this sweet child? She hated to interfere more than she already had, but she couldn't let him go on causing Emily so much pain. She'd give him a piece of her mind tonight after supper.

If only Thomas had a wife already, a softer feminine influence to balance out his crankiness and nurture Emily, then Lovina wouldn't have to worry so much. West Kootenai's single lady selection was slim, but Lovina knew that God could bring the right woman for Thomas.

She'd just have to look a little harder.

Chapter Fourteen

WEDNESDAY, AUGUST 30

Despite the abundance of late summer sunshine breaking across the blue Montana sky, Thomas couldn't shake the gray cloud that seemed to follow him all day long. He'd barely slept the night before, thinking about all the work ahead of him in the next week or so when the social worker came to do her first check. Between worrying about that and the continuous loop of his father's voice that played in his head, his brain constantly buzzed with activity, and Thomas was a man who needed peace and quiet.

There was no escaping the ongoing noise. The Grabers' house was a beehive of activity, and he'd never heard a family laugh so much. The Log Works bustled with the sounds of the saws and other machinery, plus the never-ending chatter of the young men who worked there.

And then there was Emily.

Granted, his experience with young children was limited, but he had no idea such a small person could generate so much noise. She hummed and sang and danced and talked—to him, to her dolls, to no one in particular—all with such volume, it nearly pierced his eardrums.

His afternoon walk back to the Grabers' was his one chance to be alone with his thoughts and talk to the Lord a little. That was a new discipline for him. *Dat* had never encouraged a personal relationship with God, but since his father's passing, Thomas had been curious. What if he talked to God a little more one-on-one, not just at meals and bedtime and church, but like the Bible said, without ceasing?

However, since Emily's arrival, his time alone with God had decreased, and Thomas could feel a difference. He was less content, more easily irritated, and definitely, as Emily had said at breakfast, "a grump."

Thomas hated feeling so prickly. He reminded himself so much of his own *dat* every time he scolded Emily or snapped at someone else. The one thing he feared most of all was that, deep down, he was the same as his father.

That's why he had decided a long time ago to stay single. He couldn't bear to live in a marriage like his parents had, and he definitely didn't want to raise children the way *Dat* had raised him.

And he was becoming more like his father every day he spent with Emily.

Heart heavy, he descended the hill from the Log Works. He tried to pray but his brain filled with static and the words wouldn't come. He tried reciting one of the psalms he'd learned. *The LORD is my light and my salvation; whom shall I fear? The LORD is the—*

"Thomas, just the man I was looking for." Jonathan Martin's voice broke through his meditation.

Having spent his growing up years harboring a distrust of the bishops and elders in Belleville thanks to *Dat's* constant criticism of their decisions, Thomas fought the urge to grimace.

Jonathan Martin brought his horse and buggy to a stop and climbed out. He extended his hand to Thomas.

"Brother Martin. What can I do for you?" Thomas tried unsuccessfully to keep the wariness out of his voice.

"I wanted to see how you were getting on with the little *Englisch* girl that is visiting you." Jonathan's voice held a pompous edge, and his smile didn't quite reach his eyes.

Thomas breathed deeply before responding. He just wanted to get back to the cabin, not deal with this old man's questions. "*Ach*, my *niesse* Emily is doing well. As you probably know, she lost both parents in a terrible accident and her mother—my sister—wanted me to raise her should something so terrible occur. I'm working toward getting permanent custody of her." Though his own words surprised him, it felt right to say them.

"I see." Jonathan stroked his salt-and-pepper beard. "It seems to me that you would be in a better place with all this custody business if you had a wife."

There it was.

His jaw locked in place, Thomas stood mute. He had known to expect this advice. It was the Amish way of thinking. Grow up, get baptized, get married, and start a family. And Thomas had dared to skip one of the most important steps. Wasn't that one of his main reasons for leaving Belleville?

He knew he had to respond to Jonathan's comment, but the right words eluded him.

Unfortunately, Jonathan seemed to take Thomas's silence as an invitation to continue dispensing advice. "I don't know much about the *Englisch* court system, but it stands to reason that a judge would rather place Emily in a home with two parents. Besides, that's the way we Plain people live anyway. Just like I said in my sermon Sunday, it isn't good for man to be alone." He clapped Thomas on the shoulder and gave him a sly smile.

"Yes, Brother Martin, that is what the Bible says." Thomas didn't mention Paul's advice that the unmarried ought to stay that way and if they do marry, they should love their wives like Christ loved the church.

"I wondered if you had given any thought to choosing a wife.

Since you're new in town, you might not know many folks, but I would be glad to introduce you to some young women that would make *gut* wives."

Thomas seethed silently, unwilling to be openly disrespectful to Brother Martin. "I appreciate your concern, but right now, I've got my hands full with Emily. I'm not in the right place to take on a wife too." He hoped that would placate the older man but guessed that it would take more than that.

"I realize you have many things to consider right now. That's just more reason to get married. A wife can help you." Jonathan Martin would not be easily deterred.

"Brother Martin, I appreciate your concern for me," Thomas said through gritted teeth, "but I'll deal with my personal life on my own. Just pray for Emily and for me, and that will help us so much."

"Certainly. Just know that my prayer will be for you to find an acceptable wife as soon as possible. The elders and I have discussed it, and we really don't see another way. We'll talk again in a few days and see if the Lord has changed your heart on the matter." Jonathan extended his hand to Thomas, who shook it unenthusiastically.

A picture of Lovina Graber flashed in his mind.

She would make an excellent wife, but Thomas wouldn't subject such a *gut* woman to marrying him. He'd do nothing but disappoint and hurt her, like *Dat* did *Mem*. Lovina deserved a husband who would treat her like royalty. And he'd seen the disappointment in Lovina's eyes that morning when he'd been so cross with Emily.

Thomas headed on toward the Graber farm, replaying memories he'd wanted to keep buried. He'd considered marriage once, but that had ended badly and cemented his decision to remain single. He didn't want to live like his *mem* and *dat* had— stuck living with a person he didn't love or couldn't trust, just because it was the way things were done. Both of them were miserable together, and yet, when Thomas turned twenty-one, they'd decided it was time for him to repeat the same mistake they'd made.

They set him up with Katrina Troyer, a young woman in their Belleville community, and *Dat* made it clear that marriage was expected. Thomas half-heartedly courted the girl, who was pretty to look at but had a sour disposition. She always seemed more interested in gossiping with her friends than getting to know him better.

Still, he persisted with the ruse of courtship since *Dat* expected it and he didn't know another way around the situation. He was supposed to pick her up one night to go to a singing. When he arrived, he found her wrapped in the arms of Amos Stolzfus, his best friend since they were *kinner*.

Thomas confronted the two of them and broke up with Katrina. He took the long way home that night, dreading telling *Dat* and *Mem* about the breakup. He rehearsed the words in his head, but when he had to actually say them, he lost much of the conviction he had stirred up.

His father's response came as expected. "Thomas, you're twenty-two years old now. It's time for you to grow up and get married. Irving Troyer and I have all the details squared away. You'll put this misunderstanding behind you and marry Katrina as we planned."

"*Dat*, I'm not marrying a girl who would cheat on me with my best friend." Hearing the words felt like a punch to his gut. He didn't want to marry someone he didn't love, but he couldn't marry someone he didn't trust. "I don't need a wife. I won't marry her—or anyone." Thomas's heart dropped to his belly as he braced for his father's retort.

Dat glared at Thomas, but said nothing at first, then balled his fists up at his side and clenched his teeth so hard Thomas thought he might break a tooth. Tension-filled moments passed, the silence saturating the air like a heavy fog.

Thomas glanced at his mother, who watched her husband for any sign of agitation. *Dat*'s blowups set *Mem*'s nerves on edge. It was worse when Anna Ruth was home, because she always fought back, whereas Thomas usually just let *Dat* rage and stayed out of his way.

That was, until that night.

"You smug, ungrateful boy. You never think of anyone but yourself. Of course you'll get married. How else will you be able to manage the farm?" His father spat the words at him like venom.

Mem's silent eyes pled with Thomas to yield to his father's requests.

But on that night, Thomas couldn't. Years of obedience and bending to his *dat* had built up to that moment. The words came out of his mouth before he could stop them.

"I don't want to run the farm, *Dat*."

Dat lunged at Thomas, grabbing the collar of his shirt and slamming him up against the wall. "Listen to me, you ungrateful good-for-nothing. You'll marry Katrina Troyer and you'll run the farm, or you'll leave this house." He released Thomas and stepped backward, still eyeing Thomas with disgust.

"But *Dat*—"

"There is no room for discussion on this. You will do as I say, or you will leave. I'm going to bed now. It's been a long, disappointing day." He turned on his heel and stormed off to the bedroom, slamming the door behind him.

Mem remained on the couch for a moment, silent but trembling. Pain filled her eyes as she rose to follow her husband to bed. Before she left the room, she turned to Thomas and spoke a single word.

"Please."

Thomas knew what he had to do. He knew that he couldn't break his mother's heart and leave like Anna Ruth did. But how could he put his own feelings aside and do what *Dat* wanted? Katrina had embarrassed and hurt him, and he knew nothing could ever come of their relationship now.

He spent a long, sleepless night, tossing in his bed and coming to terms with his future.

He woke from shallow sleep to hear a piercing scream come from his parents' bedroom. Thomas had dashed down the hall to find his mother standing beside the bed and his father lying motionless, not breathing. A massive stroke, the doctor had later told them.

Even now, three years later, Thomas couldn't help feeling guilty for contributing to his *dat*'s death. If they hadn't argued, maybe *Dat*'s blood pressure wouldn't have skyrocketed and he wouldn't have had the stroke. Common sense told him otherwise, but his conscience taunted him with shame. Still, it meant that he didn't have to answer *Dat*'s ultimatum.

Eventually, he'd been able to sell the dairy farm and leave Belleville, and for that, he was grateful.

Greeted by the fragrance of evergreens, Thomas looked up to see the hills lined with Henry Graber's prized Christmas trees. He sighed, trying to clear his head of the unpleasant thoughts and recollections that filled it as he approached the Grabers' house.

Lovina's and Emily's laughter drifted out the windows of the home. If he could stand up to his father and refuse to marry Katrina, surely he could refuse Brother Martin's demands that he marry someone now.

Chapter Fifteen

MONDAY, SEPTEMBER 4

L ovina stretched and yawned as the sun crept above the horizon. A day off from all—well, most—responsibilities didn't come along often, but Labor Day marked the unofficial end of summer, and in West Kootenai, families celebrated by closing their businesses and basking in the glory of nature before the chill of fall set in. This was the last reprieve for Lovina and her family before the busy Christmas tree buying season began, so they liked to pack a picnic and take a hike in their own personal pine forest.

The hike had been a tradition ever since *Mem* and *Dat* first moved to the farm, but as the family grew, they added on a picnic and games. How much fun this year would be with Emily there to indulge *Dat's* youthful spirit.

Lovina dressed quickly and made her way downstairs to start breakfast and prepare the picnic basket. She entered the kitchen and gasped when she noticed a visitor waiting for her at the kitchen table.

"Emily! How did you get in here?"

"Good morning, Lovie! I was too excited about the hike to

sleep, so I decided to come over and help you get ready." Emily smiled up at her from the table where she sat scribbling in one of her coloring books.

Lovina bit back a chuckle. "I see that. Does your *oncle* know that you are here?"

"Nope. He was being a lazy daisy." She put her crayons back in the box and got up from the table. "What are we having for breakfast? I'm starving."

"Wait. Was *Oncle* Thomas still asleep when you left?" Lovina could just imagine the panic that would set in when he noticed that Emily wasn't in the cabin where she was supposed to be.

Emily put her hands on her hips. "Yup. He was snoring too."

Lovina knew Thomas hadn't been sleeping well since Emily had arrived, so she smiled at the knowledge that he was enjoying a little sleep-in today. However, she needed to make sure he knew that Emily was safe before he—

The back door burst open. "Lovina, have you seen Emily?" Thomas—hair disheveled and still in his sleeping clothes—entered, his eyes wild and breath coming in ragged bursts.

Too late.

Thomas, in his full-fledged hysteria, stood in her kitchen, taking in the sight of his niece standing at Lovina's side. He exhaled, but his face blazed red.

"I'm right here, *Oncle*. I'm ready to go hiking." Emily bounced on her toes, her light-up sneakers flashing.

Emily was safe, so Thomas could relax. Yet, the vein that bulged in his neck hadn't settled. Lovina locked eyes with Thomas, signaling to him that everything was fine. She breathed evenly, hoping he could follow her lead and rein his anxiety in.

"Emily, you can't just—"

Lovina shot him a sharp look. He was working so hard at not overreacting to Emily's behavior since the day his *niesse* had proclaimed him a grump. Lovina had prayed diligently to see that change, and God was clearly softening Thomas's heart. She'd complimented his patience and kindness whenever she saw it. She prayed in that instant that he wouldn't blow all the progress he had made with one angry outburst.

He started again. "Emily, it scared me when I woke up and you weren't in your bed. Next time, make sure I know where you are before you leave the cabin, okay?"

Lovina smiled at him, then turned her gaze to Emily, prompting her with a look to respond apologetically.

"Okay, *Oncle*. I'm sorry I scared you. But I was just so excited about today I couldn't sit still one more second!"

Lovina's heart warmed at the way the two had worked their situation out. A week or two ago, it would have ended in yelling, followed by door slamming and tears. The hike and picnic would have been overshadowed by Thomas's brooding and Emily's hurt feelings.

Crisis averted.

"Now that we've cleared that up, why don't you go back to the cabin and get ready for breakfast, Thomas. My helper and I have things under control here."

Confused, Thomas looked down at his long linen sleep shirt and matching drawstring pants. Color rose in his cheeks as he excused himself. Lovina couldn't help but fight back a giggle at the glimpse of a different side of Thomas she'd just seen. He was normally so buttoned-up and rigid, it was a relief to know he was human too.

Emily and Lovina worked quickly to put together the breakfast for the family and then assembled the picnic lunch. *Dat* and *Mem* joined them at the breakfast table just as Thomas returned.

After the silent blessing, Lovina told her parents about coming down to find Emily waiting for her at the table. *Dat* cackled at Lovina's description of Thomas's hair and surprised facial expression. Thomas blushed but smiled.

"Emily, you never told me. How did you get in the back door?"

Emily eyed Lovina with exasperation and shrugged. "You keep a key under the frog on the back porch. I just used that."

Everyone erupted in laughter.

Once *Dat* regained his composure, he turned toward Emily. "Of course, Emily. You don't miss a trick."

Once breakfast was finished, *Mem,* Lovina, and Emily cleaned up the kitchen and double-checked the picnic basket, while *Dat* and Thomas rounded up some hiking gear from the barn. At last, they were ready to go, much to Emily's excitement.

The sun provided a little warmth on the late summer morning, but soon the five of them were building up a sweat as they ascended the trail behind the Graber home. Emily's exuberance quickly waned, and their pace became more leisurely, which suited Lovina. Her hip already ached.

As they climbed higher up the hill, the path became more crowded with evergreen trees. The fresh scent invigorated Lovina, enabling her to move a bit faster, but Emily dawdled along, stuffing pinecones in a bag Lovina provided so she could use them for crafts this afternoon. *Dat* pointed out the different types of trees, explaining what made each unique.

"See this one, Em? It's a juniper. See how it is more like a shrub than a Christmas tree? Some of them have little yellow cones and others have bright berries that you can eat. If it had more space to grow, it could be big and tall. Still, it's a pretty handy tree to have. It makes *gut* fence posts that won't rot."

"*Oncle* Thomas, could you build me a cradle for my baby dolls out of it?" She flashed him a wide grin, batting her eyelashes. "Pleeeease?"

Thomas chuckled at her attempt to sweet-talk him. "Junipers aren't great for furniture building, but I bet I could find some wood at the Log Works that would do. I've never made a cradle before. It sounds like a fun project."

Lovina smiled at the easy banter between Thomas and Emily. Finally, the two of them seemed to be growing comfortable with each other.

As they journeyed on up the hill, *Dat* pointed out Douglas firs, with their soft needles and triangular shape that made them the ideal Christmas tree, and the droopy yew trees, warning Emily of their poisonous berries.

"You must never eat a berry unless you are absolutely sure it is safe to eat. Always ask an adult," Lovina cautioned. The woods held many dangers and she hoped that Emily could strike the proper balance of appreciation and reverence of nature.

"I'll just get my berries from the store, thank you very much," she replied, as though eating wild berries was the most absurd concept in the world.

They walked on a bit farther. "See this?" Thomas pointed to a clump of droppings speckled with red berries.

Emily scrunched her nose. "Eeew. What is that?"

"Bear . . ." He paused awkwardly, shooting Lovina a questioning glance.

She thought for a moment before supplying an appropriate word that Emily would understand. "Bear scat."

"Gross! Ew!" Emily screwed up her face in disgust before fear flashed over it. "Are you saying there are bears in the woods?" Her knees trembled, as did her voice.

Thomas placed his hand on her shoulder. "These woods actually belong to the bears. And the mountain lions, elk, deer, and wolves. I brought bear spray with me today." He patted his pocket. "The mountains are beautiful, Emily, but they can be dangerous. I need you to remember that and only come into the woods with a grown-up who is prepared."

Emily glanced around furtively, as if expecting a bobcat or bear to jump out right then. When nothing happened, she exhaled deeply and nodded. "Not to worry, *Oncle*. I won't come back up here alone. It's too scary."

"Don't be scared. Just be aware," Lovina cautioned. "We're almost to the overlook. Come on!"

The trees began to thin out and the path led them to a craggy ledge overlooking the Graber farm. Thomas reached for Emily's hand to help her climb atop a rock so that she could see better, sending another swell of warmth to Lovina's heart.

"Wow!" Emily gasped. "I can see the house, and the barn, and look, there's the chicken coop! Good morning, ladies!" She marveled at the scenery for a moment then hopped down from the rock, landing hard in the dirt. "We've hiked enough now. Let's play some games."

Everyone laughed at her proclamation.

Thomas shrugged off the backpack he had carried and unpacked two blankets, as well as some games. Lovina got everything set up and they spent the next hour or so playing card games like Dutch Blitz, until Emily announced that her belly was grumbly and she needed lunch.

As Lovina helped *Mem* unpack the picnic basket, she couldn't ignore the fluttering feeling in her stomach. Perhaps she was just hungry—but this felt different. Her cheeks hurt from smiling so much.

Mem noticed too. "Lovina, you certainly are chipper today. I worried that your hip might bother you, but you haven't complained once."

"I can't explain it, *Mem*. I just feel . . ." She searched for the words. "My heart feels so light, like I could float away. Thomas and Emily are getting along so well. It's like I'm full of sunshine and it's beaming out of me."

Mem nodded. "I've never heard it put quite like that before."

"Heard what put like that?" Lovina cocked her head.

"Why, you've just described what it feels like to fall in love," *Mem* responded, avoiding eye contact with Lovina, whose grip on the bag of potato chips she was holding went slack, sending chips scattering all around her.

Love?

Lovina's face heated at the mention of the word. Could *Mem* be right?

Chapter Sixteen

Thursday, September 7

For the last few days, Lovina had done her best to avoid thinking about *Mem*'s comments—and she tried to avoid Thomas, as well.

Aside from pleasantries exchanged at the meals they shared, Lovina had been successful, but she still felt a strange breathlessness when she looked at him. By Thursday, though, she still had a long list of things to discuss with him as they prepared for the social worker's visit the next day, so Lovina knew she would have to work up the courage to get over whatever this was she was feeling.

Lovina and Emily began the day's work outside, where the fresh pine scent wafted down the hill, masking the less pleasant barnyard odors. Much of Lovina's time was spent tending the Grabers' small farm—just a few chickens that she treated more like pets than livestock and, of course, her garden patch. Northern Montana's beautiful blue skies started pouring snow sometimes as early as mid-October and could continue until late April. Only the hardiest plants could grow here.

"Good morning, Priscilla. Aren't you looking beautiful this morning?"

Emily giggled when Lovina greeted and doted on each of her hens. After the girl had filled her egg basket, she helped Lovina clean and refill the water dispenser and feeder. Every day held a similar rhythm for Lovina, who found comfort in routines and repetition.

According to Emily, who had grown up in the suburbs of Cincinnati, the closest she had ever come to farm life was visiting the petting zoo at the pumpkin patch each fall. Lovina had patiently taught her how to care for the chickens and tend to the garden and was pleased with the progress the little girl had made in such a short amount of time.

While Mondays were the usual laundry day at the Graber house, the Labor Day hike and picnic had cut some of their Monday chores short. Emily, having only known an electric washer and dryer, was fascinated by the Amish laundry process, so she was thrilled to have a bonus laundry day, as she called it.

The two sorted the clothes in the basket and placed the whites into the basin. Emily carefully scooped some of Lovina's homemade detergent from the bucket, spilling a bit.

"Oh, Lovie! I've made a mess," Emily said, covering her face with her apron.

Lovina grabbed a broom and swept the detergent up. "Now, now, Emily. There's no sense crying over a tiny spill. It's all cleaned up and no one will ever know it was there."

"But Uncle Thomas gets so angry when I spill or waste something." Her words came out in hiccups as she cried.

"I'm sure he isn't angry, Emily. He's just frustrated and sometimes he doesn't know how to express his feelings." Lovina made a mental note to talk with Thomas about this later. She knew he tried to be gentle with his niece, and he had come so far from where he started, but he still struggled when she didn't meet his unreasonable expectations.

Lovina handed Emily the heavy pitcher of water to pour into the washer, showing the girl she still trusted her to do a good job.

Emily eyed her uncertainly. "Are you sure, Lovie? What if I spill it?"

"Then we'll fill it up again, but somehow I think you will do just fine."

Emily chewed on her bottom lip as she carefully tilted the pitcher to allow the water to flow out. She didn't spill a drop. Her gap-toothed grin warmed Lovina's heart.

"Well done, Emily Grace!" Lovina praised the little girl then turned on the diesel-powered generator to operate the old-fashioned machine. Later, they would hang the clothes on the line to dry, which was Emily's favorite part.

"Are you interested in a walk to the store, Emily?"

The little girl nodded eagerly, her self-confidence seeming fully restored. "Can Gus come too?"

"Sure. If you will promise to watch him very carefully, you can hold the leash," Lovina replied, much to Emily's delight.

The two of them stopped in the house to gather up mail that needed to go out and see if *Mem* needed anything from the store, then they were on their way. It was still mid-morning, so Lovina hoped to miss both the lunch and breakfast rush.

Holding Gus's leash carefully, Emily followed Lovina on the short walk to Kootenai Kraft and Grocery. Gus looked proud as he trotted beside the girl, surely enjoying the September breeze blowing through his coat. Thanks to the stiffness from missing this month's physical therapy appointment, Lovina moved slowly. Finally, the trio entered the store to find it nearly empty and Lovina breathed a sigh of relief.

"Good morning, ladies. And good morning to Sir Gus too." Annie greeted them from behind the counter, giving a little curtsy to Gus. As the owner of West Kootenai Kraft and Grocery, she had her finger on the pulse of the area. Her kindness and obvious faith in God made her a friend to the Plain and *Englisch* alike.

"Hi, Miss Annie. Do you have any popsicles in the store?" Emily hadn't been pleased to learn that the Grabers' deep freeze was empty of frozen treats, and Lovina had promised to make that right today.

"I sure do, sweetie. They are in that cooler over there." Annie gestured. "Go grab one from the open box for now and then you can take a box home too."

"May I, Lovie?" Emily looked to Lovina.

Lovina nodded and Emily scampered to the cooler to pick her favorite flavor. "Thanks, Annie. I have some things I need to mail this morning. I will need to buy a few stamps." After plunking down a few dollars, Lovina slid several envelopes across the counter. Annie stamped them and placed them in the outgoing mailbox, her blonde braid swinging as she did.

"I'm glad you came in today. Something came to the store for you yesterday and I haven't had a chance to bring it over." Annie spoke just above a whisper. She reached below the counter and pulled out a thick manila envelope and handed it to Lovina.

Lovina scrunched her nose and turned the package over in her hands. It was addressed to the Western Wildflower, in care of West Kootenai Kraft and Grocery.

She clutched the envelope to her.

"What makes you think this is for me, Annie?" Lovina tried to keep her voice calm but she knew the fire in her cheeks betrayed her.

"I'm not wrong, am I?" Annie returned.

"But how—"

"I see just about everything going on here in West Kootenai, and I know everyone. You come in for a stamp every week and mail an envelope to *The Budget*. The last few weeks, that envelope has gotten fatter. Part of it is your column, I'm sure, but you send more than that. When this letter came in, I took my best guess. And I was right." Annie didn't look a bit smug. Her face held her usual sweet, encouraging smile.

"Annie, you can't tell anyone! I mean it. Not Ike, not Jenny, not my *mem*, no one!" Lovina's panicked voice screeched out the plea. "I had been getting the mail at the library in Whitefish, but I haven't had time to make a trip there since Emily came, so I asked them to send it here. I assumed they would address it to me personally, not the Western Wildflower."

"Oh, sweet girl. Your secret is safe with me. But why wouldn't you want anyone to know you are the Western Wildflower? Your advice letters are the most buzzed-about part of *The Budget*. You have a gift," Annie declared.

"Do you think the church elders would agree with you? I've already heard Brother Martin is trying to figure out if the Western Wildflower is from around here. He thinks my writing is too fancy. I just write the words God puts on my heart. West Kootenai is a pretty liberal Amish community compared to others, but I don't think some folks are ready for an unmarried woman doling out advice."

Annie looked pensively at Lovina. "You are probably right. Some of the old-fashioned ideas these men like to hold onto around here drive me positively crazy."

Emily returned to the counter with her popsicles. "Look, Lovina, I got a red one for now and a whole box to put in your freezer for later."

Lovina smiled at her, stuffing the envelope into her bag. "Well, we had better pay for those and hurry back home before they all melt. Thank you, Annie, for all your help today."

Lovina paid Annie for the popsicles and ushered Emily and Gus toward the door. They waved to Annie and headed toward home.

Emily chattered as they walked back to the Graber home, but Lovina's mind was a million miles away. Had she been foolish to have mail sent to the store? Was this too big a risk to take?

The worries swirled in Lovina's head but would have to wait. Lovina and Emily needed to hang the laundry and start another load in the washer, tend the garden a bit, then fix lunch. In the afternoons, when the morning's chores were caught up, Emily usually asked Lovina to read her a story or two before the little girl curled up for a nap. Plain life provided a lot more physical work than *Englisch* life did, and her little body was learning to adjust.

"Do you think they have laundry in heaven?" Emily's inquisitive nature made Lovina smile.

"I certainly hope not. I think we don't have to do any work in heaven, just sit around and enjoy Jesus."

"But laundry is fun, Lovie!" Emily could find joy in the simplest tasks, and the Plain life was new and exciting to her now.

"When it's wintertime and we have to hang things to dry and our fingers nearly freeze off, it is much less fun." Lovina's words held warning but she was sure her eyes sparkled with glee. "Feeding the chickens isn't as much fun then either."

Emily considered this for a moment, then handed Lovina another clothespin. "We'll just have to make a big batch of cocoa to drink when we come in from chores then."

Lovina laughed at Emily's practical solution, but her heart sank. If all went according to plan, by wintertime Thomas would be married and Emily would be helping some other woman hang the laundry and do the chores. While Lovina knew this was the right thing to do—the best thing for Emily and Thomas—it still hurt to think of facing the day without Emily beside her.

A lump formed in her throat, making it hard to speak. Finally, she eeked out a few words. "Yes, Emily, hot cocoa makes everything better."

If only hot cocoa could soothe the ache in her heart that surfaced every time she thought of Thomas and Emily forming a family with some other woman. She bit back tears and silently scolded herself for letting jealousy bubble up.

Lovina knew the right thing to do. She just didn't know how hard doing it would be.

Chapter Seventeen

THURSDAY, SEPTEMBER 7

"O*ncle* Thomas, pleeease? I'm making a family and building them a house." Emily batted her dark eyelashes at Thomas, effectively turning him into a giant marshmallow. His anger dissolved when she gave him one of those looks.

He glanced at the playdough creation she built in the Grabers' kitchen floor. A mother, a father, a child, and a home. Just what she deserved to have.

Emily stifled a yawn. It was time to put her to bed. The social worker was coming tomorrow, and she needed a good night's sleep.

"Clean up your playdough, Emily. You need to get to bed." Thomas meant for his voice to sound light, but Emily still winced at his tone.

"Let me take care of that. You go on to bed, and I will see you in the morning," Lovina interjected. Emily gave her a hug and waved goodnight to her.

Lovina had been strangely distant since their hike on Monday. He wasn't sure if she was feeling under the weather or overwhelmed. Thankfully, tonight, she'd seemed a little warmer and more like herself.

Thomas and Emily walked in silence across the lawn to the cabin, the late summer sun dipping low behind the mountains.

"*Oncle* Thomas, can you sing me a song tonight?"

She had first asked for a bedtime song on the second night she was here. Anna Ruth had a special one she sang to Emily every night, and when Emily described it to him, he realized that it was the same one his *mem* had sung to him as a boy. It touched him that Anna Ruth would continue a tradition from her Amish life, but the song made Thomas too emotional. He couldn't sing it without tearing up.

He usually distracted her by offering a story from her Bible storybook that Anna Ruth had read from, but tonight she was insistent on the song.

"I'm not sure I remember it," he dodged.

"It's easy, *Oncle* Thomas. *Schloof, bobbeli, schloof,*" she sang, obviously expecting him to fall in. He hesitated, but she reached out and took his hand, giving it a gentle, encouraging squeeze.

"Why don't you run and get your pajamas on and I'll see if I can remember the words."

Emily usually took her time getting ready for bed, but the promise of a song tonight seemed to motivate her to move at lightning speed. Within minutes, she stood at the bedroom door.

"Did you remember it?" Her voice, full of innocence, stirred tenderness within him.

"I think so, but you might need to help me. Hop in bed and we'll see if I can sing it."

She scrambled into the bed and pulled the quilt up under her chin, watching Thomas with expectation.

He took a breath and closed his eyes. "*Schloof, bobbeli, schloof.*" His voice wobbled with emotion as he sang the old familiar tune. The Pennsylvania Dutch words came back to him easily. He chanted the words in rhythm with his niece.

"Schloof, bobbeli, schloof!
Der Daadi hiet die Schoof.
Die Mammi hiet die braune Kieh
Und kummt net heem bis Marriye frieh.
Schloof, Bobbeli, schloof!"

"Do you know what the words mean?" Thomas asked.

Emily shrugged. "Sleep, baby sleep, then something about the sheep and the cows, I think? My mommy thought it was funny because we didn't have sheep and cows."

"You are right. The first verse says,

"Sleep, my baby, sleep!
Your Daddy's tending the sheep.
Your Mommy's taken the cows away.
Won't come home till break of day.
Sleep, my baby, sleep!"

Thomas sang the verse over a few times until Emily's eyelids drooped and her breathing became deep and even. He continued holding her hand and humming the tune until he was certain she was asleep.

He moved into the living area to tidy up and make one final pass over the paperwork Lovina had put together for the social worker's visit tomorrow. He looked through the folders on the dinette table, not seeing them. He slipped out the cabin door and back across to the Graber house to see if he had left them there.

He knocked gently on the back door and Lovina appeared, a stack of papers in her hand. "I figured you might need these. I was just ready to head over to the cabin and hand them to you."

He took the paperwork from her, his shoulders instantly relaxing with the knowledge that Lovina had everything under control.

"Is Emily asleep?" Lovina asked.

Thomas nodded. "I sang her a couple of verses of a lullaby tonight and she was out like a light."

She opened the door a bit wider and motioned for him to come in and sit. "You sang?" Lovina's eyes went wide with shock, and her lips spread into a smile.

Thomas felt a deep blush creep up his neck and color his face. He grinned sheepishly. "I'm not much of a singer, but Emily insisted on hearing a song that Anna Ruth used to sing to her. It was one that our *mem* sang to us."

Thomas wasn't sure what prompted him to share this with Lovina, but something about her invited him to relax. He spent so much time keeping his emotions bottled up, it was refreshing for him to let his guard down for a moment.

"That's so sweet that Anna Ruth would share a Plain song with her *Englisch* daughter. It means that her Amish upbringing still meant something to her, don't you think?" Lovina's soft brown eyes brimmed with tears. Thomas appreciated her empathy.

He nodded. "Anna Ruth had her own faith practices, Emily has told me, but pieces of our beliefs were still important to her. I thought when she left . . ." He trailed off, unsure of what to say next. In his family, they didn't share much information with outsiders, or even with each other. As odd as it felt to talk about his past, something about Lovina told him she was a safe person to open up to.

"I didn't mean to pry, Thomas. I'm sorry." She smiled apologetically at him, revealing dimples in her cheeks he hadn't noticed before.

"You didn't pry. I've just never talked much about Anna Ruth to anyone. Ike knows a little of the story, but just the highlights. I've spent the last twelve years pretending that I didn't have a sister, and now I have to face the future knowing she's truly gone. It's just strange."

Lovina nodded sympathetically but remained quiet. He

appreciated her willingness to let him tell the story at his own pace.

Thomas cleared his throat. "Anna Ruth was my only sibling. We were six years apart, but she was always the more rebellious one. Our *dat* was headstrong, firm in his beliefs. He never saw anything other than black and white, right and wrong. The two of them clashed for as long as I can remember."

He took a long pause before continuing, thinking back to the day Anna Ruth left them. He'd been a twelve-year-old boy, self-conscious, awkward, and withdrawn. Not much about that had changed in twelve years. Anna Ruth and *Dat* fought often, but, unlike Anna Ruth, Thomas could never forget exactly what that argument was about, and how he was at fault for everything.

"The night before she left, I found her dressed in *Englisch* clothes, ready to sneak out." He slipped back in time, remembering every detail—her in jeans, a sweater, cowboy boots, and a full face of makeup.

"*Dat* would have killed her if he had seen her. Anna Ruth made me promise not to tell him, then she asked me to do a favor for her. We owned a dairy farm and had daily chores *Dat* made us do, on top of everything else. She was supposed to water the calves in the back pen and give one its medicine the next morning. She offered me ten dollars to do it so she could sleep in a little."

He'd grumbled a bit, like any pre-teen boy would, but ten dollars sounded like a million to him. All he had to do was set his alarm a little bit earlier, and *Dat* would never know that Anna Ruth had delegated the job to him.

Anna Ruth slipped out the back door and disappeared into the night. Thomas went to bed thinking about all the things that ten dollars would buy him.

"The next morning, I got up to do my chores as usual, completely forgetting about my promise to Anna Ruth. It wasn't until *Mem* called us all to breakfast that I realized I hadn't kept my end of the bargain. I tried to find an excuse to go back out and take care of the calves before *Dat* saw what happened, but it was too late."

Thomas remembered that argument between his *dat* and his *schwester* almost verbatim.

"Anna Ruth, did I not tell you to tend to the calves in the back pen this morning?" *Dat*'s angry voice boomed across the table. His accusing eyes narrowed at Anna Ruth.

Panic-stricken, his sister hopped to her feet. *"I-I-I forgot, Dat. I'll go do it right now."*

"Yes, you will, and you'll do it every day for the rest of the month. 'The soul of the sluggard desireth, and hath nothing'. That's what you'll have—no breakfast for the rest of the month."

As though that settled the matter, *Dat* shoved a forkful of breakfast casserole into his mouth.

Anna Ruth stomped across the kitchen toward the back door, seething. *"This is ridiculous, Dat. I just forgot. There's no reason to starve me. That's child abuse."* She'd slammed the back door as she headed to tend the calves.

Thomas stared at the table as he relayed the events to Lovina. "I'd never seen *Dat* that angry before. He threw his napkin down and followed her out the door. *Mem* and I finished our breakfast in silence, but I could hardly chew my food. It was my fault he was mad at Anna Ruth. I'd been lazy, forgetful, selfish.

"Before long, Anna Ruth and *Dat* returned to the kitchen. Her face was swollen from crying, and she went straight to her bedroom. *Dat* gave me a cold, hard look that warned me not to say a word, so I went out to the barn to finish my chores before I left for school. Guilt sat in my belly like a brick. If only I had remembered to do this one little thing for Anna Ruth, *Dat* wouldn't have been so angry.

Lovina's face reflected sympathy as she listened to Thomas tell the story. "What a burden for you to carry," she whispered.

Thomas swallowed hard and continued, his eyes holding a faraway look. "I took extra care in the barn, finishing my chores and making sure that everything was neat and in order— the way

Dat liked it. As I walked back to the house, I heard a car coming down the road. It screeched its tires as it came to a stop in front of our house. I hid behind a tree so I could watch what happened without being observed."

"A door slammed, and I saw Anna Ruth run across the yard. Dressed in *Englisch* clothes and carrying a backpack, she looked back toward the house for a moment before getting in the car. I wanted to run after her, tell her I was sorry for causing this mess, but I was frozen in place. I watched the car dart down the road. That was the last time I ever saw her."

"Oh, Thomas." Lovina reached across the table and placed her tiny hand atop his. "That had to be so hard for you."

His eyes drifted to their hands, resting together so affectionately. They sat like that in the dim quiet of the kitchen for a moment before Lovina drew back her hand.

Thomas continued his story. "It was, especially because I've had to live all these years knowing it was all my fault."

Lovina's eyes went wide. "Thomas, that's just not true. You were a child, and you made a mistake."

He shrugged. "It was my fault *Dat* got so mad. It was the final straw for her, I guess. I missed her so much and regretted what I'd done every single day. *Dat* wasn't very understanding of my grief. Life had to go on. Our dairy farm struggled to stay profitable and *Dat* was determined to make it successful, even though we encountered every obstacle imaginable."

"A dairy farm? I had no idea you were skilled with livestock. I guess I assumed you'd been a woodworker back in Belleville."

Thomas laughed wryly. "I'm not skilled with livestock! I was the worst dairy farmer on the earth. And *Dat* frowned on woodworking—called it frivolous. But *Dat* had instilled a sense of duty over all else, so I tried my best to learn how to run the farm. *Dat* passed away unexpectedly about three years ago, and I kept running the farm even though I hated the dairy business. Then *Mem* got sick a year ago. She encouraged me to decide what I really wanted to do with my life, so after she passed away, I sold the farm and moved out here to start over."

"Thank you for sharing that with me. I can't imagine what a shock it was to learn about Anna Ruth's passing and Emily's existence just as soon as you moved here for a fresh start." Lovina's kindness warmed Thomas's heart.

Thomas nodded. "I'd spent a quarter of a century as Charles Smucker's son, failed dairy farmer, brother of a runaway. I was ready to be anonymous in West Kootenai. I thought I could live in the bachelor camp, work with my hands, and never have to look over my shoulder to see if someone was waiting for my next spectacular failure. That obviously wasn't what the Lord had planned."

"He certainly does have a way of pushing us out of our comfort zone, doesn't He?" Lovina asked.

"It's probably really easy for you—you're so confident and outgoing."

Lovina shook her head, her cheeks reddening, emphasizing the scar on the left. "Oh, gracious, no! Why, I love to help others, but I hate to be in the spotlight. Having this limp and then the scar drew more attention than I could handle when I was younger, so I try to work in the background when I can."

"Can I ask you about the limp and the scar? I've wondered, but it didn't seem like an appropriate question."

"I was born with one leg shorter than the other, so I've always had the limp. Sometimes it hurts, but it's more of a nuisance than anything else. I've always hated it because it made me stand out. I could never keep up with others or do the same things they did."

She tucked her head. "The scar came later. My twin sister Josie and I were doing some chores around the house while *Mem* and *Dat* were at work on our tree farm. It was cold and the fire in the fireplace was dying down, so Josie wanted to get it going again. Now, Josie sometimes acted before she thought, and this was one of those times."

Lovina's voice shook as she recounted the tale. "Of course, we had kerosene lamps all over the house, but Josie didn't know how they worked. Instead of asking our older sister Amanda for help stoking the fire, she thought it would be easier to just pour some oil from the lamp onto it. I walked in just as she did, but I wasn't fast enough to stop her. The fire blazed up. I tried to put it out, but a flame shot out and burned my face. That's where the scar came from. If I thought the limp made me stand out, the scar was like a spotlight that followed me around."

Thomas nodded. "Yeah, that would be tough for a *kind*. No one likes feeling different. To be honest, you are so good with Emily, so competent at everything around here, I don't even notice the limp or the scar most of the time."

"They are my version of Paul's thorn in the flesh." She sighed. "I've adjusted to them. I've accepted my limitations and how they fit into God's plan for me. He made me to be a single woman who will care for my parents as they age."

Thomas blinked, shocked by her revelation. "Surely you don't mean that!"

"I do. It's something I've known for a long time. Don't give me that pitiful look, either. It doesn't bother me anymore." Lovina dropped her gaze to the table, refusing to meet his.

He didn't know how to respond to her.

She was selling herself short, but she obviously didn't want to hear that from him. He wanted to lavish praise on her and tell her just how perfect he thought she was, but he didn't want to make a fool of himself. "Well, I'm glad you spoke up that day in the store. We'd have never made it without you and your family supporting us. Can you imagine Emily bunking at the bachelor cabin? That would have lasted about three minutes!" He laughed at the thought.

Lovina chuckled too. "Three minutes seems generous. I doubt that any of the guys would be willing to have princess tea parties or let her bedazzle their lunch boxes. No, God knew what He was doing, placing me in the store that day to be in just the right place at the right time."

Thomas rose and made his way to the door. "I had better get back before Emily wakes up and can't find me." He paused before stepping out the door. "Good night, Lovina. And thanks, for everything."

He walked back to the cabin, his heart feeling a bit lighter than usual. Sharing his story with Lovina, hearing her tell him that he wasn't to blame for Anna Ruth leaving, made him think she might be right. He offered up a prayer as he slipped back into the cabin as quietly as possible.

Father, You always know what we need before we even ask. Lovina is the answer to a prayer I didn't even know I was praying. Help her to see herself as the generous, capable, lovely woman she really is.

The words surprised him, but he couldn't deny their truth. He *did* see her as generous, capable, and lovely. He thought for a moment about how gently she'd touched his hand as she listened to him tell about his father. His heart sped up when he pictured her kind eyes and sweet smile, then it dropped to his stomach. What he felt for Lovina Graber was much more than gratitude— and it terrified him.

Was he falling in love with Lovina?

Chapter Eighteen

LATE THURSDAY NIGHT, SEPTEMBER 7

Lovina tossed and turned in her bed. Something she had done today had aggravated her hip. She'd used some of her homemade liniment and that helped, but now she was wide awake. Over and over in her head, she replayed the same image—her hand sitting atop Thomas's strong one. Why had she reached out and touched him?

She shook her head to clear the image. She needed a distraction

Because today had been so full of preparations for the social worker's coming visit, Lovina hadn't had time to read through the newest package of letters for the Western Wildflower column. She sat up and lit the kerosene lamp on her nightstand, then reached for her tote bag and pulled out the envelope Annie handed her earlier.

She skimmed through letters asking for advice on curing a baby's diaper rash, what to do with a bumper crop of beets, and how to convince your parents to let you get a dog. At the bottom of the stack was another letter, and reading it made her heart beat like a jackhammer.

Dear Western Wildflower,

I live in a small community where nothing much ever happens. That is, until a few weeks ago when a new bachelor moved to town. Shortly after that, he was joined by a young girl he has to care for. He needs help raising the girl but doesn't seem interested in courting or marrying anyone. In fact, he has a spinster lady that helps him with the child, but due to her physical ailments, she is not fit to be a wife and mother.

Perhaps where he came from, it wasn't frowned upon for a bachelor and a spinster to spend so much time together, but in our town, it has caused people to talk. I'm afraid it is going to ruin his reputation and that of the little girl as well.

Furthermore, the little girl he is caring for desperately needs a motherly example in her life. She plays too rough, has no manners, and does not follow our community's dress rules. Do you think the elders of our community should speak to him and encourage him to marry a suitable young woman? Perhaps even make a match for him with one of the acceptable eligible young ladies?

Sincerely,

A Concerned Neighbor

Lovina blinked, unable to believe the words she read. She flipped the letter over, looking for any trace of the identity of its sender, but there was none. However, in her heart, she just knew. This letter had to be about Thomas and Emily. And her.

Her heart continued to hammer in her chest. Who in West Kootenai would write such a mean-spirited letter? She had only one suspect in mind.

Dorcas Martin.

If it was indeed Dorcas, had she guessed Lovina was the Western Wildflower? Or did she simply hope Lovina would read *The Budget* and know this letter was about her? Surely it was the latter.

Lovina reread the letter, feeling an ache in her heart that hurt infinitely more than her hip did. *A spinster lady that helps . . . not fit to be a wife . . . it has caused people to talk.*

The words on paper stung as though they were fresh wounds, even though she'd heard them many times before. She'd heard them from her teacher. Then when Dan Herschberger broke off their very brief courtship, she heard them from him.

"Lovina, you're a nice enough girl, but you can't really expect me to want to marry you. I mean, my dat is the bishop and I hope to be bishop someday too. Even if you didn't have that scar on your face, I couldn't marry you. You could never do all the work an Amish wife needs to do, let alone support your husband as the bishop. You're damaged, and I can't risk my reputation. I should have never given you false hope. I'm sorry."

Damaged. Hearing that at age sixteen had caused her to cry for days.

Now, it fueled her.

She couldn't remove the scar or undo the limp, but she could push herself to exceed everyone's expectations. Dan was right when he said she wasn't cut out to be a wife, but she could still be valuable as a helper to others.

Lovina flinched at the memory, still painful nine years later.

She didn't have time to wallow in the past. She needed to write her response to the letter, but her hands balled up into fists and her heart thumped in her ears. Just once, she wished she could respond to the hateful words rather than tuck her tail and hide from her offenders.

She seethed for a moment until a realization occurred to her.

Maybe she couldn't respond, but the Western Wildflower could.

Since Dorcas—or whoever it was—had asked for the Western Wildflower's advice, that was exactly what she would get. She whipped out her pencil and notebook and started scribbling away.

> Dear Concerned Neighbor,
> Mind your own business. The Bible says for us to aspire to live quietly and mind our own affairs. Perhaps you should take that advice.
> Sincerely,
> The Western Wildflower.

Lovina reread her words and crossed them out. Too sassy. *The Budget* probably wouldn't even publish a letter that was so direct. She sighed deeply and started again.

> Dear Concerned Neighbor,
> If I were in your shoes, I would not speak to the elders about this situation. Give the bachelor and the girl some time to work out how to live together. Perhaps the spinster you mention is more capable than you suspect. You should not judge her based on appearances.
> Sincerely,
> The Western Wildflower.

That was less aggressive, but still lacked the poetic wisdom readers expected from the Western Wildflower. She scratched that response out, too, and put the letter aside. She dashed off answers to a couple of the other more run-of-the-mill questions.

The Thomas letter required a delicate—yet still truthful—answer. While her first answer helped ease the sting of the insulting words, it was rude. She knew the best response would have to be tactful and well thought out. She tapped her pencil on her knee, urging her brain and heart to cooperate.

Dear Concerned Neighbor,

Thank you for being a caring friend to this bachelor and his young charge. My first piece of advice is to step back from the situation and pray for everyone involved. Ask God to show you the steps to take to help this family.

My second piece of advice is to bear in mind that you are only seeing one side of the issue. This young girl who seems ill-mannered to you may be experiencing trauma and needs support to heal her heart and mind. Perhaps she simply needs more time to adjust to her home and kind friends in the community to help her.

As for the relationship between the bachelor and spinster, you should not make assumptions about them. When you hear others gossip, do what you can to put an end to the rumors.

We are told in the Bible to bear the weaknesses and burdens of others. In this situation, the best solution is to pray, watch, and wait for the Lord to move. He works out all things for the good of those who love Him. Be a friend to the people in this situation. Involving the elders or matchmaking for the bachelor could cause more problems.

Sincerely,

The Western Wildflower.

There. While the first paragraph dripped with syrupy sweetness, she recalled *Mem*'s saying. *You catch more flies with sugar than you do with vinegar.* So, she was as tactful as she could be. And it was a sound answer. Satisfied that she'd replied well, Lovina packaged the responses up and slid them into an envelope.

Lovina lowered the wick of the lamp until the flame nearly disappeared, then blew it out. Exhausted from writing such an emotionally draining letter, she rolled to her side, sure sleep would come quickly.

But instead of sleep, her brain whirred with a thought that just occurred to her. While barbs from the letter writer and Dan were hurtful, Lovina had long since come to terms with the way others saw her. Why did this letter cut so deeply?

She wrestled with the question for a while, until it was overtaken by a whole swarm of questions that she wasn't sure she wanted to know the answers to.

While Lovina had claimed to be looking for a wife for Thomas, she hadn't actually taken any action toward that goal. Why not?

Why had no one met her impossibly high standards? Why had no one seemed like a good match? Why had no one come along as an answer to her shallow prayers?

An answer began to crystallize, and Lovina filled with shame.

Mem was right—she was falling in love with Thomas.

Chapter Nineteen

LATE THURSDAY, SEPTEMBER 7

Over the past few weeks, Thomas had learned to function on limited sleep. He never seemed to be able to have a full night's rest anymore. Too many things weighed on his heart and mind.

After he left Lovina's kitchen for the second time that night, he tossed and turned on the couch for a while before falling into a fitful sleep. Sometime later, he woke to the sound of crying from Emily's bedroom. She'd struggled with nightmares the first few nights she was here but those had almost disappeared. He bolted upright on the couch, listening carefully to see if the crying continued.

"*Oncle* Thomas!" Emily called. He hopped to his feet, crossed the living space in three big steps, and threw open the bedroom door.

"What's wrong, Emily?" He looked down at the tiny form trembling in the bed, her sheets all askew. Her face was wet with sweat and tears and her sandy blonde hair was matted to her head.

She sobbed so hard that only hiccups came from her mouth. He sat down next to her on the bed and waited for her to calm herself. Emily launched herself into his lap, encircling his neck with her arms.

Unsure of how to soothe her, he patted her back almost robotically.

After a while, he felt her relax in his arms and her breathing became regular again. "It was a dream, Emily. It wasn't real. Just a dream," he soothed. Lovina had told him to wait until daytime to discuss the nightmares and try to get Emily to go back to sleep as soon as possible. She had read a book about it when he mentioned that Emily had been having them and had lots of good suggestions that helped him. He tried to remember what else she'd told him.

"I dreamed about my mommy again. But this time, that social worker, Ms. Williams, was there, and she took me away from my mommy and daddy and from you, too." She sniffled and buried her head in Thomas's neck.

Clearly, Emily had picked up on his anxiety about the social worker's coming visit. He needed to reassure her that everything would be fine—even if he wasn't completely confident in that himself.

"I'm sorry you had a bad dream, Emily. I don't think Ms. Williams wants to take you away. She just wants to make sure that everything here is going well. Everything will be just fine. Now, let's get you back to sleep so that you have lots of energy when she comes." He handed her one of her special dolls and gestured to the pillow.

"I want Lovie!" Her bottom lip trembled.

Instinctively, he clenched his jaw. "Lovina is asleep." He hated the sharp tone his voice took when he was frustrated, but even more he hated the hurt look in Emily's eyes. Why didn't Emily rely on him the same way she did Lovina Graber? Probably because Lovina was kind and patient and never lashed out in exasperation.

Thomas had learned so much from Lovina, though, and he

was responding to Emily with more tenderness than he had before. He couldn't let every annoyance derail him.

What would Lovina say?

He tried again. "We can't wake her up tonight, but you will see her in the morning. Besides, what would Lovina do that I can't do?"

Emily rolled her green-blue eyes. "Well, first of all, she would get me a drink of water and maybe a wet washcloth to clean up my face."

"I can do that," Thomas responded, waiting for further instructions. "What else?"

"And then she would read me a story from a book or tell me a story about when she was a little girl."

Thomas didn't have many sweet stories from his childhood, but he could read her a Bible story, he supposed. "I'll go get a washcloth and some water for you while you pick out a story from the Bible storybook for me to read."

He went to the bathroom to get what he needed for his *niesse*, thankful the Grabers had been progressive enough Plain people to include indoor plumbing in their cabin. He'd grown up with an outhouse and a water pump and didn't miss either of those one little bit.

Thomas remembered one time when he was not much bigger than Emily, when he decided to pull a prank on his big sister but got his *dat* instead. Anna Ruth hated the outhouse even more than young Thomas had, and Thomas almost really got her one time.

As he returned to the bedroom, Emily's voice broke through his thoughts. "*Oncle*, I don't want a Bible story. I've heard all of those. Tell me about when you were a little boy."

Since the outhouse story was so fresh in his mind, Thomas decided to share it. "Okay, but this story is a little bit gross."

Emily squealed in delight. "I'm pretty tough. Tell me!"

He continued. "Have you ever seen an outhouse? An outside toilet?"

"Like a porta potty?" Emily wrinkled her nose.

"Sort of. We had one at our house instead of a bathroom inside. Your mother hated that thing. She was so embarrassed that we had an outhouse. As you can imagine, it could really stink sometimes. I think some of the other *kinner* at school made fun of her for having one."

"That's not nice," Emily declared, narrowing her eyes.

"No, it wasn't. Well, we kept a bucket filled with lime in the outhouse. It kept the smell from getting too bad if you sprinkled it whenever you . . . went."

"Ew!" Emily replied.

"I know. It was very 'ew.' Anyway, when I was about your age, I decided to play a trick on Anna Ruth. One of my buddies had a plastic snake that looked very real. I borrowed that and wrapped it around the lime bucket before I went to bed, thinking Anna Ruth would find it in the morning, since she was usually the first one up."

"*Oncle* Thomas! That's naughty, but a little bit funny. Did you get time out?"

"My *dat* didn't do time out." Thomas shuddered when he thought about the way his *dat* handled punishment. "Anyway, I was so nervous about her finding the snake the next morning that I barely slept that night. I could see the outhouse from my window, and it was a full moon, so I kept sneaking a peek to see if she found it yet. Finally, I heard the back door snap closed and I thought it was her. I went to the window and watched but it was my *dat*, not Anna Ruth."

Emily's eyebrows shot up, and she covered her mouth with her hands. "Did you get in big trouble?"

Thomas laughed and shook his head. "For once, no. *Dat* didn't even notice the snake. I sprinted down the stairs and to the outhouse and grabbed the snake before anyone else found it. I never tried another prank after that. I wasn't ever very good at them anyway."

"We should think of a prank to play on Lovina. She would love that."

"She might not like it as much as you think she would," Thomas warned, though Lovina did have a wonderful sense of humor, just like her father had. "Anyway, it's very late and we have a big day tomorrow. To bed with you, young lady."

"Can you tuck me in again? And maybe do my song?" She batted her long eyelashes to persuade him.

He smiled, needing very little encouragement. "Yes, but you must go back to sleep after one round of the song, okay?"

"Okay," she agreed, settling herself under the sheets.

He sang, watching her eyes grow heavy with each word. What could have been a catastrophe tonight turned into a sweet moment he would treasure. It filled his heart with hope for the future.

Maybe Ike was right—Anna Ruth's faith in him wasn't misplaced, and he could be a father to Emily. As he settled back onto the couch to catch a couple of hours' sleep before his busy day began, he pulled the quilt around his shoulders and offered up a prayer of thanks.

While none of this fit in the plan he'd concocted for a new life in West Kootenai, he couldn't deny that meeting his *niesse*—and Lovina Graber—had made his life fuller and less lonely. He'd never thought family life held anything other than friction and heartbreak, but what he was beginning to experience with Emily encouraged him to believe that more was possible.

When the social worker visited, would she see how much progress Thomas and Emily had made together? Or would she notice all the ways Thomas still fell short?

Chapter Twenty

Thomas pushed the eggs around on his breakfast plate, his stomach too full of butterflies to eat much of anything. Between jitters about the social worker's visit today and the feeling he got when Lovina smiled at him, he could hardly sit still. He inhaled the steam rolling from the cup of tea Lovina had brewed for breakfast in place of *kaffe*, hoping the fragrant herbs would warm him and clear his mind.

"What did you call this blend, Lovina?" He blew on the hot liquid before taking a long sip. Her knack for creating healing teas was just one of her many gifts. She seemed to be able to anticipate what he might feel even before he did. Not only that but she knew how to set him right.

"It is Well With My Soul." Her smile reassured him that things would go well today. "I figured we might all need a little boost of serenity this morning. It has chamomile, which has calming properties, and then a little lemon balm and lavender, but not too much. I don't want you falling asleep on Ms. Williams today."

Henry laughed and stood. "No, sir, I don't think that would

be the impression you want to give. Now, Rose and I will be working on the tree farm most of today, so we'll be out of your way. Is there anything we can do for you before we head out?"

"Just keep us in your prayers," Thomas said. He stood up from the table and looked at Emily. "You ready to head back to the cabin and help me tidy up?"

Emily's shoulders sagged. "Can't I hang out with Lovie 'til the lady gets here? Pleeeease? Gus will need a walk pretty soon."

Thomas found her whining more annoying than usual this morning, but he also knew that if he didn't agree to let her stay, she'd pout. It was easier to agree than to fight. Pick your battles, Lovina had told him, and she, as usual, was right. "You can stay for just a little while, but don't get into anything messy and be ready to come back to the cabin as soon as Ms. Williams arrives." He shot Lovina a questioning look.

Had he done the right thing?

Lovina nodded back at him. "We'll just clean up the kitchen, walk Gus, and then I might work in my garden just a little. Emily will stay spic and span, won't you?" She pointed her forefinger at Emily, who nodded enthusiastically.

"Cross my heart, *Oncle*." Emily held two fingers up to her lips, kissed them, then made an X over her heart.

He couldn't help but smile at his *niesse* as he helped Lovina clear the table. She was definitely her mother's daughter. Headstrong and charming in equal amounts.

After Thomas had brought all the dishes to the sink, Emily opened the pantry door, pulled her little apron off a hook, and slipped it over her head. "Can you tie this for me, *Oncle*?"

Thomas made a sloppy bow with the strings. Emily turned around and slipped her arms around his neck, giving him a quick peck on the cheek.

"What was that for?" Thomas asked, bewildered at her sudden show of affection.

"You looked like you needed a hug," she answered with a shrug before scampering off to Lovina's side.

Lovina made eye contact with him, giving him a look full of wonder. He returned a grin then excused himself to go make final preparations for the social worker's visit.

He was grateful to have a few minutes to himself to gather his thoughts before Ms. Williams arrived. Emily's spontaneous hug had left him shaken and filled with a sudden urge to show Ms. Williams just what a good father he would make.

When Ms. Williams had left Emily with him three weeks ago, she'd given him a list of tasks to complete. With Lovina's help, he had worked through several folders full of paperwork and had pulled together most of the necessary documents. He had a plan for the ones he hadn't completed yet. The issue that worried him most was that Emily still needed to find a therapist to talk to, and West Kootenai had none. They'd found one in Whitefish, but the first available appointment wasn't until mid-October. He hoped Ms. Williams would understand the limitations of living in a rural area and extend some grace, especially in light of how well Emily had adjusted.

He walked across the Grabers' backyard and could hear the giggles coming from the kitchen. Lovina had a way of making Emily happy that Thomas aspired to have someday. Being able to soothe her after last night's bad dream gave him hope that he was on his way, but he still needed to curb his temper and tame his tongue when he spoke to her.

Thomas entered the cabin and looked around. Everything seemed to be in order. The stack of documents Ms. Williams would go over sat on the dinette table. Lovina and Emily had cleaned the cabin yesterday, and the fresh scent of Lovina's homemade solution lingered in the air. Lovina had also arranged some wildflowers in a vase and placed those on the kitchenette's counter. Emily's toys were all put away and her bed was neatly made.

The clock on the wall read 7:45. Miss Williams would be here by 8:30.

Thomas sat down with his Bible and read his daily psalm.

Today's was Psalm 29. He read through it, stopping at the last verse. *"The LORD will give strength unto His people; the LORD will bless His people with peace."* He read it over and over, saying it aloud a few times as well. His heart pleaded with the Lord for strength and peace, no matter what today's visit brought.

A knock at the door interrupted his prayer.

He looked up at the clock again. 8:23. He'd been sitting longer than he realized. He closed his Bible and walked to the door, taking a deep breath before opening it.

Ms. Williams stood in the doorway, dressed in a fancy black pantsuit and heels. She pushed a pair of sunglasses back on her head, sweeping her sleek dark brown hair out of her face.

"Mr. Smucker, how do you do?"

"Good to see you again, Ms. Williams. Won't you come in?" He stepped aside to make room for the social worker to pass, then peered around the backyard for evidence of Emily. She and Lovina must have taken the dog on a walk. When they returned, they would see Ms. Williams's car in the driveway and Lovina would bring Emily back to the cabin.

Thomas gestured for the social worker to have a seat at the dinette table. He sat across from her and waited for her to initiate the conversation. She opened her briefcase and pulled out several folders, arranging them in front of her on the table.

He wished he had a cup of Lovina's calming tea right now.

He drummed his fingers on the table. "I—uh—have done a good bit of the paperwork you left for me," he croaked.

She cocked her eyebrow as she glanced at the pile of papers on the table. "I see that. That's a good step. Now, let me find my checklist and we'll get started." She shuffled through a folder for a moment until she pulled out a packet of stapled papers.

"Do you have your financial statement? We can start there."

Thomas looked through his stack and pulled the form. "There you go."

She skimmed over it and placed it facedown on the table. They repeated this with different forms for a few minutes.

Thomas glanced at the clock on the wall. Emily and Lovina should have been back from walking Gus by now.

"While you are reviewing those, I'm going to pop over to the Graber house and see if Emily is ready to come back over. She was helping Lov—uh—Miss Graber with some chores this morning while I prepared for your visit. I'll be right back."

The social worker nodded and continued reading through the paperwork. Thomas sprinted across the yard and knocked on the Grabers' back door. No one answered. He walked around the side of the house to find Lovina tending her garden patch but no sign of his *niesse*.

"Where's Emily?" Thomas squeaked out, his heart thudding in his chest.

"Isn't she with you?" Lovina placed her hand over her eyes to shield them from the sun.

His blood ran cold. Ironic, since he felt hot all over. "I left her with you! Of course she isn't with me!" Lovina had promised she would watch her—that she would return Emily to him. "Where did she go?"

"Thomas, I'm sure—" Lovina's voice was soothing but Thomas didn't want to hear it.

"How could you be so careless?" Thomas paced around the yard, calling for his *niesse*. "Emily! Where are you?"

Lovina dusted her hands on her apron and stood, panic sweeping across her features. "I sent her back to your cabin when we came back from walking Gus. I saw that Ms. Williams was here, so I told her to go on back. Then I came around here to tidy the garden. I can't imagine where she might have gone off to."

Ms. Williams emerged from the cabin. "What's all the yelling about?"

Thomas exchanged a glance with Lovina, silently warning her not to answer, but she ignored him.

"Emily is playing a little trick on her *oncle*, I'm sure. She's playing a game of hide and seek." Lovina's voice sounded unnaturally peppy. Her scar flared, hot and red. Thomas wondered if the social worker would notice.

"Now is not the time for games, Miss Graber. Does Mr. Smucker often have trouble keeping control of his niece?"

"Oh, no, Ms. Williams. Emily is very well behaved," Lovina responded. "Let me just check the barn to see if I can coax her out of hiding."

Lovina hobbled toward the barn. Thomas followed close behind.

"Emily?" Lovina's gentle voice shook only slightly as she threw the barn door open.

"Lovie?" A small quiet voice rose from the hay.

"Emily Grace Spencer, come out of there right now," Thomas boomed.

Emily scrambled out of the hay, dusting stray pieces off her dress. "I was cutting through the barn to come back to the cabin and I saw a kitten." She held a small orange cat that was purring happily in her arms. "He let me catch him, and I wanted to hold him for a while. I must have fallen asleep."

Relief flooded Thomas, followed quickly by shame.

He'd lost his temper with Lovina and with Emily, and the social worker was there to witness it. Last night's victory of comforting Emily after her nightmare was a distant memory, completely overshadowed by his most recent bumble. He turned and trudged out of the barn, Emily and Lovina following behind him.

Ms. Williams stood outside in the yard waiting for them. "Well, hello, Miss Emily. You were playing hide and seek, I hear?"

"Not really. I just found a kitten and took a little nap." Emily produced the kitten for Ms. Williams to see.

The social worker put her hands in front of her and took a step back. "I'm highly allergic! Don't get that near me, please."

Thomas realized that his future with Emily was in the balance. An overreaction here could put an end to his guardianship. He pressed his lips shut and breathed in through his nose, attempting to slow the frustration rising within him. Again, he wished he had a to-go mug of Lovina's calming tea.

Thankfully, Lovina took the kitten from Emily's hands. "How about I take this little fluff ball back to the barn. She probably has a mama cat looking for her. She's awfully little to be on her own."

"Miss Graber, when you are finished dealing with the cat, I would like you to join us so we can complete our interview today." Miss Williams nodded at Lovina, then headed back to the cabin.

Thomas looked from Emily to Lovina. "I'm sorry I reacted that way. I was scared when I couldn't find Emily."

"I know. It was a natural reaction, Thomas. Go on and talk with Ms. Williams." Lovina smiled at him, her soft brown eyes radiating the grace that she so generously dispensed, then headed back to the barn while Thomas and Emily went to the cabin.

Thomas exhaled, the first real breath he'd let out since he'd realized Emily was missing. Ms. Williams sat at the table, jotting down notes on a legal pad. Thomas wondered just what she was writing and prayed that it wasn't anything negative, though he worried that it could be.

"Let's get back to work, Mr. Smucker. I'm not seeing your medical form or a statement from a therapist for either of you. What seems to be the problem there?"

"Emily, you need to go wash up and change after being in the barn," Thomas advised. He was glad he had prepared an answer to this question. "We don't have a doctor or therapist here in West Kootenai. I've made appointments for both of us with folks in Whitefish but the first available aren't until October. Will that be a problem?"

"Not a problem, per se, but I will need you to have the forms faxed or emailed to me as soon as you complete the visits." Ms. Williams made a note on her pad.

"I'm sure we can make that happen," Thomas said, meaning

he was sure Lovina could make that happen. She'd taken the lead on scheduling appointments and, well, everything.

"See that you do. Now, since we don't have those papers, I can't call this an official and complete home visit, which means I'll need to come back in October after you have your paperwork in order. What I will do today is interview you and Emily, and Miss Graber since she seems to have such a large role in Emily's life."

As if on cue, Lovina opened the cabin door and entered. She greeted Thomas and Ms. Williams, then stepped into the kitchenette, out of the way.

"I'm glad you could join us, Miss Graber. I have some questions for the two of you I'd like to ask before Emily comes back in the room. I don't understand Amish traditions, so I'll be direct. Are you two romantically involved?"

Thomas swallowed hard and felt his cheeks fill with heat. Just as he opened his mouth to explain that Lovina was just a friend, Emily bounded in from the bathroom.

"*Oncle* Thomas and Lovie are going to get married."

Chapter Twenty-One

FRIDAY, SEPTEMBER 8

Lovina froze at the stove. *What?* Where had Emily gotten that idea?

"That's wonderful news, Mr. Smucker. That will really help your case when we go before a judge later this year. A two-parent family is always preferred when available." Ms. Williams finally smiled as she jotted down more notes on the legal pad.

"Wait just a moment, Ms. Williams," Thomas said. "I think there's been a misunderstanding."

Indeed there had been, and Lovina wanted to get it cleared up immediately. "Mr. Smucker and I are only friends. I love helping him with Emily, but I assure you, there is nothing romantic between us." Nor would there ever be. Not with him—or anyone else.

"Emily, why would you tell Ms. Williams that? You know that's not true." Thomas's face blanched.

The sharpness of his voice matched the angle of his jaw, Lovina thought as she watched him grow more and more defensive by the second.

"I asked God to make you marry Lovie, *Oncle*, and I know that God answers prayers."

Lovina's tension melted as she broke into a fit of giggles. Thomas closed his eyes, and a slow grin spread across his face. Ms. Williams pressed her lips together and covered her face with her hands.

"Oh, the faith of a child!" the social worker exclaimed.

Emily crossed her arms. "Don't laugh at me. God does answer prayers. They will get married. Just wait and see." She flopped facedown on the sofa, and Lovina moved over to stroke her back sympathetically.

"Em, we aren't laughing at you. Your announcement surprised us, that's all. But you need to understand that sometimes God's way of answering our prayers isn't the way we expect. Your *oncle* and I are friends, and that's all we are ever going to be." Lovina's heart broke a little saying the words, knowing that deep down, she wished they weren't true.

"We'll just see," Emily insisted.

Lovina raised her eyebrows at Thomas, who promptly changed the subject. "So, Ms. Williams, you want to do some interviews with us. Who would you like to speak to first?"

"I can start with Miss Graber, so when we're finished, she can go on about her day. Why don't we speak at your house?"

Lovina nodded and led the social worker out the door and across the yard to the Graber home.

"Could I fix you a cup of tea? Water?" Lovina offered, gesturing to the table for Ms. Williams to sit.

"Water would be wonderful, thanks."

Lovina filled a glass with ice and water and brought it to the table, then sat across from Ms. Williams.

The social worker took a long sip. "I'm interested in getting your perspective on how Mr. Smucker is managing with his niece. How would you describe him as a caregiver?"

Lovina thought for a moment. "When I first met Thomas, he was painfully shy and withdrawn. He spent nearly a month in the community without making any friends except Ike Sommers. Then Emily came to live with him and things started to change."

"Tell me more about that change," Ms. Williams probed.

"Well, I suppose that having Emily here forced him to be around my family, and we're a pretty rowdy bunch at times." Lovina chuckled. "It's impossible to be a wallflower around my *dat*. The more time Thomas spent around us, the more he came out of his shell. He and Emily really warmed up to one another too. At first, he seemed almost afraid of her and she seemed to smell his fear. She challenged him, and he didn't know how to respond. He could be short-spoken with her, but he and I discussed it, and he seemed to turn that around too. He's much more patient with her now, and when he does snap at her, he's willing to apologize."

Ms. Williams nodded and took some more notes. "That's good to hear. Instant parenthood is challenging, and I had many concerns about his ability to respond. Has he ever been physically violent with her?"

"Absolutely not." Lovina shook her head.

"Good, good. I've read that corporal punishment is a widely accepted practice in many Amish communities, so that was a particular worry for me. Speaking of the church, how does Emily seem to be adapting to life as an Amish girl?"

"At first, it was a bit of a struggle for her. She had some electronics withdrawal and wanted to wear her princess dress to church." Lovina smiled at the memory. "But she made some young friends and has embraced wearing Amish dresses, as long as her dolls can match her. She's learned a good bit of Pennsylvania Dutch too. We play a lot of games that entertain her without a device and she's endlessly fascinated with life on our little farm."

Ms. Williams grinned. "As evidenced by her new feline friend. All of this information is a credit to Mr. Smucker's ability to parent. Anything else you think I need to know?"

Lovina could think of a million things to add to what she'd told Ms. Williams. How Thomas's greenish-blue eyes would light up when Emily showed him her artwork. How perfectly Emily's tiny hand fit in his large one. And how soft his gruff voice became when he helped Emily with a task.

She didn't say any of those things, though. She feared they might reflect more on her admiration of Thomas than on his ability as a parent. And if she spoke those words out loud, her feelings for Thomas would be impossible to deny.

"Sometimes Thomas lacks confidence when it comes to Emily, but I think you can encourage him. A little praise goes a long way with him. I don't think he's heard much of that in his life. Tell him what he's doing well, and if you find things that need improvement, give him very specific steps he can take to right them. He will be a good *dat*. He just needs to experience a little more success to believe in himself."

Ms. Williams nodded and closed her folder. "I think your assessment is spot on, Miss Graber. One last question. I'm a bit concerned about what will happen when Mr. Smucker and Emily move out of your family's cabin. You've been such a key source of support. I wonder how well the two of them will do on their own."

"They are welcome to stay here as long as they need. I figure they'll stay at least through the summer until Emily starts school. By then, who knows? Thomas may have found the perfect woman to marry." She dropped her gaze to the floor. The thought pierced her heart.

"That's a good point. I'm sure that they'll be fine, given enough time. Might I use your bathroom before I go back to the cabin?"

"Certainly. Down the hall on your right."

Lovina was washing up Ms. Williams's glass when a shrill scream came from the bathroom. Panicked, she limped down the hall to see if the social worker was all right. At the door, she heard laughter.

Confused, she rapped on the door. "Is everything well, Ms. Williams?"

When the social worker opened the door, she was laughing too hard to speak. In her right hand, she held a small black plastic snake. When she finally caught her breath, she said, "When I went to wash my hands, this was hiding under the hand towel."

Lovina covered her mouth with her hand to keep laughter from spilling out. "Oh, Emily Grace. You *lappish maedel*. I think this was a prank meant for me. I'm so sorry, Ms. Williams."

"No apology needed, Miss Graber. This prank makes one thing very clear. Emily is a normal, healthy five-year-old girl with a sparkling sense of humor. She's thriving here, thanks to Mr. Smucker's efforts and, of course, your help."

"I heard a scream" Thomas appeared, interrupting the scene in the hall.

The two women looked at him in surprise then burst into laughter again.

"I think Emily tried to play a prank on me, but she got Ms. Williams instead." Lovina nodded at the other woman who held the snake up for Thomas to see.

His eyes went wide, and the color drained from his face. "That is my fault. I told her about a prank I tried to play on her mother when we were *kinner*. She thought you would enjoy it, Lovina. I'm so sorry, Ms. Williams. I should have warned her not to pull pranks."

Lovina watched his posture go rigid, like it did every time he made what he perceived as a mistake. Her heart sank. She exchanged a glance with Ms. Williams, who nodded in return.

"Mr. Smucker, let me assure you, all this tells me is that Emily is a happy little girl who is comfortable enough to play tricks on the people who care for her. That's completely normal behavior. You are doing a wonderful job, even for a single man. Now, let's get back over to the cabin and finish up our interviews before Emily gets any more ideas." She started down the hall and motioned for Thomas to follow her.

He shrugged at Lovina and headed back to the cabin.

Lovina wandered back through the house and sat again at the

table. She pulled the envelope full of Western Wildflower letters she'd carried all morning out of her apron pocket. She held it to her chest, more convinced than ever that she had to submit her response.

As pleased as Ms. Williams was with Thomas's progress, she still indicated that the judge would favor a two-parent home. Thomas was so close to creating a home for Emily and himself. There was just one piece missing from the puzzle, and Lovina was determined to help him find it.

Chapter Twenty-Two

Tuesday, September 12

Surrounded by the smell of sawdust, Thomas unpacked his lunch pail, carefully unwrapping each item before he started eating. Last week, he had made the mistake of haphazardly opening one of the packages tucked into the pail. He had ended up covered in glitter, which, he soon learned, clung fiercely to the gritty sawdust that covered every square inch of the Log Works. Emily thought it would be sweet to add what she called "a little pizazz" to his day.

That little girl was so much like his sister that he often felt that he had been transported to Belleville, Pennsylvania, circa 1999. Anna Ruth had resisted the Plain life even at a young age. She preferred vibrant colors and patterns to the subdued pastels and neutrals that made up her sparse wardrobe. The light-up tennis shoes that Emily wore would have thrilled five-year-old Anna Ruth beyond words.

Ike Sommers, with his brown hair that stuck up in all directions, pulled up a chair next to Thomas in the break room at the Log Works, an oasis of relative quiet in the midst of the never-ending shrill of buzz saws. "No glitter bombs today, Thomas?"

Thomas laughed. "Just plain old ham and cheese, it looks like. And some fruit salad left over from lunch yesterday." He unwrapped the final parcel and sniffed it, smiling at the scent of cinnamon that tickled his nose. "And some oatmeal raisin cookies." He offered one to Ike, who gladly accepted.

"The Graber ladies are feeding you *gut*. I think you've picked up a pound or two since you came to town," the older man ribbed Thomas.

"The Grabers are fine cooks and generous people," Thomas said soberly.

No matter how many times Henry, Rose, and Lovina reassured him that he owed them nothing, he couldn't shake the notion that he was in debt to them. The feeling wouldn't go away, no matter what they said.

Ike took a bite of his turkey sandwich and washed it down with a gulp of milk. "How did the social worker's visit go? That was Friday, right?"

"*Ja*," Thomas replied, his mouth full of fruit salad. "It went well, except when Emily fell asleep in the barn and I couldn't find her. Oh, and when she announced to the social worker that Lovina and I were getting married. And then there was the moment Ms. Williams found a plastic snake Emily had planted as a prank on Lovina."

Ike raised his eyebrows at Thomas's statement. "A plastic snake! I bet the social worker was mad."

Thomas shook his head. "Not at all. In fact, she said that it showed just how happy and well-adjusted Emily was."

The conversation lulled between the two as they chewed their food. Thomas could sense that something was weighing on Ike, but he didn't know how to draw it out of the man.

Thomas never considered himself a conversationalist. His *dat* had been a man of few words and prided himself on privacy. Opening up and sharing wasn't something the Smucker men knew how to do.

Fortunately, Ike Sommers was more engaging and forthright.

He cleared his throat. "Well, now that your first social worker visit is over, what's your next step with Emily?"

Thomas appreciated his friend's no-nonsense way of cutting to the heart of the issue, but he didn't have an answer for Ike.

"I suppose we just keep going on, checking off boxes on all the paperwork we have to do and wait to see if the social worker approves me for adoption. Her main concern was that our living situation with the Graber family is temporary. She's worried about what would happen if Emily and I moved out on our own, which I suppose we ought to think about doing someday if I am going to raise her. The social worker didn't seem convinced that I would do such a good job of raising Emily without a wife and family for support. To tell the truth, she's not wrong."

"Looks to me like you are doing a fine job so far, especially with the help of Lovina Graber." Ike raised his eyebrows and smiled slyly at Thomas.

The oatmeal raisin cookie now in Thomas's mouth turned to chalk. He feared this—that others could sense his deepening feelings for Lovina. He wasn't fit to be a husband to such a wonderful woman. He had nothing to offer her. He could hear his *dat*'s voice again. *"Never let anyone else see your weaknesses."*

And his feelings for Lovina were definitely a weakness.

If Ike saw it, did others?

Ike's eyes lit up. He snapped his fingers. "Why didn't I think of this before?"

Thomas washed the cookie down with a final swig of milk that curdled at Ike's words. "Think of what before?"

"The solution to your problem is right in front of your nose, Thomas. You have all the tools you need to make a family for Emily. You just have to use them."

Thomas's heart dropped into his stomach. Surely Ike wasn't suggesting that Thomas marry Lovina. "I'm not sure I'm following you, Ike. What do you mean, *make* a family?"

"I know I'm not in much of a position to speak about this,

but the Bible does tell us that it is not good for man to be alone." Ike, a middle-aged bachelor himself, was right on both counts, and Thomas fought the urge to say so.

Thomas avoided eye contact with Ike, instead carefully stacking the reusable containers into his lunch box. He had no desire to discuss this issue with his friend. It wouldn't be right to marry Lovina out of convenience or a sense of obligation to Emily. Lovina deserved a love story out of one of Emily's fairy tale books—a husband who was just as special as she was.

In spite of knowing better, Thomas let his mind drift for just a moment. He could see Lovina fixing his lunches and baking her butterscotch pie just for him in the coziness of their own little home. He allowed himself to consider the happiness she would bring to his life.

Suddenly, the scene in his head turned ugly. He was berating Lovina, just as his *dat* had always done to his *mem*.

No, Thomas wouldn't make a good husband to anyone.

Ike forged ahead with the conversation. "Look, I know when you first came here, you said you weren't looking for a wife. But things have changed now. You have Emily to consider."

"That's exactly what I'm doing, Ike," Thomas spat at his friend. "I am not fit to be anyone's husband. I'm probably not fit to raise Emily, but that's what Anna Ruth wanted, so I'll give it my best. As for marriage, I'm a bachelor and that's how I'll stay."

Ike shook his head. "You keep saying that. I don't know what you mean. You are a *gut* Amish man, Thomas. You're baptized in the church, you have a good job, and people like you. What else is there?"

Thomas could list all the ways he failed at being husband material. He owned little more than the clothes on his back and what fit into his rucksack—no house, no property, no livestock. He had spent most of the meager profit from the sale of his *dat's* dairy farm on the move out west. And he only knew how to be the same kind of husband and father *Dat* had been.

He thought back on the Sunday morning when he had lost his temper with Emily just because she wouldn't wear what he wanted her to wear. He had no redeeming qualities in the family department. Why couldn't Ike understand that?

"Ike, what was your father like?"

Ike furrowed his brows. "He was like every other Amishman. He worked hard, had a big family, and raised us to follow the *Ordnung*. What's that got to do with anything?"

"If you had known my *dat*, you would understand. He took hard work, family, and following the *Ordnung* to the extreme. It's as though he thought he could earn his way to heaven by being the hardest worker and having a family that followed the rules more closely than anyone else. *Dat* didn't have much flexibility in him. That's why Anna Ruth left us, why I never knew I had a niece until she died. He cost me a sister." Thomas bounced his knee as he spoke.

The last words surprised even himself, but it was true.

Ike looked down at his lunch, picking at the last few bites of his sandwich. He chewed slowly, remaining silent as Thomas stewed in his thoughts.

Thomas stared at the sawdust-covered floor. Tears pricked his eyes. He clenched his jaw as he fought them back. He hated feeling like this—exposed and vulnerable.

At last, Ike swallowed his food and offered Thomas a shrug. "But Thomas, I know you. You aren't your *dat*. You are kind and your heart is open to new people and places. Look how quickly you've made a home here in West Kootenai."

"My father was one of the least kind people I've ever known." Thomas attempted to hide the quiver. "I hear his voice in my head every time I have to make a decision. It takes every ounce of will that I have to resist acting just like he would. I saw the pain he inflicted on my *mem* and Anna Ruth. I know how he made me feel, and I don't ever want to do that to another person." Thomas's eyes welled up again, but he bit back the tears that threatened to flow.

Dat would have called him a sissy for crying in front of another man. For showing any emotion at all.

"And you won't. Because you lived that experience, you won't repeat his mistakes." Ike's voice was no more than a whisper. "God has created you to be so much more than a duplicate of your *dat*. He's equipped you with a sharp mind and a kind heart. He doesn't want you to live in the shadows."

Thomas considered Ike's words. *Living in the shadows.* That's exactly what he had been doing since he was a little boy. He had chosen a life of solitude, one where he didn't risk hurting anyone else—or being hurt.

Could Ike be right? Had God designed him for more?

He closed his eyes and pictured a life where he didn't have to give up Emily. He allowed himself to imagine raising her as his own, with Lovina by his side. She loved Emily and took such wonderful care of her. Would she be open to the idea of marrying him so they could take care of his niece together? Or would she want more?

She'd told him that God's plan for her was to be single. What if she was hiding from something, too, just as Thomas was?

The picture in his head grew clearer. Emily, Lovina, and he stood together in a green field under the blue skies with the Montana sun shining down on the three of them, with Lovina's little dog Gus nipping at their feet, no shadows to hide in.

Peace filled his soul.

Then the sun dropped from the sky and everything became dark. He could hear his father's voice. *"Who do you think you are? You quit the dairy farm when it got hard. Do you think raising a family is easy? You're too soft. You don't have what it takes."*

"Thomas, are you all right?" Ike asked.

Dazed, Thomas opened his eyes. He tried to focus on Ike and get the dark image out of his head. "Yeah, I'll be fine. I just don't know, Ike. You made some good points. I'm going to have to think about this some more. I just don't think I have what it takes to be a husband and probably not even a makeshift father. It's going to take a miracle to change my mind."

"Be careful what you ask for. He just might provide one." Ike slapped Thomas on the shoulder before walking away.

Chapter Twenty-Three

Tuesday, September 12

The scent of cinnamon wafted throughout the Graber kitchen as Lovina loaded up a basket full of goodies to deliver to various community members. She and Emily had baked several loaves of friendship bread yesterday and had made up fresh batches of her Feel Better blend tea.

Lovina reviewed her mental list of folks to visit to make sure she had everything she needed. "Let's go get the horse and buggy ready, Emily. You can see if your kitten is still out in the barn."

"Are we going to see Miss Susanna today?" Emily asked.

Susanna and her husband lived next to Mrs. Milner, Susanna's *mem*, so she got to visit with Susanna's little sisters.

It warmed Lovina's heart to see Emily so eager to see her friends. She smiled at Emily. "I think we have time to drop in on them."

"Can I bring my kitten to show Sarah Jane, Dorie, and Marigold?" Emily stuck her bottom lip out and looked up at Lovina with pleading eyes.

"I don't think that's a great idea, Em. We have several stops to make and the kitten might get restless. I would hate to lose . . . What did you decide to call her?"

"Pumpkin Spice Latte," Emily responded, as though that were the most typical name for a kitten in the world.

Lovina suppressed a grin and headed on out to the barn, Emily and Gus close on her heels.

As Lovina readied the horse and buggy, Emily searched the barn for Pumpkin Spice Latte, and much to Lovina's relief, the kitten remained well hidden. They loaded up their basket into the buggy and headed out for a morning full of visits.

Finally, after making deliveries to Ruth Sommers, the *Englisch* widow Millie Arnold, and Mrs. Deborah Shelter, whose daughter Evelyn was recovering from the flu, they brought the buggy to a stop in front of the Milner home. The girls were playing in the yard, so Emily ran to join them while Lovina pulled out two loaves of bread and several sachets of tea and ambled out of the buggy toward the door.

Mrs. Milner answered the door and welcomed Lovina in. "Do I smell friendship bread? That's my favorite! Come on in and have a seat. Susanna is out on the back porch breaking up some green beans. I'll tell her you are here."

"Oh, don't bother. I'll go out and give her a hand." Lovina was anxious to relay the events of the social worker's visit to her friend. She made her way through the house and out the back door.

"Lovina! I was hoping you would stop by today. How did it go with the social worker last week?" Susanna sat breaking beans on the bare porch floor, her legs crisscrossed like a *kinder* might sit at school. She extended her hand to Lovina, a silent request for help standing.

Lovina took Susanna's hand and pulled her friend to her feet, Susanna's growing belly making it hard to keep her balance. "Emily is in the front yard playing with your sisters. I came back here to help you with the beans."

"I'm finished with them, so just take a seat and tell me what's going on."

Lovina smiled at her persistent friend. "The visit went really well, I think. The social worker thought Thomas had made some excellent progress with his parenting skills, and she was so impressed with how well-adjusted Emily seemed to be, despite all the trauma she's endured."

"So you think he will get to keep her?" Susanna's eyes lit up at the thought.

"I do. She had some concerns about what would happen when the two of them move out of the cabin and live on their own." Lovina chewed at the inside of her lip.

Susanna nodded sympathetically. "I can tell that's something you aren't looking forward to either."

"They aren't mine to keep, Sus. Part of helping them is preparing them to be independent. I figure when Emily starts school and doesn't need me to take care of her, they'll find their own place. It's part of the process." Lovina shrugged.

"It doesn't have to be that way. I've told you before, I think you and Thomas are a perfect match."

"And I've told you, that's not my path in life." Lovina needed to redirect the conversation. "I have to tell you what Emily did while the social worker was there." She launched into the details of Emily's escapade in the barn with the kitten and the snake in the bathroom prank.

Susanna tried to keep her laughter in but was unsuccessful. "She's a hoot. I hope the social worker was amused, not angry."

"Ms. Williams was a good sport about the whole thing. She said that it indicated how safe Emily feels and how well-adjusted she is. She seemed quite entertained, especially when Emily announced that Thomas and I would be getting married."

"What?" Susanna gasped.

"Oh, yes. Thomas and I clarified that we are only friends, but Emily insisted that we would get married. Guess how she knows?"

"Because she's a smart little girl?" Susanna posited, a knowing smile crossing her lips.

Lovina shook her head and rolled her eyes. "No. Because she's been praying for it. As if getting what you want is that easy."

"Isn't it?" Susanna returned. "I mean, can't it be?"

"God isn't a wish granter, Susanna. You know that as well as I do." Lovina didn't mean to snap at her friend, but they'd discussed this same topic at least twenty times before.

"I know that, but I wonder, have you prayed about your relationship with Thomas? Or are you just assuming that you're still meant to be single forever?" Susanna asked, pricking Lovina's heart with her words.

She had prayed that God would help her take care of Emily and Thomas. She had prayed that God would lead them to the right woman to be Thomas's wife. And, she had prayed that God would take away the feelings that kept bubbling up inside her for Thomas. However, she'd never asked God if He had placed Thomas and Emily in her life for any reason other than to help them. Why? Perhaps because she was afraid of the answer.

Considering the possibility of making a family with Thomas and Emily would mean Lovina would have to open herself up to rejection again. The pain from her teen years was as fresh as ever, even if she pretended that she had moved beyond it. She couldn't bear that again. Her feelings for Thomas were so much stronger than they had been for Dan.

If he rejected her, she wasn't sure she could ever recover.

"Susanna, I know it must seem silly to you, but I have to believe that everything that has happened to me in my life—my limp, my scar, Dan's rejection—all of it was to prepare me for a life alone. Otherwise, what was the point of all that suffering?"

Susanna took Lovina's hand and squeezed it. "I can't pretend to know the pain you've suffered. But remember the verse I love so much. *And we know that all things work together for good to them that love God, to them who are the called according to His purpose.'* He can still take all the broken pieces and make something beautiful."

"I know, Sus. You're right." That was the easiest way Lovina had found to put an end to these conversations. Agree—and move on. "I'll pray about it. Now, I've got to get Emily back home so we can fix lunch. I'll see you soon."

Lovina said her goodbyes to Susanna and her mother, then went out to the front lawn to coax Emily back into the buggy.

Susanna's words played over and over in her head as the two rode back to the Graber home. Lovina was glad she hadn't mentioned the Western Wildflower letter to Susanna. She'd dropped it in the mail today, and Susanna would see it when it was published. Lovina anticipated another of Susanna's lectures after that.

She considered what Susanna had said about that verse from Romans. Yes, she believed that God worked all things to the good of His people, but she had trusted God so completely before with Dan and look how that turned out. Instead of being an answer to a prayer, he'd turned her world upside down. The path she was on now was the one God had put in front of her and, most of the time, it suited her perfectly fine. She would just have to keep praying for the feelings she had for Thomas to go away and for God to place a wife for him in his path.

A wife that wasn't Lovina Graber.

Chapter Twenty-Four

WEDNESDAY, SEPTEMBER 20

I n the week and a half following the social worker's visit, Thomas had grown more confident in his parenting skills and relied less often on Lovina for help with basic chores, like dressing Emily or fixing her hair.

The three of them had established something of an evening routine. Thomas and Emily lingered after dinner at the Graber home to play games or read together. Sometimes he would whittle while Lovina and Emily had imaginary tea parties.

While Thomas and Emily had established a more affectionate relationship, Thomas still struggled to entertain his *niesse*, lacking Lovina's creativity.

They sat at the Grabers' kitchen table, involved in a heated game of Chinese checkers this evening.

"Your turn, Lovie," Emily said after hopping her marble across the star-shaped board.

The back door opened and Henry Graber escorted Rose into the kitchen, the two taking seats at the table as well.

Henry removed his hat and wiped sweat with a bandana from

the bald spot inside his halo of salt-and-pepper hair. "Shew! I finally got those new smoke detectors installed in the cabin and replaced that torn window screen."

"Hmmph. It's a shame it took this long to get that taken care of. I believe someone mentioned it back in the spring." Rose inclined her head toward her husband, a questioning smile creeping across her face before leaving the table to get glasses of lemonade for everyone.

Henry raised his thick eyebrows and returned his wife's smile. "Who could she be talking about, Miss Emily? Was it you?"

"It was her, Mr. Henry. Are you getting forgetful?" Emily giggled.

Feigning offense, Henry shook his head. "I forget nothing! Mind's like a steel trap, I tell you." He shifted his attention to the newspaper on the table. "Thomas, have you read this week's edition of *The Budget*?"

Thomas grimaced. *The Budget* had been a source of great contention in his home. *Dat* said it was nothing more than a gossip rag and forbade the reading of it. *Mem*'s cousin would sneak copies to her every now and then, which *Mem* read cover to cover then burned in order to avoid *Dat*'s ire. Toward the end of *Mem*'s life, she had her own subscription, which she relished.

"I haven't read *The Budget* since I left Belleville." He strained to keep his tone even.

Henry stood and dusted his pants. "You're welcome to read our copy any time if you'd like to keep up with the news from back east."

Thomas uttered a curt word of thanks, then fiddled with the marble in his hand. It was a kind offer. Henry had no idea what a point of controversy the newspaper had been in the Smucker home.

Oblivious, Henry continued. "This new column from the Western Wildflower writer sure has taken off. People send advice letters, and the writer answers them."

Thomas followed Henry with his eyes as the older man took the platter of cookies his wife extended to him. Henry placed it on the table and sat back down, taking a long draw from the glass of lemonade Rose also handed him.

Thomas grabbed a cookie and nibbled without responding. The older man apparently took Thomas's silence as an opportunity to continue his commentary.

"In fact, one of the letters this week sounded like it was written about you." Henry shook his head and laughed.

Red flags rose in Thomas's brain. Had someone asked for advice about him? "What do you mean?" His eyes shifted across the table to Lovina, who fixated her gaze on the checkerboard. He watched her clench her jaw tightly.

"Rose, find that letter about the bachelor fellow that was in the newspaper and read it to Thomas."

Lovina's head snapped up. Her cheeks flushed a deep red, her scar radiating like a lantern. "Why, *Dat*? I'm sure Thomas isn't interested in that nonsense." She fidgeted in her chair.

"Actually, you've piqued my curiosity," Thomas admitted as Rose sat again and searched through the pages of *The Budget* for the right section.

"Ah, here we go. Dear Western Wildflower . . ." Rose read the letter from "Concerned Neighbor."

Henry chuckled. "See what I mean? Right down to the spinster that helps the bachelor out." He used air quotes when he said spinster.

"What's a spinster?" Emily piped up. All eyes turned to her. She had been sitting so quietly, Thomas hadn't realized she was listening.

Rose gently responded. "It means a woman who has never married, but it's not a nice thing to say."

Emily nodded and her mouth made a soft *O* shape.

"*Ach, Dat*. There are plenty of Amish bachelors in the world. I'm sure it wasn't talking about Thomas," Lovina's shaky voice lacked its usual confidence. She rose and got the teapot off the stove and filled a cup for Thomas.

"So, how did this flower-person answer?" Anger bubbled up in Thomas's chest, squeezing so tight it was hard for him to get the words out. He took a long swallow of the scalding tea.

"He, or she, as it may be, gave some sound biblical advice. Pray for these people and be a friend, and trust God to do the hard work," Rose said.

"In other words"—Henry laughed—"keep your nose in your own business. "

Thomas failed to see the humor in the situation.

Lovina had a point that it could have been about someone other than him. However, it felt awfully close to his situation. It rankled that someone would write an anonymous letter to get advice from some know-it-all mystery columnist. He was starting to see *Dat*'s point about it being a gossip rag.

Rose stood and looked out the back door. "Henry, you *are* getting forgetful. You left the barn door wide open. Let's go close it, and I'll make sure Emily's kitten has food." The two of them headed out the back door and left Thomas and Lovina sitting in silence.

Thomas drained the rest of the tea. "You ready, Emily? Let's get home and get ready for bed." He held his jaw so tight the words could barely eek out.

"Thomas, you're a million miles away," Lovina teased. "What are you thinking about?"

He certainly couldn't confess the truth to her. He paused to generate an acceptable response. "I, uh, was just wondering if that letter your *dat* mentioned was really about me."

Color rose in Lovina's cheeks. "Surely not. I mean, who would be so bold as to write that letter?"

"It doesn't take much boldness to write an anonymous letter, or an anonymous response, for that matter." His words came out more tersely than he'd intended, but Thomas could feel the frustration building up again. He regretted mentioning the letter to Lovina.

"What do you mean? You don't like the Western Wildflower?"

"I've never read the Western Wildflower. I just don't care much for people who pretend to be something they aren't." He stopped himself from saying more, but his mind immediately brought up an image of the deceitful Katrina Troyer.

"Lots of writers use pseudonyms for a variety of reasons. I don't think the Western Wildflower is pretending as much as she—or he, I suppose—might be protecting herself. Maybe she doesn't want fame or attention."

Lovina's defensive tone caught him off guard. She had a point. It wasn't very Plain of a person to strive for attention. The Amish preferred to lead humble, unassuming lives. But even he knew Plain people who liked the spotlight every now and then.

"Maybe you're right and this Western Wildflower doesn't want the attention. If that's the case, why doesn't he or she just quit writing? Getting involved in the advice-giving business is flat meddlesome, especially when people are just prying in other people's lives like this 'concerned' neighbor is." His lip curled in a snarl when he spat the word *concerned*.

Lovina balled her fists up and thrust them to her sides, chin tilted up at Thomas and an icy stare emanating from her eyes. "Meddlesome? That's what you think? The Western Wildflower gave a solid biblical response. Yes, the neighbor may have been nosy rather than concerned, but the author redirected that meddling and encouraged them to pray. I can't believe you would condemn that!"

With that, Lovina spun on her heel, stalked across the kitchen, and put her teacup in the sink. She paused to collect Gus and plant a goodnight kiss on Emily's head. Just as her *mem* and *dat* came back in, she shot Thomas a scathing look and stalked up the stairs.

Thomas sat at the table, rubbing his forehead in complete

bewilderment. What had he said that had prompted that kind of response from Lovina? He'd never seen her that full of vinegar before. Emily and the Grabers looked equally stunned.

"Son, I don't know what you did, but it looks like you just poked the bear," Henry said. "You might want to figure out how to make it right before the morning comes."

Chapter Twenty-Five

L ovina stomped her way through the house and up the stairs to her bedroom, slamming the door firmly behind her. She flung herself across her bed, burying her face in the pillows.

That stubborn man. Calling her meddlesome and suggesting that she was seeking attention. Nothing could be further from the truth.

Well, saying that about the Western Wildflower, anyway. They were one and the same.

But he didn't know that. Almost no one did.

Uncertainty flooded her. Was she doing something wrong by writing under a pseudonym? Should she confess to being the writer? Or should she stop writing altogether? Why didn't she know what was right in this situation?

She flopped over onto her back and stared at the ceiling, breathing in and out carefully like her physical therapist had shown her. Her whole body was tense, making her hip even tighter and more sensitive. She was letting her emotions take over.

When Thomas criticized the Western Wildflower, he wasn't

criticizing her. He had no idea how the words would sound to her. It was a misunderstanding, plain and simple.

Quitting writing was out of the question. God had called her to write. She would simply need to develop a thicker skin.

And she would need to help Thomas see that the advice of the Western Wildflower wasn't intended to be meddlesome.

Sufficiently calmed, she swung her legs over the side of the bed and opened her nightstand drawer and pulled out her notebook. She flipped to the first blank page and scooted back onto the bed so she was supported by pillows as she wrote.

As far back as she could remember, well before becoming the Western Wildflower, writing had been her way of making sense of things. Sometimes she just wrote what was in her head in one long paragraph. Sometimes she made lists. Other times, she wrote poems.

Today, she started with a word.

PRIDE.

That was Thomas's concern—that the Western Wildflower was proud. On the other hand, avoidance of pride drove Lovina to keep her identity hidden. But Thomas was guilty of being proud, too.

She tapped her pencil on the paper as an idea began to germinate in her mind.

Pride
When one is too stubborn to accept another's help,
Pride brings destruction.
When a lie is easier than the truth,
Pride makes a mockery.
When one is wise in his own eyes,
Pride creates a fool.
But when one puts another's needs before his own,
Humility gives rise to love.

She read the words back to herself, surprised at how it refreshed her to pour her feelings out onto paper. She tore the page from her notebook and shoved it in her pocket. Now that she had sorted her feelings, she could handle doing her nighttime chores.

She headed downstairs to clean up the kitchen for the evening and enjoy a cup of her Deep Sleep blend tea. She had a feeling she would need it.

Mem sat at the kitchen table, reading *The Budget*. Lovina cringed. Had *Mem* connected the dots and realized Lovina was the Western Wildflower?

"Care for a refill, *Mem*?" Lovina asked.

Mem raised her cup for Lovina to fill it, then inhaled the aroma steaming from the tea. "Ahhh. You did a good job on this batch. You've nailed the blend of herbs so that the bitterness of one is counteracted by the sweetness of another."

Lovina sipped from her own cup. "Indeed." That comment made Lovina think of how she and Thomas balanced one another in caring for Emily. Lovina could be the silly, fun, nurturing one, while Thomas was firm and more practical.

Mem folded the paper and set it on the table. She sat in silence, sipping her tea. Unspoken words hung in the air between the two.

The tea soured in Lovina's belly. She hated keeping secrets. She never meant for the Western Wildflower thing to get so out of control. But she wasn't ready to share it with the world yet either.

Mem finally broke the silence. "Do you think the letter in *The Budget* was really about Thomas and Emily and, well, you?"

Lovina took a deep breath. "I think it's awfully coincidental if it wasn't about us. And I don't usually believe in coincidences."

Mem nodded. "I feel the same. But who would write such a letter? While it didn't say anything directly unkind, the tone definitely was hurtful. The way the writer referred to the woman helping the bachelor as a spinster who wasn't fit for marriage and family . . ." She trailed off, clenching her jaw.

"But, *Mem*, I am a spinster. It's not an insult, just a fact."

"Lovina Harriet Graber. You are not a spinster. Just because many Amish girls marry at very young ages, that doesn't mean that your ship has sailed. If you would just open yourself up to the idea of getting married, I'm certain that God would bring you just the right man. In fact, he may already have."

Lovina sighed.

At least *Mem* had moved on from the Western Wildflower. Now she was fixated on her favorite topic—Lovina's nonexistent love life. Lovina had tried, obviously to no avail, to redirect *Mem* from this line of conversation many, many times over the last several years. *Mem* just couldn't accept that Lovina was destined to remain single and that she was quite satisfied to do so.

Well, she had been until Thomas Smucker and his niece came along.

Before Thomas, not even Lovina's vivid imagination could produce a vision of her as a wife and a mother. She knew her place in the world and had accepted it. Now, though, something had shifted.

A smile tipped her lips as a new vision became clear.

It took little effort to imagine being married to Thomas. She was already cooking his meals, washing his clothes, and raising his niece. She could picture doing all of that in a little cabin of their own somewhere, sleeping next to him every night and waking up beside him every morning.

She shook the image out of her head.

Her situation had not changed. She was still the crippled, eccentric spinster that the people of West Kootenai overlooked and underestimated. She was still the outcast who preferred to stay in the background. The only change was that now, she wasn't sure she would be content remaining alone forever.

Lovina rose from the table and took her cup to the sink. She filled the basin with hot soapy water and washed the glasses and plates that had collected after dinner.

Mem brought her dirty teacup over to the sink and wrapped an arm around Lovina.

"Lovina, do you trust God's plan for your life?"

"Of course, *Mem*. I always have."

"Do you trust it enough to let go of your own plan and let Him lead?"

"*Mem*, I'm not holding on to anything. Nothing has changed."

"Hmmmph. Tell that to the Lord, Lovina. Things have changed in a big way in your life. Take a step back and look at it from my point of view."

Lovina looked at her mother, confused. "What do you mean?"

"When I hear you talk, you sound like you don't think you are worthy of a husband and a family. As your mother, I look at you and see a masterpiece of God's creation. Just because one *dummkopf* called you 'damaged' doesn't mean that God never meant for you to love and be loved. He was just the wrong man, that's all. Just because you limp a little and have a scar on your cheek doesn't mean you are disqualified from being a mother. Think of all the things you've learned because of your struggles. Don't you think that those lessons would be wasted if you didn't have *kinner* to share them with?" She patted Lovina on the shoulder and gently kissed her cheek. "Goodnight, sweet daughter of mine."

Lovina gripped the edge of the sink and whispered a goodnight in reply. Tears burned her eyes. She didn't want to cry. Crying would be like admitting that *Mem* was right.

Was *Mem* right? Had she sold herself short all these years? Was she worthy of more?

Lovina shuddered at the thought.

To distract herself, she drained the sink, then rinsed it out and wiped it dry until it sparkled. She tidied up around the kitchen, getting things ready for the next morning. She grabbed a couple of cookbooks from *Mem*'s shelf to pick something to make for the upcoming church service that they would be hosting. She slid into a chair at the table and leafed through a few recipes, dog-earing a few pages of interest.

She closed the cookbook and pulled out the poem she had written earlier. She reread the words, trying to see this situation from someone else's perspective. Was it that she was too proud to humble herself to become a wife?

Or was the problem much simpler? Was she too scared of being hurt to take the risk?

Frustrated, she folded the poem back up. She was ready to toss it in the trash when she heard *Dat*'s footsteps coming down the stairs. She shoved the poem back into her pocket.

"*Ach*, Lovina! I didn't know you were still down here," *Dat* said, pantomiming a heart attack.

"Just getting things ready for tomorrow, *Dat*."

"I forgot to get a glass of water to take my medicine." He filled his glass up and kissed her on the head. "Goodnight, Lovina. Sleep well," he called over his shoulder as he headed back upstairs.

She doubted good sleep would be possible tonight. As her mother's words ricocheted through her mind, Lovina allowed the picture of herself as Thomas's wife and Emily's *mem* to enter her thoughts again, and this time she didn't dismiss it. She walked upstairs to her room, letting the what-ifs take root. Letting Thomas and Emily overtake her mind wasn't difficult.

They already had her heart.

Chapter Twenty-Six

THURSDAY, SEPTEMBER 21

The smell of crispy, fried bacon mingled with *kaffe* wafted through the air in the Graber kitchen, making Thomas's mouth water.

Rose's and Lovina's meals, while simple and traditional, nourished Thomas's body and soul. Most mornings, he could count on a bounty of meat, eggs, and always a side of grains—either biscuits, cinnamon rolls, or oats—as well as uplifting conversation.

Today, the women had prepared the oatmeal by baking it with sugar, spices, and berries. But this breakfast at the Grabers' was an unusually quiet affair. The lack of chatter unsettled him. He knew he had upset Lovina last night, but was everyone angry with him?

He glanced around the table at Henry and Rose taking turns yawning. Rose's eyes were red rimmed, and Henry's usually twinkling eyes held only a distant stare. And Lovina was in another world altogether. Perhaps they'd struggled with sleep. He hadn't slept well himself last night after arguing with Lovina about the Western Wildflower. He regretted speaking so forcefully about the letter and its response. It had clearly upset her and that hadn't been his intention at all.

"I love this baked oatmeal. Don't you, Emily?" He attempted to stir up a little conversation.

Emily didn't take the bait. She simply nodded and shoveled another spoonful of the sweet, gooey, syrup-covered oats into her mouth.

Rose must have sensed Thomas's discomfort. She, too, tried to engage the others. "This was my *mem*'s recipe, Emily. I think she got it from her *mem*. It's an old one but always delicious, especially since Lovina's raspberry bushes yielded such sweet berries this summer. We froze lots of them. It was her idea to add them into the oatmeal."

"I love them!" Emily enthused.

Lovina pushed the oatmeal around in the bowl but didn't seem to hear her *mem*'s words.

Thomas tried again. "What else did you freeze or can from your garden, Lovina?"

Rose elbowed her daughter, whose head snapped up. Dark circles hung underneath her usually sparkling brown eyes. "Hmm?"

"Thomas asked about what you put up from the garden," Henry offered.

"Oh, ummm, let's see. I canned a variety of jams and jellies, stewed tomatoes, some green beans, and sauerkraut. Then I froze berries, corn, carrots, and spinach." She took a bite of the oatmeal and turned to Emily. "Do you like the raspberries in the oatmeal?"

Emily gave her a confused look. "I just said that I did, Lovie. Do you need another cup of coffee?"

Everyone at the table giggled, snapping them out of whatever trance they'd all been in.

"I suppose I do." Lovina blushed and stifled a yawn.

Thomas pushed his chair back from the table. "Here, hand me your cup, and I'll get you a refill."

"That's not necessary, Thomas. I can get it in a minute."

"I insist." Thomas reached for her cup before she could protest. A shiver ran up his arm when their hands briefly touched. She dropped her eyes to the table and withdrew her hand.

He filled up Lovina's coffee cup, added a splash of cream and a spoonful of sugar as he had seen her do before. Thomas set the cup in front of Lovina. She glanced up at him and gave him her gentle smile. Little crinkles spread around her eyes, and a hint of dimples formed on her cheeks.

His eyes locked on hers. The sound rushed out of his ears and for a moment, all he could hear was his heart pounding.

A shriek followed by a bowl crashing to the floor broke the spell.

Thomas's head snapped up. Emily stood beside the table, covered in sticky remnants of maple-syrup-doused oatmeal, surrounded by ceramic chunks and Lovina's dog licking up the mess.

His first instinct was to respond as his father would have. "Emily Grace! How clumsy of you!" The instant the shout left his lips he regretted it.

His niece's lip quivered then she burst into tears, her shoulders slumping in shame. "I'm so sorry, *Oncle*. I'll clean up this mess, I promise."

"No worries, dear," Lovina soothed. "It was an accident. Now stand very still while we get these sharp pieces picked up." She stooped to the floor and collected the pieces of the broken bowl, shooting Thomas a stinging look.

He had stuck his foot in his mouth again.

"It was an accident, Emily." Thomas tried to smooth over the mistake he had made. "You didn't mean to break the bowl. You just have to remember to be very careful."

"She *was* being careful, but she tripped over Gus when she stood up." Lovina's caustic tone smarted. "That's why we call it an accident, Thomas."

Whatever had passed between them moments ago—or whatever he had imagined passing between them—was gone.

Henry and Rose excused themselves to do chores on the Christmas tree farm and slipped out of the tension-filled kitchen. Lovina finished cleaning up the mess and sent Emily back to the cabin to change.

Thomas stood silently, arms crossed, watching Lovina's efficiency in the kitchen. Sometimes it seemed like the issues with her leg slowed her down. Other times, usually in emergencies and crises, she moved with surprising grace. The woman was a true wonder.

And he had a way of infuriating her.

"Lovina, I shouldn't have spoken so harshly to Emily. I'm sorry."

"You don't owe me an apology. Tell it to your niece," Lovina said without looking up from the table she was wiping down.

Since Emily had arrived, Thomas had learned the value of a sincere apology. His father, who had been wrong more often than not, would have never apologized to him or Anna Ruth. Not to *Mem* either. And look where it landed him—he died isolated from his only daughter and grandchild, with a wife who was miserable and a son who had no idea how to be a proper husband or father.

"Has anyone ever told you that you are a stubborn man, Thomas Smucker?" Lovina asked, putting the rag down and looking him in the eye.

Thomas thought for a moment. No one had ever said it, but he was sure people back home thought it. He didn't know how to answer, so he turned the conversation around. "The same could be said for you, Miss Graber. Only a stubborn woman would insist that a stranger and his niece be taken into her home."

She blinked, then shrugged. "I guess that's true. And aren't you glad I did?"

"Yes, I am. I truly don't know what I would do without you." He hoped to coax another smile out of her, one that warmed and healed him even more than her tea could. "Stubbornness isn't such a bad trait, I suppose."

"You're right. But sometimes I cling to old ideas and beliefs because I'm scared of what change might look like. Is that what you do?" She gripped the back of the dining room chair and stared at him, her brown eyes piercing his heart.

Frustrated that his tactic hadn't put an end to the conversation, Thomas let out a huff. How could Lovina go from giving him that sweet smile a few minutes ago to calling out his worst traits so quickly? Every conversation with the woman confounded him more. She was a mystery.

"I'll take that as a yes," she said when he didn't answer her. She turned her back to him and went to the sink and started the dishes. "Your lunch is in the refrigerator if you aren't too stubborn to take it. Have a good day."

He'd been dismissed.

He wasn't at all sure how to win this battle with her. He stalked to the refrigerator and grabbed his lunch. He wasn't too stubborn, and he wanted to make sure she knew that. On the other hand, stubbornness *did* prevent him from engaging in a conversation that made him uncomfortable.

He would never understand women. What a terrible husband he would make—just like his father had been.

After he ducked out the back door of the Graber home and started his walk toward the Log Works, he met Emily coming out of the cabin.

"Bye, *Oncle*, have a good day at work," she offered meekly. Her voice lacked her trademark exuberance.

Had he dampened her spirits so much by raising his voice to her?

"Come here, Emily," he said gently.

She turned toward him, her chin tucked.

He squatted down until he was eye level with her, then tilted her chin up so that her eyes met his. "I'm sorry for speaking to you that way this morning. I know that it was an accident, and there wasn't anything you could have done differently. Do you forgive me?"

Emily threw her arms around him in an embrace.

"Of course I forgive you, *Oncle*. I'm glad you aren't mad at me. I don't like when you are mad. You get all quiet and pouty."

Thomas laughed and squeezed Emily tighter. "I do no such thing. I'm a ray of sunshine all the time!"

Emily pulled back and cocked one eyebrow. "Thou shalt not lie, *Oncle* Thomas." Then she burst into a fit of giggles.

He waved goodbye, and she blew him a kiss then skipped back to the Graber house.

He walked on to work, considering the different women he had known in his life. From his niece to Lovina Graber, young Anna Ruth to his *mem*, it didn't matter the age. Thomas had learned that understanding women was a challenging task for him. Poor *Mem* had spent forty-five years being misunderstood by *Dat*, and he saw how miserable she had been.

If he was going to raise Emily and give her the life Anna Ruth would have wanted her to have, he was going to have to stretch himself and learn how to interact with the mysterious creatures, for everyone's sake.

Chapter Twenty-Seven

THURSDAY, SEPTEMBER 21

Lovina had watched out the window as Thomas and Emily embraced. She swallowed a triumphant smile. He had taken her advice. Maybe she had been too hard on Thomas just now.

At any rate, it worked.

She finished up the dishes as Emily came bounding into the house.

"What shall we do today?" Emily always liked to know what was on the day's schedule. Lovina had learned that the girl loved order. She supposed it made Emily feel safe.

"We have some barn chores, of course, and we need to do some mending. Your *oncle* is rough on his pants! Two pairs have thinned spots at the knees that will tear if I don't reinforce them. *Dat* has some shirts that need repair too. Do you think you can help me with that?"

The little girl nodded eagerly. Emily was a sponge, soaking up every piece of knowledge that Lovina shared with her. And academically, she was advanced, as Anna Ruth had clearly spent time preparing her daughter for school.

"Do we have any baking to do today?" Emily's eyes sparkled when she asked. Baking had become her favorite household task, other than laundry, of course.

"As a matter of fact, we do. We will have church here at our house this Sunday, and I was going to prepare some butterscotch pies. We can make pie crusts today, and tomorrow we can work on the filling. Oh, and we'll need to go to the store to get the cheese we will serve on Sunday."

The two busied themselves with collecting the eggs, refreshing the chickens' feed, and pampering their hens a bit, and then quickly finished up the other chores. Lovina wanted to miss the lunch rush, so they put Gus's harness and leash on, and headed to the store.

Lovina's trip to the store held a second purpose. She had a package to mail to *The Budget* offices, and she anticipated having mail waiting on her too. Every time she did this, the butterflies in her stomach felt more like stampeding cattle. What if someone saw her pick up mail addressed to the Western Wildflower? How could she explain that without lying? She simply prayed that no one would ask.

Emily and Gus ran a bit ahead of Lovina as they made the short trek. Lovina reckoned Gus adored the little girl almost as much as she did. She smiled, remembering their first meeting at the store all those weeks ago, and seeing how far Emily had come in such a short amount of time.

Lovina caught up with the two at the steps to the store and followed them in. Annie, decked out in a western, red-and-yellow plaid shirt and stiff dark blue jeans, was helping a customer at the counter, so Lovina didn't approach to do the mail swap just yet. Instead, she and Emily and Gus picked up the items they needed from the small grocery section and wandered around for a bit.

Finally, Annie was standing alone at the register, and Lovina quickly moved to catch her attention. "Hi, Annie. I have some things to send out if you don't mind taking care of those for me." Lovina spoke quickly and softly to her *Englisch* friend, casting a quick glance around to make sure no one was looking when she pulled the envelope out of her bag and slid it across the counter.

"Sure thing, Lovina. You know, I've really been enjoying your pieces in *The Budget*. I think knowing that it is you makes them even more special." Annie took the envelope from Lovina and discreetly placed it in the outgoing mailbox behind the counter.

Lovina could feel her cheeks heat up at the compliment. "*Ach*, Annie. *Danke*. I can't believe you read them."

Annie laughed, her long blonde braid swinging as her shoulders lurched. "It's not every day that I'm an accomplice to one of the most notable writers in the Amish world. Of course I'm going to read it!"

Lovina smiled at the thought of Annie as her accomplice, like they were partners in some scandalous heist. "Has any mail come for me lately?"

"I'm glad you mentioned it. I almost forgot. They are in my desk drawer for safe keeping. Let me ring you up here, and then I'll run and get them."

Lovina paid Annie for the items she had purchased and then called to Emily to get Gus ready to go. They were inspecting the homemade cupcakes on display, Gus licking his lips as if in anticipation of a sample. Patty Cakes were a treat that Lovina had a tough time turning down. As good of a baker as she was, she could never match Sarah Shelter's artistry at cupcake baking.

Annie returned quickly, the heels of her boots clicking across the wood floor, and handed Lovina a large envelope that she quickly shoved into her tote.

Just then, the bell over the door rang and Lovina looked up to see Dorcas Martin and her mother enter the store, each carrying a box of jelly jars.

When Dorcas noticed Lovina, Emily, and Gus standing a few feet away, she gave an exaggerated huff. "Annie, I thought you told me you weren't going to let animals in the store anymore. I told you how allergic I am to them and, besides, it can't be hygienic. I would hate for the health department to shut you down." Dorcas glanced disgustedly at Lovina and her dog.

"Gus is not an animal, ma'am. He is our friend." Emily's voice was laced with fiercely protective barbs.

Dorcas pursed her lips as she pushed past the trio and plopped the box on the counter. She put her hands on her hips and turned to face Emily. "Some of us have been raised to know that it is good manners to leave our pets at home. We also know not to talk back to our elders."

Annie and Lovina exchanged a look and, Edgar, the older *Englisch* man who worked in the store, stepped out from stocking shelves and took Emily aside to teach Gus a new trick.

Annie engaged Mrs. Martin in conversation about the jelly jars, leaving Dorcas to stand aside and shoot spiteful glances at Lovina. A shame really, Lovina thought. Dorcas could be a pretty girl if she were less hateful.

"No need to worry, Dorcas," Lovina commented awkwardly, attempting to smooth Dorcas's ruffled feathers and soothe her own frustration. "We're just on our way home."

"It may be *your* home, Lovina, but it isn't *hers*," she spat, narrowing her eyes at Emily. "And it isn't Thomas Smucker's either. You'd do well to remember that."

Confused, Lovina drew closer to Dorcas. "What do you mean? I'm just helping them out."

"Keep telling yourself that, Lovina. Everyone else can see the truth. You want Thomas Smucker to forget you're a crippled spinster that no one else wanted and fall in love with you. Well, that's not going to happen. Soon enough, he won't need you anymore and then he'll be able to see that what he really needs is a young, healthy, normal Amish girl."

Lovina's chest tightened.

Was this what people really thought she was doing? Using Emily to make Thomas fall in love with her?

Clenching her fists, she looked over at the little girl who thankfully hadn't heard a word of the conversation that had just occurred. "Come on, Emily. Let's get Gus home and away from Miss Martin. I wouldn't want to give her an allergy attack." Lovina clenched her jaw, biting back the words she really wanted to say.

She started toward the door with Emily and Gus on her heels, but Dorcas Martin had to get one parting shot in.

"What's that envelope sticking out of your bag, Lovina?"

Lovina's blood ran cold.

She stopped in her tracks without looking back at Dorcas. Had Dorcas seen the envelope, or was she just fishing to see what Lovina would say? Lovina refused to take the bait.

She finally turned to face the vindictive girl. She forced a smile and prayed that her voice wouldn't betray her. "That's just some mail for a friend. I need to go drop it off now. Have a nice day, Dorcas, Mrs. Martin."

She pushed the door open and ran out as quickly as she could. Carelessly, she fled down the steps, with Emily calling to her to stop. Not accustomed to moving so quickly, she got the heel of her shoe caught in the hem of her dress and missed the bottom stair.

Lovina went sailing to the hard ground. She landed on her hands and knees and felt a fierce throbbing in her right forearm. Afraid to bear weight on her arm and push herself up, she turned over and sat on the ground, inspecting her wrist. She could make circles with it and open and close her palm, so it was probably sprained, at worst.

Not unlike her pride.

Chapter Twenty-Eight

SATURDAY, SEPTEMBER 23

T homas wiped the sweat from his brow as he unloaded the bench wagon. Tomorrow, the Graber family would host the community for church services and he finally felt like he could help them rather than just be a recipient of their good will. He wished they could have done the hard work earlier in the morning before the sun rose and the temperature shot up to the mid 80s, unseasonably warm for the end of September.

The Graber women, along with other ladies from the community, worked inside the house, preparing food and cleaning the house from top to bottom.

Thomas had noticed Lovina had not been using her right hand and was rubbing her wrist, which puzzled him. She had been exceptionally quiet as well, leaving Thomas to wonder if she was still upset with him for his careless tone toward Emily or the disagreement they had about the Western Wildflower.

He shook his head to rid himself of the thought. He'd apologized to Emily, and there was nothing more he could do. Certainly he couldn't go back in time and behave differently, but going forward, he vowed to be more mindful of the words he said and the way he said them.

Henry Graber stood with some of the other men from the community and directed Thomas where to place the benches within the house. While some traditions varied from community to community, the basic structure of worship services remained the same.

Thomas had found comfort in the familiarity when he moved to West Kootenai. In fact, he enjoyed the services here even more than the ones back in Belleville. He loved the way everyone came together to create a family-style environment for worship. He prayed that Emily would come to appreciate it as well.

Thomas placed the final bench as directed by Henry, then walked out to the porch to grab a drink of water. Lovina stood there, refilling the water pitchers and putting out more paper cups. She filled one for Thomas, then handed it to him.

Their hands touched briefly, sending a spark through his arm and straight to his heart. Lovina met his eyes and smiled softly at him. He returned the smile and took a moment to appreciate her chestnut-colored eyes and the warmth of her gaze.

"Mr. Smucker." A voice interrupted Thomas's thoughts.

Lovina jumped back from him and busied herself with sweeping the porch.

He glanced up to see Jonathan Martin and Benjamin Yoder standing in front of him. "May we have a word?" Elder Martin asked.

It felt less like a request and more like a demand, so Thomas simply nodded and followed them to stand near the barn. His heartbeat sped up. What could the two older men possibly want? He took a long swallow of the water to soothe his parched throat. "How can I help you gentlemen?"

Elder Yoder cleared his throat. "We hear you've had a visit from the social worker regarding your *niesse*." The man cocked his head sideways, inviting Thomas to respond.

Thomas wasn't sure what to say. Yes, Ms. Williams had paid

him a visit, but what did that matter to Yoder and Martin? "*Ja*, I did." A simple affirmation was all he could muster at the moment.

"And what did she say, Mr. Smucker?" Jonathan Martin's sharp tone revealed his impatience with Thomas.

"*Ack*, well, we simply have some paperwork to complete to make my guardianship legal. Just some hoops to jump through, as they say." Thomas tried to de-escalate the men's curiosity.

"Mmmmph," Mr. Yoder grunted. "I heard that the social worker had some concerns about your ability to take care of the girl."

"Not concerns, really. She just needs to ensure that Emily is being properly cared for. She did have questions about how the Plain lifestyle might impact Emily's well-being but Lovina was able to put her at ease."

The two men exchanged a look. Jonathan Martin crossed his arms. "That's what we wanted to discuss with you. From what we hear and what we just saw, you and Miss Graber have gotten mighty cozy taking care of your niece. Are you courting her, Thomas?"

Thomas couldn't speak. His blood boiled, but he had to keep a cool head for Emily's sake. After collecting his thoughts, he swallowed hard. "Not that it is your business, Mr. Martin, but I am not courting Lovina. I'm not courting anyone. Lovina is a friend. I could not have cared for my niece to this point without her. I assure you nothing romantic is going on."

While Thomas's words were true, he felt the sting of guilt when he spoke, and he hoped that the two elders didn't detect the dishonesty lacing his words. There was nothing romantic going on with Lovina, but he couldn't deny that the feelings he had developed for her were more than platonic. However, he knew he couldn't act on them, no matter how badly he wanted to, so the elders' accusations were ridiculous.

Jonathan Martin nodded at Thomas. "Have you given thought to courting anyone? As I mentioned before, it would probably help your custody case if you had a wife, or at least the prospect of one."

Thomas clenched his jaw so hard, he worried he might break a tooth. "I appreciate your concern, brothers, but let me set your minds at ease. I'm not planning to get married. Not now, not ever."

"Now see here, Thomas." Jonathan Martin pointed his finger as he spoke. "As I've mentioned to you before, it is the duty of an Amish man to marry and to multiply. This is the Lord's will for us. You certainly don't question that, do you?"

Again, Thomas chose his words with care. He thought back to the conversation they'd had a few weeks ago and the way Jonathan had weaponized the Bible against him. "I agree that is usually the case. However, sometimes the Lord calls us to remain single. Paul even says that in First Corinthians, doesn't he?" Thomas could see that he had thrown Mr. Martin's argument off track.

The two older men weren't making the progress they had apparently hoped for in this conversation.

Mr. Yoder tried again. "Don't you think Emily needs a father and a mother both?"

"I think that would be ideal. However, she has had so much upheaval and trauma in her short life, I think she would be better off to stay with me than to move to yet another home."

"And you plan to raise her Plain?" Jonathan Martin asked.

"*Ja*, I think that is the best upbringing for a child." Thomas almost felt smug in his response to the elders. However, he couldn't help wondering if they didn't have another trick up their sleeves.

"If this is how you feel, Mr. Smucker, we think it is only fair to tell you that the community has some concerns about your lifestyle that need to be clarified before we can support your raising of this child." Mr. Martin's voice dripped with condescension and false concern.

Thomas narrowed his eyes at the man. "And what concerns might those be?"

"Allow me to speak plainly. Your relationship with Miss Graber is inappropriate. If you are not courting her and do not plan to marry her, you need to put some distance between yourselves. People in this town talk, Mr. Smucker. You don't want to raise Emily in an environment that is shrouded in rumors and questions, do you?" Jonathan Martin's syrupy sweet tone cut to Thomas's soul.

"There is nothing going on with Miss Graber and myself, Mr. Martin. I resent the accusation. And might I remind you that bearing false witness is a sin, as well." Anger swirled in Thomas's head. He sought to contain it and remain calm, but with each word from Jonathan Martin, his grip on civility loosened.

"Nonetheless, Thomas," Mr. Yoder added, "you must think of how it looks to the rest of the community. Miss Graber is a spinster. She's always wanted a husband and now she has you living in her family's cabin and indebted to her for the help she provides. Because of the damage to her face and the limp she has, she's not a desirable candidate for a wife. Perhaps she sees you as her last chance. You must do what is right and separate yourself from her."

"Lovina Graber is not trying to marry me, gentlemen. She is helping me. No strings attached. As far as her so-called disability goes, she is one of the most capable people I've ever met. Her limp may slow her walk a bit, but she more than makes up for that with her intelligence and resourcefulness. And her scar sure doesn't stand in her way. Now, if you will excuse me, I have to help Henry in the barn." Thomas turned toward the barn, but Mr. Martin stepped in his path.

"You will need the support of the community if you choose to adopt your *niesse*, Mr. Smucker. It would be in your best interest, as well as hers, if you would listen to our advice and make some changes in your situation. A *kinder* needs a *dat* and *mem*, Thomas. You can't deny that. You can't give the girl all she needs. She would be better off in a proper Amish home, even a good *Englisch* foster home, than with an *oncle* who doesn't truly believe in our ways. Maybe that's still a possible route. I can ask the social worker if you'd like."

The threat shot through Thomas's heart like an arrow. "Exactly what are you saying, Jonathan?" Thomas used the older man's given name to put himself on equal ground with the elder.

"I just think a man in your position should be careful. Every choice you make affects the *kinder*. The social worker will be around the community asking questions of us all. We've had adoptions happen before. As one of the elders in our community, my statement will have the power to make or break your case. If you heed my advice and I can see you trying to be a *gut* parent, then I will share that with the social worker. If you don't, I will have to share my concerns. Choose your friends wisely, Mr. Smucker." With that, the two men walked back to the bench wagon and left.

Thomas's heart was crushed.

Perhaps Jonathan Martin was right. Thomas didn't have the means to take proper care of Emily on his own, and he knew he would never get married. He had seen what an unhappy union looked like and he wasn't putting Emily through that.

But was it selfish to avoid marriage?

Was he more worried about being a bad husband or the challenge of being a good one? Of losing his heart to someone again and being betrayed?

And was he being unfair to Lovina—taking so much of her help without offering anything for her in return?

He drank deeply from the cup still in his hand, wishing the water could wipe out the doubt he felt in his gut. While his physical thirst was quenched, he still had a deep burning inside that he knew was going to take more to douse.

Chapter Twenty-Nine

On the morning of the Sunday service, Lovina rose extra early to finish preparing their home for the community to arrive.

Lovina dreaded few things more than hosting church service at her family's home. For one Sunday, sometimes two, each year, all eyes turned to the Graber house, and Lovina couldn't escape the attention.

This year, with Emily and Thomas living in the cabin, her anxiety climbed even higher. After the conversation she overheard yesterday between Thomas and Elders Martin and Yoder, she knew the town was abuzz with gossip about her relationship with Thomas. She thought Dorcas's comments had just come from the younger woman's jealous heart, but clearly, rumors did exist. And Dorcas suspected that Lovina was the Western Wildflower.

She hated that Thomas was being scolded for letting her help with Emily. And that Jonathan Martin, threatening to give a bad report to the social worker that could cause Thomas to lose Emily—that really infuriated her. How dare he?

Even more, it'd stung when she overheard Thomas say that

185

he, like Lovina, planned to stay single. He would make some woman a *gut* husband, and Emily needed a *dat* and *mem.*

A few times, hope had crept into Lovina's heart and she allowed herself to imagine a change to the calling she had long ago accepted for herself. Perhaps *she* could be that wife and mother, after all. But hearing him voice his desire to stay single crushed every bit of optimism she had ever held.

Lovina knew that her *mem* needed help with the Sunday lunch that followed the service, but she hoped she could do all her serving from the kitchen and stay out of sight. If people were talking about her, her best option was to conceal herself.

West Kootenai was enjoying a bit of Indian summer in late September, which was welcomed, since next week could bring snow. Because the Grabers had such a lovely lot, everyone would enjoy today's meal outside, so Lovina would take care of the indoor chores and stay away from those who liked to gossip.

As she waited for the cheese atop the breakfast casserole to finish melting, Lovina sat at the dining table and leafed through a notebook that held some of her recent writings. She jotted down a Scripture that she had thought of many times.

Psalm 18:6: In my distress I called upon the Lord, and cried unto my God: He heard my voice out of His temple, and my cry came before Him, even into His ears.

Lovina knew that all she needed to do was call upon the Lord today and He would hear her. He could calm her anxious heart. She'd done that many times, and God never failed her. However, right now, in these circumstances with Thomas and Emily, it felt impossible to surrender her thoughts to God.

What was different about this situation? She would ponder on that a little later and see if she could work it into a poem or something. For now, she needed to finish up the preparations for the day.

Mem and *Dat* came downstairs together, both dressed and ready for the long day's events.

"Good morning, Lovina," *Dat* said. "Is that your cheesy-sausage bake I smell?"

Lovina nodded just as Emily and Thomas came in through the kitchen door and joined them. Emily made a dash directly to Gus to supply him with his morning belly rubs. Thomas sat down at the table in silence, not even meeting Lovina's eyes. He'd been quiet at dinner last night too.

She supposed that he had let the elders' scolding get to him. On top of it hurting his pride, it probably embarrassed him too. Hearing that people thought Lovina, the damaged *aldi maed*, was chasing him down and trying to trick him into marrying her had to be humiliating.

Lovina would have to be more intentional about avoiding Thomas when others were around. She certainly didn't want rumors going around about him that might interfere with him finding a proper wife. That was still her goal for him—to find a kind, lovely young Amish woman for him to marry, one whose body and face weren't so hard to look at, one that would take good care of him and Emily. The feelings she had for him wouldn't interfere with that.

The preparations seemed endless, but at last, buggies began arriving and the service got underway. Lovina quietly entertained Emily with coloring books and small toys throughout the lengthy service. Dorcas Martin and Frannie Yoder sat behind them, and Lovina could feel their eyes boring into the back of her head. They whispered and giggled and generally made Lovina miserable.

Today, Abe Sommers preached. His sermon centered on Romans 8:28, Susanna's favorite verse that she had quoted to Lovina last week. *"And we know that all things work together for good to them that love God, to them who are the called according to*

His purpose." Abe's voice boomed the familiar words in Pennsylvania Dutch.

"What's he saying, Lovie?" Emily whispered in her ear. The little girl had started to pick up some Pennsylvania Dutch phrases here and there, but the Scripture was read in German, so she was clueless.

"He read a verse that says things work together for the good of people who love God and do His work," Lovina whispered back.

Emily looked confused. "What does that mean?"

Lovina sought some child-friendly words to satisfy Emily. "If we love God and do what He wants us to do, we can trust Him to work things out for us."

Emily seemed to contemplate Lovina's answer for a moment, then resumed coloring.

Abe continued. "God has called each of us according to His purpose. We must choose to submit to that purpose in order for things to work for our good. If we are fighting God's call on our lives, we will miss the blessings He has in store for us."

Lovina's heart pounded in her ears. She felt like he was speaking directly to her.

Had she strayed from the purpose God had called her to? Was that what was giving her such trouble? Had she let her desire to be loved by Thomas distract her from her mission of singleness? She wished she had her notebook now. She wanted to wrestle with these questions later when there weren't people around to watch her squirm.

Abe relayed a few more stories and Scriptures to round out the sermon, but Lovina didn't hear another word he said. She was so fixated on the questions that swam in her head, there wasn't room for new thoughts.

As soon as the service was over, Lovina sent Emily to play with the *kinner* and dashed straight to the kitchen where she busied herself getting the food out of the refrigerator.

Mem whizzed into the kitchen to retrieve a dish. "Lovina, if you'll just bring things to the door, I'll grab them and set them out. I know your wrist hurts and you seem to be favoring your left leg a little more than usual. You can just stay in and wash up as the dishes come back, okay?"

"Thanks, *Mem*. I'm going to make myself a cold pack for my wrist. It's a little puffy still. I'll be glad to take care of the dishes." There were two huge pluses to staying inside: she would be able to avoid the judgmental eyes of Dorcas and Frannie, and she wouldn't have to worry about tripping and spilling all the food.

The meal was well underway, and Lovina was tucked safely out of sight in the kitchen. Every now and then, *Mem* came to the door to ask for more of something or to return an empty dish for Lovina to wash. As she did the dishes, she kept an eye on Emily through the back window and occasionally caught a glimpse of Thomas too. She felt absolutely ridiculous—hiding in her own kitchen and pining over a man she could never have.

Despite her frustration at her own behavior, Lovina knew she was doing the right thing by staying out of the way. Thomas needed time without her hovering around to meet people—young women—in the community. As long as she was in the mix, he was unapproachable.

As she dried a platter, she saw Thomas talking to Maggie Shrock. She was not a bad choice. Maggie had courted one of the bachelors last year and that had ended badly for her. Still in her *Rumspringa*, Maggie had been rumored to run around with *Englisch* boys now and then, but that was just gossip. Lovina couldn't give any weight to those rumors if she wanted people to doubt the ones circulating about herself.

Still, she thought Thomas deserved someone better.

She scanned the crowd and noticed Dorcas and Frannie huddled together whispering and pointing in Maggie Shrock's direction. Lovina gave thanks that those two hadn't sunk their fangs into Thomas, even though she knew Dorcas was interested.

Lovina closed her eyes in silent prayer. *Lord, forgive me for being selfish when it comes to Emily and Thomas. I want to remain in their lives even though I know Your plan for me is to remain single. I am thankful for Your plan for my life, even when I don't understand it. I trust You, God. Everything You do for me is for my good and Your glory. Help me to keep following and obeying You. Forgive me for being petty and jealous when it comes to Dorcas and Frannie. Help me see them as You see them. Amen.*

The back door slammed closed and Lovina's eyes jarred open. Dorcas Martin stood in the kitchen, lips snarled. "I came after my *mem*'s platter. Is it clean?"

Lovina sighed and pressed her lips into a forced smile. She hadn't expected God to give her an opportunity to show love to Dorcas so soon. "They are all clean. Which one was it?" Lovina asked softly, pointing toward the table full of clean, dry plates, pans, bowls, and platters.

Dorcas scanned the table then lifted an off-white, oval ceramic platter off the table. She turned up her nose as she inspected the platter.

Lovina smiled, trying to remember to practice what she'd just prayed. "Well, there you go. Have a good afternoon, Dorcas." She hoped the younger woman would turn and leave.

She should have known better. Dorcas never skipped a chance to belittle Lovina. And she had the best setup right now—no witnesses and no way for Lovina to escape her razor-sharp tongue.

"I wanted to ask you what you thought of last week's edition of *The Budget*. How did you feel about that Western Wildflower person's little column?" Dorcas towered over Lovina.

"I'm a little behind on reading *The Budget* just yet, what with all the preparations for having Sunday service here." Lovina had little ability to bend the truth, and the excuse sounded hollow, even to her own ears.

"Well, let me summarize. Someone wrote a letter asking for advice. They were concerned about a single man in their community raising a child on his own with only the help of some old spinster. Now, doesn't that sound suspiciously familiar?" Dorcas tapped her bony finger on her chin as though she was thinking about where she had heard such a story before.

Lovina didn't respond at first. She knew it was a trap. No matter what she said, Dorcas would trick her into admitting that she was the Western Wildflower. She clenched her jaw tight and backed away from Dorcas,

"Please, Dorcas. I don't know what you think has happened but..."

"Oh, Lovina. I suspected it was you but when I saw that envelope in your bag, it all clicked for me. I think it's time that we pull the mask off the Western Wildflower. What a perfect day for it. The whole community is together . . . what luck! Soon everyone will know, and you'll get all the credit you deserve." Dorcas headed out into the yard, running toward none other than Thomas Smucker.

Chapter Thirty

SUNDAY, SEPTEMBER 24

That Western Wildflower letter had kicked matchmaking into high gear.

Thomas had been approached by every single Amish woman in West Kootenai today, and not one of them held a candle to Lovina. He didn't mean to compare them all to her, but it was hard not to notice the contrasts. Where Lovina held an introspective, quiet strength and was, above all, authentic, most of these girls were flighty and immature. He couldn't imagine spending his life with a woman like that.

At least he had dodged Jonathan Martin's daughter. While his interactions with her had been limited, he had witnessed her uncharitable behavior. Emily told him that Dorcas had been ugly to Lovina about Gus just the other day. Her sharp tongue alone made him want nothing to do with a girl like her or her friend Frannie.

He stood watching Emily playing in the yard with the other *kinner* and smiled. With the Christmas tree farm in the background and the sun blazing in the blue sky overhead, they looked like something out of a magazine. She had settled into the Plain life so well. She still insisted on wearing her light-up princess shoes but had adjusted to the rest of the community's standard clothing, even the *kapp*. Lovina had been instrumental in convincing her to wear Amish apparel, even allowing her to design her dresses and accessories.

Lovina was one of a kind. The longer Thomas knew her, the more certain he was of that. However, she was the kind of woman who deserved a kind, compassionate, understanding husband. She'd had a wonderful example in Henry Graber. Thomas, too much like his own *dat*, fell short in every way. He had resigned himself to singleness when he broke up with Katrina. But, he reminded himself, that was before Emily came into his life and changed everything.

Thomas stood in the yard pondering his dilemma when Dorcas Martin came charging out the back door of the Graber house, plowing directly into him.

"Oh, Mr. Smucker, I need to talk to you right now," Dorcas gushed.

Frustrated that his luck had run out, Thomas looked around for Emily and conjured up an excuse to cut out of the conversation. "I'm sorry, Miss Martin, I need to see to my niece."

Dorcas grabbed his arm.

"Wait! You need to hear this right now." Dorcas Martin's voice was abnormally loud and high pitched. All around them, people paused their conversations and activities to look in their direction.

Thomas pulled his arm free. "All right. What is it?" His words held a sharp edge that he didn't intend but couldn't quite control.

"Have you read *The Budget* lately, Mr. Smucker?"

Not that nonsense. "Look, Miss Martin, I really need to get to my niece. If you'll excuse me." Thomas moved forward but Dorcas blocked his way.

"But, Mr. Smucker, this is important. I'm sure you've heard

of the Western Wildflower who writes those advice letters." She didn't wait for him to respond. "Well, I bet you didn't know that the mysterious writer is from West Kootenai."

Thomas blinked at her, not sure how to respond. "That's . . . *wunderbar*, I suppose."

She smirked. "For sure and certain, it is. Wouldn't you like to know the identity of the writer?"

"Actually, I am not interested in such things, but I have a feeling that you are going to tell me, so go ahead. My niece needs my attention." Thomas's patience had reached its limit. Dorcas Martin's attitude grated on his nerves.

"Why, it's none other than your very good friend, Lovina Graber!"

Speechless, Thomas stared at the young woman, sure she was mistaken. Out of the corner of his eye, he saw Lovina standing in the doorway, her face red and eyes downcast. All other eyes in the crowd were focused on Dorcas Martin and Thomas.

A cold sweat enveloped his body. His ears buzzed and his chest contracted. Confusion overtook Thomas's thoughts. How could Lovina be the anonymous Western Wildflower?

He thought back to the conversation they had had a few nights ago when she called the anonymous writer brave while he termed the Western Wildflower "meddlesome." At the time, he thought she had overreacted. Now, her response made so much more sense. She was the writer and viewed his critique as a personal attack.

He closed his eyes and breathed in deeply.

Thomas couldn't decide which bothered him more—her deception or the fact that he had been fodder for her work. He felt so exposed, especially since all of West Kootenai suspected that the bachelor she had written about was him.

He spun around to see Lovina standing beside him, her eyes silently pleading with him not to react to this news in front of everyone.

"I can't believe—" Words escaped him. What couldn't he believe? That Lovina had written about him for every Amish person in America to read? Or that she'd done it by lying about her identity?

His father's words rang in his ears. *"Let no man deceive you with vain words—Ephesians 5:6."* That's exactly what Lovina had done—not just to him, but to the whole community. She knew how much he valued honesty, and yet, she had used his situation to gain acclaim as a writer in the Amish world.

Lovina appeared so humble and selfless, but the truth was that she was a fraud and she had betrayed his trust.

Again, he thought of another of his *dat*'s favorite proverbs. *"Whose hatred is covered by deceit, his wickedness shall be shewed before the whole congregation."* That's exactly what was happening to Lovina now—everyone could see the truth of who she was.

Disgusted with both Lovina for her deception, and himself for his gullibility, Thomas wanted nothing more than to run to the cabin and hide, but his feet were fixed in place. Members of the community gaped at him, and he felt trapped. He hated the swirl of emotions that moved through him.

"Thomas, I can explain." Lovina's soft voice broke through his thoughts. "I never meant for the writing to go this far. I know you must think that I'm nothing but a coward for writing anonymously, and you are right. I never wanted anyone to know I wrote those pieces. I'm so embarrassed."

Dorcas Martin stood beside Thomas and Lovina, a manufactured look of injury on her face. "I can't believe that shy little Lovina Graber would be so dishonest with us all. We look like such fools!"

Thomas shifted his attention to Dorcas. "Miss Martin, thank you for this information, but I think you should mind your own business now."

Lovina's *dat* came alongside his daughter and wrapped his arm around her. "Yes, Dorcas, we can handle this from here.

Friends, finish up your lunches. My family and I will be inside ironing out the details of this revelation."

Dorcas Martin's face held a look of shock and derision. Thomas was certain she had more to say on the matter, but Henry Graber had put an end to the public side of the conversation and whisked an inconsolable Lovina back into the house.

Before Thomas could follow them, Jonathan Martin strode over to him. "I hope this doesn't ruin your chances for keeping your niece, Mr. Smucker," the older man sneered.

"This has nothing to do with me retaining custody of Emily. Lovina Graber was simply helping me take care of the girl. There was nothing more to our relationship." Thomas pulled his shoulders back and crossed his arms, as though he had settled the matter.

Clearly, Jonathan Martin held a different position. "On the contrary, Thomas. Allowing the resident gossip columnist to have a hand in raising your niece won't look good. It isn't as if Miss Graber is simply the traditional *Budget* scribe we all thought she was. That's a time-honored position. No, the real problem is the advice she doled out while she kept her identity hidden." He clicked his tongue on the roof of his mouth, placed his arm on Dorcas's shoulder, and led her away.

By then, most of the crowd had turned their attention away from Thomas and were whispering among themselves, no doubt about Dorcas's revelation that Lovina was the Western Wildflower.

Despite feeling deeply betrayed by her, he couldn't fight the urge to defend her against the judgments of people like the Martins. No matter what Thomas thought of her decision to write under a pseudonym, he couldn't deny her talent as a writer.

Thomas moved toward the back door to join the Grabers in discussing Lovina's deception. Maybe hearing her explain her reasoning would change the way he felt.

He doubted it.

His parents, at least his father, had drilled into him from a very young age the importance of honesty and keeping his word.

Katrina's deception had ended their relationship and ruined his friendship with Amos Stolzfus. Would what he had learned today put an end to his friendship with Lovina?

Chapter Thirty-One

L ovina sat at the dining table, her tongue incapable of making words. Her mind raced with concerns—her identity was now known to all, and Thomas would be so angry. How could she have let all this happen?

Mem patted her on the knee but offered no platitudes. *Dat* paced the perimeter of the kitchen.

Finally, *Dat* placed his hand on her shoulder gently. She stared ahead, her face feeling like stone, and took a deep breath. "*Mem, Dat,* I'm so sorry I kept this from you. I never meant for this Western Wildflower thing to get this big."

"*Ach,* Lovina, you should have told us," *Mem* said, stroking Lovina's back. "We would have supported you. Your writing is a gift from God."

Dat added, "For sure and certain, it is. And I understand why you might not have wanted everyone to know that you were the writer, but you could have trusted us with your secret."

"I know that now. I regret that I didn't tell you. While I couldn't stand the idea that I might get attention from the community for the writing, I did enjoy hearing people talk about the advice I was giving. Then, I felt guilty of pride. I was afraid, and I still am, that the elders might discipline me in front of everyone. I was confused," Lovina admitted.

Mem nodded. "All of that sounds reasonable, and I don't think they will hold this against you. However, there is the matter of the advice letter. Did you suspect that it was about Thomas when you responded?"

The back door squeaked open and Thomas entered. "I would like to know the answer to that myself." He stood stiffly just inside the door, his hands shoved in his pockets and his face a deep crimson.

Lovina buried her face in her hands. She wasn't sure how to answer that question. Truth was her only option, she supposed. "I didn't know for sure that it was about you, but I strongly suspected. There were too many similarities for it to be about anyone else."

"Then why didn't you admit that you were the writer the other night when we discussed it? You could have saved us all this embarrassment." Thomas's voice had a cold edge to it that she hadn't heard before.

"I-I-I was too self-conscious," she stammered, tears threatening to fill her eyes. "I worried that everyone would think I had an ulterior motive. The letter basically accused me of using Emily to get you to marry me. My response told the writer to back off. If folks knew it was me writing, it would sound like the writer was right and I was just jealous."

Thomas rubbed his temples—considering her words before responding. "I suppose that you would worry about that. But didn't you ever worry how people would look at me if they learned you were the Western Wildflower?"

"I'm sorry, Thomas. I did what I thought was right."

Lovina shook her head vigorously and threw her hands in the air. "Why would anyone think any less of you because of something I had done?"

"It looks like I let you play me for a fool. Some people have said they think you are trying to rope me into marrying you. How naive I must be if you were writing about me right under my own nose, and I was too clueless to notice."

"Now wait just a minute, Thomas," *Dat* interrupted. "It's a big leap to think that everyone considers you a fool."

"Maybe it is. Maybe I'm too sensitive. But I will tell you this. A lie of omission is no less dishonest than if she made up a story and told it for truth. Lovina lied to me—to us all—about being the Western Wildflower. That's going to be hard for me to forgive."

Chapter Thirty-Two

SUNDAY, SEPTEMBER 24

T homas turned and walked out the back door, not giving
Lovina a chance to atone for her mistake. Lovina wanted
to melt into the floor. A painful lump burned in her
throat.

"*Mem*, *Dat*, I am truly sorry for keeping this from you. I had
no idea what a position I was putting everyone else in. Can you
forgive my selfishness?"

Mem embraced Lovina tightly. "My darling girl, we serve a
forgiving God. Just as He forgave us, we forgive you. You should
have told us, yes, but you had no intention to hurt anyone. Why
don't you go upstairs and rest while we get everything taken care
of down here."

While Lovina would normally have argued with her mother
and insisted on helping with the cleanup, there was no way she
could face the people of the community now. *Mem* and *Dat* each
exuded so much grace, she knew their neighbors would treat them
kindly. Besides, they were both much more resilient than she was.
They would be fine.

Lovina, on the other hand, felt that her whole existence was in jeopardy. She had spent most of her teen and adult life trying to help others and make a difference in the community. With a snap of her bony fingers, Dorcas Martin had thrown Lovina into the spotlight and stripped her bare for everyone to see, revealing her to Thomas as a deceitful schemer.

She needed to withdraw, lick her wounds, and pray about how she could handle this.

She trudged up the steps, leaning heavily on her good leg to keep her balance. She sank onto her bed, throwing her forearm, still tender from her earlier fall, across her eyes. The pressure of a headache niggled just behind her eyes. Perhaps she could drift off to sleep for just a bit . . .

But she couldn't. With her eyes closed, she could still see the accusing, judgmental looks of the community when they heard Dorcas reveal her as the Western Wildflower. Most of them viewed her like Thomas did—a liar and a phony.

She had suffered something like this once before—back when Dan had dumped her. It took her years to move past the humiliation she'd endured at his hands. This was infinitely worse. She didn't know how she could recover from it. Not only were the townspeople condemning her, but so was Thomas, someone whose opinion truly mattered.

A knock on her door broke through her thoughts.

"Can I come in?" Susanna asked in a gentle voice.

Lovina sat up on the bed, smoothed her dress, and straightened her *kapp*. "*Ja*, Susanna. Come in."

Susanna waddled over and plopped down next to Lovina. "Your *mem* told me you were up here. I saw what happened. I'm so sorry, Lovina." She put her arm around Lovina's shoulder, and Lovina let herself soften at her friend's embrace.

"I've made a terrible mess of things." Lovina replayed the events of the afternoon in her head. She'd gone to see a horror movie in Kalispell with her sister Josie during their *Rumspringa* days. Now she was living one.

"*Ach*." Susanna rebuffed Lovina's negative self-talk. "Nothing is too messed up for God to fix. You know that. Besides, didn't you hear Brother Sommers talk about how all things work for our good when we love the Lord?"

Lovina massaged the back of her neck. "But there's more to that, Susanna. We have to be working in God's purpose for our lives. What if my writing wasn't part of my purpose? What if it was self-indulgence? A sin, even?"

Susanna shook her head. "I refuse to believe that. God has given you a special gift. You use it to glorify God, not yourself. Why, if Dorcas hadn't made your secret public information, no one would have ever known. How could you be prideful when you didn't want people to know?"

"Maybe." Lovina shrugged. "But I've embarrassed my family, and I've hurt Thomas." When she thought about the disgust in his eyes when he realized that she had been the anonymous advice columnist, her heart broke into a million pieces. Even if he could forgive her, their friendship would never be the same.

"Will he let me care for Emily anymore?" Probably not, she figured. And could she blame him? She *had* lied when she hid her secret identity from him. She had violated his trust and that was something she could never earn back.

"Give him some time, Lovina. He knows how much you love Emily. Anyone can see that you are wonderful with her. Don't let this one moment define you. Trust God to work it out. I will come check on you later this week. I will be praying for you."

Susanna hefted herself off the bed and disappeared into the hallway. Lovina appreciated her friend's kindness but there was so much more Susanna didn't know—like how Lovina truly felt about Thomas.

The affection she felt for him could never be returned. Not that she had planned to act on it, but somehow having it as a possibility—and now having that crushed—hurt terribly. Even worse, because of the embarrassment she caused him, he might have lost the chance at a good wife to care for him and Emily.

Because she'd followed her heart and written as the Western

Wildflower, because she had indulged her pride, she had lost everything that mattered to her.

She knew what she had to do.

Grabbing her notebook, she flipped to a blank page and began writing. She quickly dashed off a letter to her twin sister Josie in Kentucky. She would mail it tomorrow and then begin the next step in her journey.

She had to leave West Kootenai.

Chapter Thirty-Three

FRIDAY, SEPTEMBER 29

In the week following the church service at the Graber home and the revelation that Lovina was dispensing advice as the Western Wildflower, Thomas resolved to take care of everything for himself and Emily. After the incident with Lovina on Sunday, he had told the Grabers he would be moving out soon and wouldn't need Lovina to watch Emily anymore. They had begged him to reconsider, but it hurt too badly for him to think about it.

He'd taken time off work to search for a new housing and childcare arrangement and to work through the list of items the social worker had asked him to complete. He hadn't made much progress. He'd made it to Friday afternoon with no plan for Monday. With each passing moment, he grew less and less certain of his ability to raise Emily on his own.

Multiple times a day, Emily asked to go to Lovina's. Every time he refused, the little girl acted out a bit more. Rose Graber had helped him out a few times when Emily needed something he couldn't do for her.

Thomas hadn't seen Lovina at all. He supposed she was

staying out of sight until the turmoil died down. He couldn't blame her—the Amish gossip mill was running rampant with stories about Lovina and her motives for the answer she gave to the letter about his situation and her motives for helping him care for Emily. No one but Thomas seemed at all curious about the identity of the original letter writer, though.

Today, Thomas was trying his hand at laundry. He'd done it at home when *Mem* was sick, but *Mem* hadn't had a gas-powered wringer machine like the Grabers'. He had just washed clothes in the sink with a washboard, rinsed them, and hung them to dry. They weren't quite as clean looking and smelling as they were when *Mem* did the laundry, but they were passable.

He stood on the Grabers' back porch, wrestling with the unfamiliar machine. He'd added dirty clothes, water, and detergent, but he couldn't figure out how to turn the blasted thing on. As he examined the machine, he heard footsteps approaching. To his relief, it was Ike Sommers.

"The guys have been missing you at the Log Works, Thomas. I thought I'd drop in and see how things were going for you." Ike scanned the mess of laundry around Thomas. He walked over to the machine and flipped the switch on the diesel generator. The machine began to hum.

"Thanks, Ike." Thomas clapped his friend on the back. "I can't seem to get things working right, no matter how hard I try."

"I had hoped by the end of this week you'd have worked things out with Lovina. I can see you haven't." Ike shook his head.

"I don't know what to do, Ike. As much as it pains me to admit it, I miss her."

Ike lifted his eyebrows. "I'm not surprised that you miss her, but I am surprised to hear you say the words."

"That makes two of us." Thomas sighed. He missed everything about Lovina Graber. Not just her efficiency and skill in caring for Emily, but her very presence, as well. Lovina was spirited and joyful and balanced out his seriousness. Well, the Lovina she pretended to be, anyway. He didn't know the real

Lovina. He knew the version she wanted him to see. The real Lovina was still a mystery. "But I'm still angry at her. I don't know how I will ever trust her again." The frustration bubbled up again. *"Thomas Smucker, you are such a fool."*

As it did any time he allowed thoughts of Lovina's deception to come back to him, his *dat*'s voice rang in his ears. That only vexed him more, sending him on a downward spiral of misery.

"Don't you think Lovina deserves some grace?" Ike asked.

Thomas considered his words. "My head understands that idea, Ike, but my heart doesn't know how to allow it. I've told you about *Dat* before. Grace didn't come easily fom him. I'm afraid I'm just like him."

Ike shook his head. "I've told you before, that is nonsense. The Lord has made you a new creation. You don't have to do things the way your *dat* did. Don't rely on your own strength to forgive Lovina. Ask God for help."

"That's easier said than done," Thomas replied bitterly.

A tense silence followed, with neither man breaking it. The sound of the generator-powered washer hummed loudly, filling the air between them.

Finally, Ike asked, "How's Emily doing with all this?"

As if on cue, Emily came barreling out of the cabin. *"Oncle* Thomas, you are making a mess. That's not how Lovie does laundry."

"I'm doing the best I can," Thomas replied curtly, then shot a helpless look in Ike's direction.

Emily had been vocally displeased with their new arrangement. She wanted to go back to spending her days with Lovina and Gus, not Thomas. He hadn't told her the whole story about why Lovina wouldn't be taking care of her anymore, but he told her enough that she knew the problem was very serious.

At every opportunity, she pointed out to Thomas how inferior he was to Lovina. He couldn't cook as well as she could, he didn't know how to play or do the voices in stories like she did, and he generally lacked Lovina's sunny disposition.

"Why don't you just ask Lovie to show you?" Emily asked, apparently exasperated with his insistence upon independence.

Ike echoed Emily's wisdom. "The young lady has a point, Thomas."

Thomas could no longer contain his frustration. "I don't need her help. I can figure this out on my own." Thomas had always been stubborn, but this situation had drawn out his obstinance.

"Miss Emily, do you remember me? I'm Ike Sommers. I'm a friend of your *oncle*. He told me you wanted him to build you a cradle for your dolls. Could you bring one out so I can measure it and know how much lumber to bring?"

Emily's eyes sparkled with excitement and she dashed back into the cabin to find a doll for him to inspect.

"Well done, Ike." Thomas congratulated his friend, but his voice was laced with bitterness. "I guess some bachelors *do* have what it takes to keep little girls under control."

Ike stroked his chin for a moment, clearing his throat before he spoke. "Thomas, I'm going to say something, and I want you to take it with all the Christian love and kindness I intend. Stop being so stubborn. You care about Lovina Graber. Talk to her. Figure out a way to move forward—together. You are acting like a *bensel*. I need to grab a bite to eat at the store and get back to work but promise me you'll think about what I've said. Tell Emily goodbye for me and that I'll work on her cradle. I'm sure I can figure out the dimensions."

Thomas nodded wordlessly and watched Ike disappear down the road. The older man was right. Thomas almost wanted to laugh at his own orneriness. It was uncalled for. It reminded him so much of his own *dat*. He wished he could shake it off, but right now, being bullheaded brought him a measure of comfort. Putting those walls up kept him safe.

Thomas heard the cabin door slam. Emily stood before him with a doll in hand.

"Where did Mr. Ike go? I brought my baby for him to measure."

"I'll measure it for you and then let Ike know what we need." He looked down to see Emily's chin trembling as she fought back tears. He still wasn't comfortable with responding to her emotional outbursts. "Emily, what's wrong? Are you hurt?"

She shook her head but didn't make eye contact. "I just miss her, that's all."

"You miss your *mem*? I know that's hard."

"I didn't mean that. I miss Mommy and Daddy all the time. I miss Lovie right now." She traced circles in the dirt of the Grabers' backyard with the toe of her light-up shoe.

He stepped down from the porch, placing a hand on her back and patting her gently. He had no wise words to share with her, so he just stood there, awkwardly trying to show her his version of comfort.

Emily turned her greenish-blue eyes toward him, peering at him accusingly. "You could fix this if you wanted to." She crossed her arms and set her jaw.

"What do you mean?"

"You could 'pologize to Lovie for being mad at her, and then I could stay with her again."

She was so much like her mother. So determined, so certain that her idea was the best. That lip jutted out stubbornly, just like he had seen Anna Ruth's do during so many clashes with their *dat*.

"Emily Grace, it isn't that simple. Besides, you knew we couldn't stay here in the Grabers' cabin forever. You need a real home. You'll start school next fall, and you won't be with Lovina all day then, so you might as well start getting used to it." The washer stopped its humming, and Thomas stooped over to retrieve the damp clothes. He angrily stuffed them in the basket and moved to the clothesline.

"I will never get used to it! She is my friend and I love her. You are mean to keep me away from her." The intensity of her gaze increased.

"You don't know everything about this situation. I'm the adult, and you have to trust me. I know what is best for you."

"You do not! You don't know anything. You aren't my daddy and you never will be. I hate you!" She stalked off to the cabin and slammed the door.

Thomas stood at the clothesline, staring after his *niesse* in disbelief. She hadn't had a temper tantrum like that in a long time. In the past week, she'd been open with him about her displeasure that Lovina wasn't in their lives anymore, but it hadn't reached this level of disrespect.

An image of how his *dat* would have handled Emily flashed in his mind. *Dat* would have cut a switch from a tree and whipped her legs until she was sorry she spoke that way. Thomas had to admit, a tiny bit of him wanted to punish her, but he knew that wasn't the way.

However, the fact that the thought crossed his mind sickened him. Becoming his *dat* was the one thing he had wanted to avoid. And yet, here he was, resorting to "because I said so" reasoning and considering physical punishment. He'd pushed Emily away, just like *Dat* had pushed Anna Ruth away.

In that moment, he knew that if he was to become a different man than his *dat* had been, his behavior had to change. Just like the day Lovina had called him out for hurting Emily's feelings, he needed to apologize to his *niesse* and make things right with her. As simple as it sounded, he couldn't even make his feet move toward the cabin where Emily was most likely crying her heart out over his hateful words.

He knew what he should do. What held him back?

The sky had been bright blue and clear when he started working on the laundry, but over the last few minutes, dark clouds had rolled in. Thunder rumbled in the distance. He considered taking the laundry in, but he just didn't have the energy. He sat down on a stump, burying his head in his hands.

Dat had often compared himself to Job, a righteous man who was condemned to suffer many indignities and losses in order to test his loyalty to God. One of *Dat*'s common quotes was *"I was not in safety, neither had I rest, neither was I quiet; yet trouble came."* *Dat* felt that, like Job, his problems weren't of his own making, though Thomas often questioned that. *Dat* considered his behavior righteous—after all, he could back it all up with a handy Bible verse, so the trials he suffered wouldn't be affected by a change in his actions.

Thomas pondered that for a while. Like his *dat*, he often saw things in either black or white, right or wrong. He was quite nearly as legalistic and judgmental as Charles Smucker had been, despite his efforts to the contrary.

Was *Dat* right? Were his problems just a consequence of the enemy tempting a godly man?

If they were, then he had no hope for mending fences with Emily or forgiving Lovina.

But if he was wrong, then possibilities existed beyond anything he had dared to hope or dream.

Chapter Thirty-Four

L ovina hadn't left her house since Sunday afternoon. She had traded all of her outdoor chores with *Mem* for strictly indoor jobs, except for her chickens. She'd managed to sneak out and care for them before anyone else was stirring, though she had noticed a light in the window of the cabin most mornings.

Mem and *Dat* had indulged her week of wallowing in self-pity, but she wasn't sure how much longer they would continue to allow her to sit in her misery, which was exactly why she had to get out and about today. She had some business to take care of at the store that couldn't wait.

She waited until *Mem* and *Dat* had gone to the tree farm to do their daily chores before she left home. Thomas and Emily had been in the backyard hanging their laundry. Her heart ached. She'd wanted to do that for them. But Thomas wouldn't even speak to her or allow Emily near her.

She understood that he was angry and hurt by her deception, but must he punish her by keeping Emily away?

She slipped out the front door and headed toward store,

praying all the way that the crowd was small today. When she arrived, there weren't any buggies parked nearby, so she heaved a sigh of relief.

Annie welcomed her in with a hug. "Pull up a seat and I'll pour you a cup of coffee. Tell me how you've been."

"That's a loaded question. Are you sure you have enough *kaffe?*" Lovina sat at the counter and recounted the tale to Annie, glad there was no audience to witness when her emotions overcame her and her voice wavered.

Annie listened intently to the whole story. "Oh, Lovina, I'm so sorry it turned out this way. I never dreamed Thomas would have this kind of reaction, did you?"

Lovina shook her head. "I knew he wouldn't like it that I had been writing under a pseudonym, but I thought it would be something he could get past. Now I don't think he ever will."

"I have to ask. Do you love Thomas?" Annie asked as she refilled Lovina's cup.

Lovina drew in a deep breath. "Is that what people are saying?"

Annie shrugged. "Some people. But that's not why I asked. I've seen how you look when you talk about him, and I can tell that you miss him more than you let on. So, do you have romantic feelings for him?"

"I don't know how to answer that, Annie," Lovina replied. She did know the answer, but she refused to admit it, even to herself. "I do care for him that way, but I know nothing can come of it. Especially now."

"Are you sure?" Annie cocked her head and gave Lovina a knowing look. "Or are you just afraid?"

Lovina sighed heavily. "It doesn't matter if I'm afraid, Annie. I know that I have violated Thomas's trust, and he can't forgive me. And I worry that I've caused problems for his custody case. That's why I'm here. Can I use your phone in the office? I need to make a couple of calls."

"Of course, honey. Go on back and take your time."

Lovina walked behind the counter to Annie's office just in the nick of time, as the bell over the door rang to indicate someone else had come into the store. She sat at Annie's desk and pulled a paper out of her pocket.

First, she called the train station at Whitefish to inquire about upcoming trips to Kentucky. She booked a ticket for next Wednesday, then called the *Englisch* driver, Wyatt, to make arrangements for transportation. Finally, she dialed the number her sister Josie had sent her. It was the phone shed at the end of her lane. She would leave a message with the information about when she needed Josie to meet her in Bowling Green.

With all of that done, Lovina felt a weight had been lifted from her shoulders.

She needed time and space away from West Kootenai. Thomas and Emily needed her to go so they could create their own sense of normal. *Mem* and *Dat* would be shorthanded, but Geneva would be home soon, and she could step up.

Lovina walked out of the office and back into the store only to see Dorcas Martin and her mother sitting at a table with an *Englisch* woman. Upon closer inspection, Lovina could see that the *Englisch* woman was Ms. Williams, Thomas's social worker. They hadn't noticed her behind the counter yet, so she slipped back behind the partition and listened carefully to their conversation.

"I'm certainly glad you wrote to let me know about this, Miss Martin. I hadn't planned to visit Mr. Smucker until later next month, but your letter convinced me to pop in on him today and see what he has to say about all of this."

All of what? Lovina wondered. She prayed Ms. Williams wasn't referring to the situation Lovina had caused. Surely a social worker wouldn't be concerned with an anonymous Amish advice columnist.

She listened some more.

Dorcas spoke, her voice even and dripping with false sweetness. "I've had concerns about his ability to care for that poor little girl all along, but now, his situation has gotten so much worse. He's looked all over town this week for someone to take care of her while he works, and no one will do it. The little dear has so many complex issues, none of us Amish girls feel up to the challenge of caring for her."

Lovina's mouth gaped open. Complex issues? Emily was a dream to take care of! What other lies had Dorcas Martin told Ms. Williams?

The social worker nodded and jotted down some notes. "I admit that I thought she was adjusting so well, especially with Miss Graber's help. Now that they've had a falling out, I do worry about how well Mr. Smucker can keep up with her care on his own. That was one of my questions on my last visit. If his living situation is unstable, perhaps foster care would be better for Emily."

Lovina couldn't stand by and listen anymore.

She bolted out from behind the counter. "Hello, Ms. Williams. I couldn't help overhearing your conversation with Dorcas. Are you planning to take Emily into foster care? I think that would be a tremendous mistake."

Panic struck Dorcas's face, and she looked to her mother for help. The usually demure Mrs. Martin spoke up. "Now, Lovina, this isn't your business. Haven't you caused enough problems for Thomas and Emily? We just want to see her well taken care of."

"If that's true, then you will leave her with Thomas. He's come so far in such a short time. They get along so well. Why, he doesn't even need my help anymore." Lovina's voice shook, but she forced a smile, hoping Ms. Williams would believe her words anyway.

"Oh, is that why he was begging every widow woman and young mother in town to take Emily while he works?" The venom had returned to Dorcas's voice. "She's a wild little *Englisch* child and needs an *Englisch* family to raise her. Ms. Williams agrees."

Lovina clamped her jaw closed and ground her teeth. She shifted her pleading gaze to the social worker.

"I want what is best for Emily, Ms. Graber. After hearing from the Martins, I believe that would be for her to live outside of the Amish community. Shifting from the world she was used to into a much more conservative culture like this has to impact her behavior and explain why Emily has had such a difficult time adjusting. It explains her frequent outbursts and tantrums."

"What outbursts and tantrums? I've spent nearly every day with Emily since she came to town and have no idea what you are talking about," Lovina said through gritted teeth.

Emily's behavior had been like any other child's might have been in this situation, and Thomas had been learning to deal with her outbursts, which were becoming less and less frequent or severe.

"When her uncle asked her to wear an Amish dress, she threw a fit. That's according to Mr. Smucker himself. I've heard she also became aggressive and threatening with Miss Martin over a dog. And don't forget her behavior on my last visit—putting a plastic snake in the bathroom to scare you and hiding with a cat in the barn after you told her to go to the cabin. Since Mr. Smucker has not managed to get Emily in to see a therapist and I'm not a medical professional, I can't diagnose anything. However, these behaviors indicate that Emily needs more extensive therapy and knowledgeable care than Mr. Smucker is providing."

"You told us those were normal behaviors for a well-adjusted child." Lovina tried to keep her voice even.

"Well, yes. But I didn't have a complete picture of the situation. These reports from Miss Martin and her father have been helpful in providing some objective information about Emily's care."

"Dorcas, how could you?" Lovina's heart sank beneath the weight of this new

development. She knew Dorcas could be spiteful, but this was a new level.

"You're just mad that he is finished with you. You used that little girl to try to get him to court you and when he found out what a big phony you were, he rejected you. Just like everyone else has."

Annie came out of the kitchen bearing a tray of lemonade and cookies. "What on earth is going on out here? Lovina, are you all right?"

"This is the social worker who oversees Thomas's custody case." Lovina gestured toward Ms. Williams. "Dorcas and her family have been feeding her lies about Emily's behavior and Thomas's inability to raise her."

The shocked look on Annie's face drew the social worker's attention. "Is that inaccurate?" Ms. Williams asked.

"Absolutely. My name is Annie Johnson. I own this store and keep an eye on pretty much all the goings on here in town. Emily is just an absolute doll. Thomas is doing a wonderful job with her, for a bachelor with no child-rearing experience. I think you'd better ask around a bit more before you make any decisions."

Dorcas's eyes flamed. "Are you saying I'm lying?"

Annie shrugged, tossing her long braid over her shoulder. "I didn't say that exactly, Dorcas. I just don't think you are painting a very complete picture." She shot a sympathetic look at Lovina.

"Well, perhaps Annie is right. I will head on up to visit Mr. Smucker and then begin some further investigations. Thank you for the information, Miss Martin." The social worker rose and strode across the room to the door. "Oh, drat. Would you look at that? It's pouring rain now. The sky was crystal clear when I arrived." She fumbled around in her bag for an umbrella and dashed to her car.

Lovina shot one last dagger-filled look at Dorcas before leaving the store, slogging her way back home. Her shoes squished in the mud, and the rain soaked her dress. She wanted to get back to warn Thomas, but there was no way a crippled woman limping in the rain could ever outrun a car.

Chapter Thirty-Five

Thomas made a mad dash for the cabin before the rain completely drenched him. He entered, doffed his hat, and shook the water out of his hair. When he wiped the rain droplets out of his eyes, he noticed that Emily had made a mess in the small living area. She had brought all of her clothes and dolls out of the bedroom and dumped them on the floor.

"What on earth are you doing, Emily Grace?" He hated a messy house, and his nerves were already on edge.

"I'm moving in at Lovie's house. You can't make me stay here with you." She sounded much older than her five years.

Thomas took a deep breath and counted to five before he responded, a tactic Lovina had taught him but he was generally too impatient to practice. "You know that you can't move in with Lovina. The social worker has approved me as your temporary legal guardian, so you have to stay with me until the court decides otherwise."

Emily sucked in her round cheeks and narrowed her eyes. "Lovina can just write her a letter explaining why I can't live here anymore." She opened the closet door, pulled out a cardboard box and began piling her belongings in it.

"Lovina's letters have caused us enough trouble." The words popped out of Thomas's mouth before he even thought. Everything he said seemed to make the situation worse. It reminded him so much of how his father handled Anna Ruth. He didn't want to make the same mistakes *Dat* had made, so instead of arguing with her, he sat down on the couch and watched her pack.

Honestly, Thomas wasn't really worried that she would leave and move in at the Grabers' home. Lovina would know how to fix this. She was the one skilled in handling children, not him. He would have to swallow his pride and apologize to her, but he knew he couldn't take care of Emily without her help.

A knock at the cabin door interrupted his thoughts. He opened it to see Virginia Williams standing there, soaking wet despite holding an umbrella. She looked less than thrilled to be here.

"Come in, Ms. Williams. I'm sorry, did we have an appointment today?" Thomas searched his mind for details.

Ms. Williams looked around the room, noting the mess and the tension that hung thick in the air. "No, we didn't, but I am allowed to drop in unannounced at any moment. Are you all doing a bit of cleaning?"

"Nope," Emily interjected before Thomas could process a response. "I'm packing my things. I'm going to live with Lovie."

"Now, now, Emily. There's no need for that." Thomas tried to keep his tone even and his face neutral even though his blood pressure nearly shot the top of his head into the ceiling.

"Is there a problem I need to know about?" Virginia Williams's gaze swept from Thomas to Emily and back again.

"Nothing we can't manage. Just a little misunderstanding." Thomas grabbed Emily's box from the floor. "Now, why don't you go put these clothes and toys back where they belong, and I'll talk with Ms. Williams."

Emily crossed her arms and planted her feet wide. She turned up her chin defiantly. "Nope. I've made up my mind."

Ms. Williams exhaled a long sigh and sat down on the couch, pulling her notebook out of her bag. She scribbled for a minute then turned to Emily. "What is it that has you ready to move, Emily? I thought you were happy here with your uncle."

"I was until he stopped letting Lovie take care of me. She was my very best friend, and just because he's mad at her doesn't mean that I am." Her lip trembled as the tough shell she'd been trying to keep in place broke.

"Mr. Smucker, am I to understand that you and Miss Graber have had a falling out of some sort and you won't allow Emily to see her anymore? Despite the many traumatic events Emily has experienced, you are choosing to take one of her comforts away from her? One rule we follow in this profession is that the child's needs come first." She scribbled some more on her notebook.

"Ms. Williams, I don't think you understand," Thomas started, then trailed off. While there was a lot more to the story, she was right. Lovina was what was best for Emily and he had been selfish when it came to his feelings toward Lovina.

"I'm going to need to talk to Emily, Mr. Smucker. I have some questions for her, and I will need you to give us some privacy." Ms. Williams's sharp eyes peered at Thomas, who realized there was nothing to do but let the social worker have her way.

Thomas looked around the room for a place to go. He didn't want to go back out in the rain, but that might be his best choice. The wet, gloomy exterior matched his interior perfectly.

Ms. Williams caught Thomas's eye. "Why don't Emily and I go back to her room while you get this cleaned up?"

He nodded and watched as the two disappeared into Emily's bedroom. He busied himself cleaning up the mess Emily had made. When it no longer looked like a tornado had hit, he sat down on the couch and sighed.

He might have tidied up the mess in the living room, but the mess he had made of his life still loomed large. He had alienated everyone who mattered to him. But what could he do to fix this?

Thomas ran through various scenarios in his head but kept coming back to the same hard truth. He had been right all along. He wasn't fit to be a husband and father. The way his friendship with Lovina had fallen apart and how Emily felt about him made that abundantly clear.

He had spent the past several weeks working so hard to complete the items on the social worker's checklist so that he could keep Emily, only to learn that he was too much like his father—too legalistic and judgmental—for it to matter.

Emily and Ms. Williams came back into the living room after their brief conversation. Emily's face was damp with tears and didn't have that determined look on it anymore.

Ms. Williams kept her well-manicured hand planted on Emily's shoulder. "Mr. Smucker, Emily had some very telling answers to my questions. Between what I've seen here today, Emily's past behaviors, and the reports I've collected, I believe it is in her best interest to be placed in foster care. She needs a well-trained guardian and access to frequent therapy."

The words struck Thomas at his very core. Ms. Williams, an expert in parents, children, and families, believed he was unfit too. "I see. Emily, is that what you want?"

The little girl shrugged. "I want to go back to the way things were when Lovie took care of me while you worked. But you don't like Lovie anymore and I don't think you like me either." She stomped her foot and crossed her arms, giving Thomas a cold glare.

Thomas looked from Emily to the social worker and back. "What makes you think that?"

"All you do is fuss at me when I make mistakes and you won't let me visit Lovie, either. You've stopped singing me my song at night. You just seem mad that I'm here."

Thomas realized that his behavior over the last several days might make Emily feel that way. It just reinforced the truth—he didn't know how to be a loving father. He was too much like Charles Smucker, and he wouldn't want another child to grow up in that kind of household.

Ms. Williams was right. Someone else, anyone, really, would be a better guardian for Emily.

He swallowed hard, stifling the sensation that his knees might buckle any second. Waves of nausea threatened him, but he steadied himself. "I guess it's decided then. When will Emily leave?"

"I think we can get her things together pretty quickly, and I'll take her this afternoon. I need to make a few calls to secure a good spot for her."

"So soon?" Thomas whispered. "Well, I can help Emily finish packing if you would like to step outside and make your calls. Will I be able to visit with Emily later on?"

Ms. Williams tilted her head. "I suppose that wouldn't be a problem. I can't guarantee her placement will be nearby, but I'm sure we can work out some kind of arrangement for visitation. We can figure that out later." She excused herself to go out to her car and make her calls.

Thomas and Emily stood in silence in the living room. He didn't know what to say to make this better for her. He glanced down at her, but her eyes remained fixed on the floor. She chewed on her bottom lip and clenched her tiny fists at her side, reminding him so much of Anna Ruth. If Emily continued living with him, she would be as miserable as her mother was. He knew firsthand how hurtful an emotionally distant father could be.

As they boxed up the dolls and clothes Emily had gathered, the tension between the two of them made it difficult for Thomas to draw a breath. He couldn't help but think of his *mem* and what joy Emily would have brought her. Why couldn't things with Anna Ruth have turned out differently?

The pain in his chest intensified until he felt that it might split open. *So this is what a broken heart feels like.*

"I can have the rest of your things sent later if you'd like," he muttered, more to break the silence than anything.

She nodded and ducked her head. Then, without a word, Emily lay on the loveseat and pulled the plaid blanket off the back and covered her head. Even though not a sound came out, the tiny form under it trembled as she shuddered with silent sobs.

The small pink T-shirt in Thomas's hand dropped to the floor. He moved to the loveseat and sank to his knees. Emotion stuck in his throat like a beaver dam clogging up a narrow river, and he struggled for breath. Emily's little hand hung off the side of the loveseat and he slowly wrapped his fingers around it. Thomas expected her to pull away. Instead, her hand clung to his with a grip that surprised him. And even though Thomas knew she was mad, he also knew she didn't want to let go.

I don't either, sweet girl. Lord, why is this so hard?

"Emily, I'm sorry this didn't work out." Thomas's breaths came in ragged gasps. "I should have known better than to try and be a *dat*—when I'm just your sorry bachelor *oncle*." Thomas pressed his lips together. "Somehow we'll make it through this." He attempted to swallow again, but his mouth tasted like sawdust. "Somehow . . . oh, dear God . . ." And not knowing what else to say Thomas's words became a silent prayer.

Chapter Thirty-Six

The rain fell with a vengeance from the usually blue Montana skies. Lovina slogged her way back home, but her pace was exceptionally slow.

Everything in her hurt, but especially her heart. She'd tried to stay strong. She'd attempted to do what was right, but in the end she'd failed everyone. She'd failed her calling. She'd failed her parents and community. She'd failed Emily. All the little girl wanted was someone to care for her and love her. Yet Lovina couldn't even do that. Her mistakes were too great.

Everyone is right. They are all right. I'm not fit to be a mother.

She took another pained step forward as her right foot slogged through the mud, followed by her left. She'd failed Thomas. And by failing him, she failed her heart. The sharp pains that shot from the center of her heart outward to all her limbs confirmed that.

Seeing her house ahead did nothing to bring hope. It could be a hundred miles rather than a hundred yards. Her shoes squished in the mud and made it hard for her to keep her already precarious balance. She'd wanted to make it back to the house in time to intercept the social worker and help Thomas set the record straight, but the parked car in front showed her she'd failed yet again.

With each step, she uttered a simple prayer. *Help them, Lord.* Thomas needed divine intervention right now. He tried to be so strong. She knew he didn't want to give up, but he reminded her so much of a wounded puppy that had been kicked so many times it refused to stop cowering in the corner.

The rain ran off her *kapp* and down her cheek, dripping over her trembling jaw. Lovina pictured Emily's little face the day she'd arrived. She'd tried to be so brave and yet fear had filled her gaze. She'd lost so much already for one so young. Did she have the same look on her face now that she had then?

The pain in Lovina's hip radiated out, but she continued on, refusing to give up. And as she remembered Emily's smile as they hung clothes together on the line, Lovina knew what she had to do.

She had to meddle.

More than that, she had to demand that Thomas accept her help, whether he liked it or not. It didn't matter if Dorcas Martin or the rest of the community gossiped. In this moment, she cared more for the little girl than she cared what they had to say. And yes, she admitted it. She cared for Thomas too. More than that. She loved him. She loved him in a way that she never thought she could love a man. She'd care for him too, in simple ways, just as she'd been doing. She'd deny her heart and her greatest desire—to be a wife and a mother. And she'd give these two people her love and her help, even if that made her the laughingstock of the community.

They were worth it. Emily was worth it. Thomas, wounded yet wonderful Thomas, was worth it.

Even though Thomas was still furious with her, Lovina hoped he would put aside his feelings and let her help him one more time.

Soaked through to the bone, Lovina finally arrived at her house to find Ms. Williams loading a box into the trunk of her government-issued car. Emily sat in the back seat, staring straight ahead. Thomas was nowhere to be seen.

Gus darted from the barn, barking. Lovina hobbled to the car with him nipping at her heels, both of them looking like drowned rats.

"Where are you taking her?" Her voice shook but was twice as loud as usual.

"I'm taking her to a foster home in Whitefish. Now, if you'll excuse me, Miss Graber, I need to get on the road. You can say a quick goodbye."

Lovina knocked on the back passenger side window. Emily's large greenish-blue eyes met hers, but they held no sparkle. When Emily rolled down the window, Lovina reached in to stroke her hair. Gus jumped and barked at the window until Lovina swept him up into her arms.

"My sweet girl, I don't know what's going on, but I'll talk to your *oncle* and see what we can do about this. You keep saying your prayers, okay?" A sob caught in Lovina's throat.

Why was Thomas letting her go?

Emily just sniffled and nodded, grasping Lovina's hand with one of her own and letting Gus lick the other.

"Miss Graber, I really need to be going." The social worker's tone bore an attempt at compassion, but her impatient words were a dagger to Lovina's heart. Emily released her hand and rolled up the window.

Lovina stood in the rain, watching the car pull away, clinging to Gus as he struggled to get down and chase after Emily.

The car disappeared in the distance, and Lovina's sorrow transformed into anger. A vein twitched in her forehead as she clenched her jaw and ground her teeth. She rocked Gus from side to side in her arms, feeling her fury expand from a flicker to a roaring fire inside. Thomas should have fought harder for Emily. She should have been able to get here quicker. Once again, her body betrayed her when she needed it most.

Lovina stormed around the side of the house and up to the

door of the cabin. Her heavy, wet dress threw her off balance, but she righted herself before slipping on the doorstep. She pounded until her hand ached. At last, Thomas opened up.

"Why did you let her go?" Her words came out as a forced whisper.

Thomas wouldn't meet her eyes. He shifted from one foot to the other before answering her. "I had to. I can't do things for her that she needs. I'm too much like my own *dat* to ever be a good father to that girl. She deserves better."

Speechless, Lovina fought the urge to grab Thomas by his shoulders and give him a good shaking. Her voice cracked when she finally opened her mouth. "You loved her. That was enough. The two of you were growing together and making a family. It takes time, Thomas. I can't believe you gave up on her. On yourself!" She reached out and placed her hand on his arm.

"I love her too much, Lovie. I want what's best for her, and I know it's not me."

"It could be you." *It could be us,* she wanted to add, but instead, she withdrew her hand and turned away, slogging back to her own house. She let the back door slam behind her as she entered and slid into a chair at the kitchen table.

Mem came dashing into the kitchen, her concern for Lovina clear. She handed Lovina a fresh dish towel to wipe her face and hands. "Daughter, what has happened?"

Lovina held the towel to her face for a moment and breathed deeply as she tried to form the words in her head before she said them out loud. "He let her go, *Mem*. Thomas let the social worker take Emily away."

Her *Mem* sat in stunned silence as Lovina relayed the story of everything she had witnessed at the store and then when she returned home.

"Emily was completely crushed, *Mem*. I don't know if she can overcome this kind of hurt, especially without us at her side. I will never understand why Thomas didn't fight harder to keep her."

"All he had to say for himself was that he was too much like his *dat* to be a good father?" *Mem* asked. "What do you think he means?"

"His *dat* was very legalistic and unkind. I guess Thomas sees himself that way too. But he was so good with Emily. He was becoming so patient and loving. He had learned so much. I can't believe he just gave up."

Mem paused for a moment before responding. "Think about what you just said."

"That I can't believe he gave up?" What was *Mem* hearing that Lovina hadn't heard?

Mem shook her head. "No. The part about how he sees himself as an unsuitable father because his own father was so harsh. Take a moment and really think about that."

Lovina still didn't follow *Mem*'s reasoning. She turned the idea over and over in her head. "I'm not sure what you mean."

"You think Thomas sees himself as unworthy because he never learned to be a good father from his own *dat*. You and I know that is wrong. We have seen how he cares for Emily and how much he has grown in such a short amount of time. Why do you think Thomas doesn't see that?"

Lovina struggled to see where her mother was going with this conversation. She tried to put herself in Thomas's shoes. "It's hard to stop believing something that you've always accepted as true, even when you have proof that it was a lie."

Her own words echoed in her ears. Was this what she was doing to herself? Did she see herself as unworthy and less than because others had seen her that way? Lovina dismissed the thought as soon as it entered her head. She knew herself well enough to know the truth.

Mem nodded. "Right. So, how can we help Thomas?"

Lovina shrugged. "*Mem*, I honestly don't know. Like I said, he's just given up."

"Maybe he hasn't given up as much as he's just afraid to keep trying. Maybe the lies he believes about himself are true. But what if they aren't? Sometimes it's more comfortable to keep believing the lie than it is to embrace the truth."

Lovina considered her mother's words for a moment. *Mem* was right, as usual. But what good did that do at this moment? Emily sat in a car that was speeding away from them, and Thomas was moping in the cabin. Right now, someone needed to act.

As though reading her thoughts, *Mem* spoke out. "You need to help Thomas confront the lie that he isn't good enough to take care of Emily."

"He isn't speaking to me right now, *Mem*. He thinks I am a liar and a phony. I'm not sure I can convince him to believe anything."

"The best way you could help him is by sharing your own experience, Lovina."

Lovina rubbed her temples and closed her eyes. The more *Mem* said, the less sense she made. "I don't have any experience in this."

"You've never believed a lie about yourself?" *Mem* probed.

Lovina shook her head. "Not like this. *Mem*, what are you trying to say?"

"You have said that the Lord didn't intend for you to marry. You were meant to stay single. Why do you think that's true?"

"I guess because I've never had luck in romance. Plus, I would just be a burden on any man I would marry."

"And where do those thoughts come from?" *Mem* wouldn't let it go.

Tired of explaining herself over and over again, Lovina threw her hands up in the air. "Experience, *Mem*. Don't you remember what Dan said when he broke up with me? I'm damaged." The pain was as fresh to Lovina now as it was when it happened. She closed her eyes and shook her head to dismiss the very thought.

"Of course I remember it, Lovina. But what if all that was just a lie? What if God made you to be a wife and mother but you were too busy believing the worst of yourself to accept the truth?"

Mem's voice rose several decibels as if trying to force Lovina to hear her.

Lovina stood up speechless before her mother. What if she was right?

"Lovina, I've watched you with Emily. You care for her so effortlessly. You are made to be a mother. And I've seen the way you look at Thomas too."

Lovina's cheeks flared with heat. "*Mem*! That's not true." But in her heart, she knew that it was.

Was it possible that she had worked so hard to believe the lies she told herself that she had blinded herself to the truth?

Her mother reached across the table and grasped Lovina's hand. "My dear girl. What is it the Bible says? It's easier to see the mote in someone else's eye even though you have a beam in your own? Go talk to Thomas. Tell him how you see him. Tell him how God sees him. And let him help you see yourself right too. Go on, before that social worker gets any farther away."

Mem got up from the table and returned to the living room, leaving Lovina to consider her advice.

As hard as it was for her to admit, maybe she *was* guilty of believing a lie about herself. As long as she professed that God didn't mean for her to become a wife and a mother, she could protect her heart from the hurt she'd experienced before.

If she could embrace the truth, could Thomas do the same? *Show me how to do this, Lord. Show me how to help him see himself as You do.*

Chapter Thirty-Seven

T homas stood at the window reliving the social worker driving away after Lovina had said a tearful goodbye to Emily. And Lovina's question. *"Why did you let her go?"* His heart ached. All of this was his fault. He knew better, even that first day that Emily showed up. He knew he could never give her the kind of life she deserved. He had only delayed the inevitable by letting her stay with him. All he had to show for his poor choice was a trail of hurt. The social worker took Emily away. He and Lovina weren't even speaking. Everything was a mess.

A mess of his own creation.

Thomas finally gave up his post at the window and sat down on the couch. He took in the sight of the quiet living area, so empty without dolls and art supplies everywhere. It looked just like his heart felt—hollow and abandoned. He used to seek out the quiet. Now, the silence was nearly deafening.

He exhaled deeply. What now?

He needed to find a new place to live, but he wasn't especially interested in returning to the bachelor camp. Perhaps Ike would know someone who had a place to rent. He looked at the clock on the wall. Ike would probably be at the store having lunch. If he left right now, he could catch him.

Thomas grabbed an overcoat and made his way through the mud to the store. The rain was beginning to let up, but it had already done its damage to the day. His laundry was soaking wet on the line, and his shoes were likely ruined. He much preferred those clear blue Montana skies to what he was seeing now.

As he sloshed along the muddy road, he tried to focus on things he needed to do to get his life back to normal, but thoughts of Emily and Lovina kept invading. Regret plagued him. How he wished he could take back all the hurt he had caused them, but like his *dat* often quoted from Isaiah, *"Remember ye not the former things, neither consider the things of old."*

Still, Thomas felt the yearning to make things right.

He approached the store just as Ike was arriving. He waved at Thomas and greeted him with a friendly smile that quickly fell when Thomas approached.

The older man gestured for Thomas to follow him into the store. "I take it you didn't heed my advice about Lovina."

Thomas couldn't speak. He just shook his head.

Ike placed a hand on Thomas's shoulder. He squeezed as if to remind Thomas that he was there and he cared. At the gesture, a quivering in Thomas's chest grew and he sucked in a breath to hold back the sob that wanted to escape. But he wouldn't cry. He wouldn't. Not here. He had to stay strong. He had to remember he was doing the right thing. The best thing for everyone.

The two walked into the store and found a booth where Ike could eat while Thomas updated him on what happened after Ike left the cabin.

Thomas ordered a black *kaffe* that he doubted he could drink, but having something in his hands made him feel a bit sturdier. The words tumbled out of his mouth as his hands tightened around the steaming mug he clung to like a lifeline.

"So, Emily's gone? For good?" Ike asked, shoveling today's roast beef special into his mouth.

Thomas nodded. "I thought it was for the best—that's what the social worker said, anyway. As much as I wish I could have been the one to raise her, like I've said all along, I'm not cut out for fatherhood. Ms. Williams assured me they would find her a loving home with people who know how to raise a little girl."

Ike swallowed, then washed down his food with a gulp of milk and wiped his mouth. "I'm going to tell you something, Thomas, and it may not be what you want to hear. I've been praying for you and Emily since she came into your life. At first, I prayed that the Lord would help you find a family that could take care of her. However, the more I saw the two of you together, the more I realized that God had placed her just where she needed to be. I saw a change in you. So, I began praying that you two would be able to stay together."

"I started praying for that, too, Ike, but this last week has shown me that I was right all along. God never meant for me to marry and have *kinner*. I'm too much like my *dat*—too black and white, too harsh, too unforgiving. I'm working on those things, but until I can be a better man, I'm not going to bring Emily up with that kind of treatment. I saw what it did to Anna Ruth, to my *mem*, and to me. I won't do that to someone else." Thomas took a swallow of the *kaffe*, now cold but still bitter. His heart ached in his chest at the realization.

"Don't you think you are being a little hard on yourself?" Ike asked.

Thomas pondered his question for a moment, then shrugged. "Maybe I am, but I also know the damage my *dat* did. I would rather be safe than sorry when it comes to Emily."

"And Lovina?"

Ike's question hung in the air. Thomas could pretend not to understand what Ike was getting at, but there was no use. Ike was too perceptive.

"I've struggled to forgive Lovina ever since I found out she wrote that letter in *The Budget*. I feel a bit foolish when I think about how angry I've been and what a big deal I've made of this, but I don't know how to fix it. Part of me wants to forget it ever happened, but another part of me can't let it go." Thomas listened to the words that came out of his mouth, surprised at the admission he just made. He cared enough about Lovina that he did want to forgive her. And forgiving Lovina was the key to keeping Emily.

By refusing to forgive, he was closing everyone he loved out of his life.

"That part of you that wants to forget about it, where do you think that's coming from?"

Thomas hesitated, but Ike could see right through him, and he knew it. "The part that cares about Lovina as more than a friend," he answered begrudgingly.

His heart pounded so loud he was sure Ike could hear it. Owning up to his feelings went against everything he thought he wanted.

Could he overcome his stubbornness and allow happiness into his heart?

"You are letting the other part win, though. The part of you that says you don't deserve a wife and a family because you are too much like your father. I want you to think about why that is," Ike responded as he flagged the waitress for the check.

Thomas rubbed his forehead, searching for the answer. "I had a girl I was going to marry. I didn't love her, but *Dat* wanted me to marry her. Then I caught her kissing my best friend. I decided right then that marriage wasn't for me. *Mem* said I would change my mind, but I watched my *dat* make *Mem* miserable. I vowed I would never do that to another person."

Ike nodded. "I understand why you might feel that way. That had to be hard to live through."

"*Ach, vell*, living with my *dat* was tough but swearing off women was easy." Thomas sat back in his seat and crossed his arms. "Between the lack of success of the dairy farm and the poor reputation that *Dat* had around town, eligible women weren't exactly beating down the door. After Anna Ruth left town, our family withdrew even more, only attending Sunday services. I courted Katrina, but that didn't work out."

"And then, you came to West Kootenai," Ike interjected.

Thomas nodded. "Right. I had no plans to marry. I just wanted to be free of the weight that came with the Smucker name in Belleville. I wanted to be anonymous, another bachelor living in the woods. But along came Emily, and that changed everything. Somewhere along the way, after she arrived, I started seeing things differently. I started to think I could be a father." His voice cracked as he continued. "And Lovina . . . somehow, she made me feel capable. She taught me how to interact with Emily without criticizing or judging me. And how did I return the favor? I shut her out of my life entirely."

Ike smiled. "I understand where you're coming from."

"I guess you would. You're the oldest bachelor in West Kootenai!" Thomas teased, but his heart didn't match his light tone.

"The oldest bachelor and the stupidest. Here I am giving you advice when I can't find a way to tell the woman I love how much I care for her." Ike's eyes wandered to the counter where Annie stood smiling and making conversation with a customer. "I've wasted too many years, Thomas, battling my worries and doubts. I urge you not to do the same."

Thomas swallowed hard. He'd had no idea how Ike felt about Annie.

After Ike settled his bill, the two men walked out of the store together. The rain had stopped, and steam rose from the blacktop road and from the roofs and treetops.

"I appreciate you taking the time to talk to me, Ike. It means a lot. You've given me some important things to consider. Keep praying for me, won't you?"

Ike clapped Thomas on the shoulder. "It would be a privilege to pray for you. Just promise me that you'll listen when the Holy Spirit tells you what to do."

Thomas shot a half smile at Ike. "I'll do my best—and you do the same."

He waved to his friend and then slowly made his way back to the Graber cabin. He mulled over the questions Ike had presented to him. Why was it that he couldn't allow himself to forgive Lovina and then pursue her romantically? Could he blame that on his father too?

The truth of the matter was that Lovina was a gifted writer. No doubt the Lord placed the things she wrote on her heart and in her mind. Her words blessed and uplifted others. Just because *Dat* wouldn't have approved didn't mean that Lovina was wrong.

Hadn't he learned that his *dat* was wrong about many things? Could it be that he was wrong about Lovina's behavior being an act of betrayal?

What a *dumbkopp* he'd been!

The Graber house came into view and Thomas sped up. It might be too late to make things right with Emily, but he could still show Lovina that he could forgive her.

Was it too late for her to forgive him?

Chapter Thirty-Eight

A rap at the back door pulled Lovina from her silent prayer. She jumped at the sound, then straightened her *kapp*, rose to her feet, and smoothed her apron. She opened the door to find Thomas standing there. Her heart dropped to her belly, a mixture of fear and disappointment washing over her. Had he come to berate her again? Could she take any more?

"Can I come in?" His voice was soft. By the conflicted look on his face, she could see that he'd been wrestling with something.

Though part of her was angry at Thomas for letting Emily go, Lovina pulled the door open and stepped aside, wordlessly inviting him in. He paced back and forth around the room before finally settling at the table. Lovina crossed the kitchen to start a pot of Feel Better tea. She had a feeling they might need it.

He heaved a loud sigh. "I need to say some things, Lovina. I know I've been unbearable. Can you forgive me?"

Lovina chose her words carefully, but she didn't mask her irritation. "Can I forgive you for being unbearable? *Ja.* Right now, I'm more upset that you let Emily go with that social worker."

"I didn't know what else to do. I am not capable of raising her. Look at what a mess I've made of things." Thomas's cheeks flooded with color, and he rested his head in his hands.

Lovina worried for a moment that he might collapse. She sat down across from him, picking up a piece of paper that contained one of Emily's many drawings. This one showed Lovina, Thomas, Emily, and, of course, Gus, standing in front of a Christmas tree. Lovina traced the lines Emily had sketched before handing the drawing to Thomas.

"But, Thomas, that's just it. You've done a fine job with her until now. Every family goes through ups and downs. Any wrong you've done, you could have chosen to fight for her and make it right." Frustration filled Lovina's thoughts. None of the words she said came out right.

Thomas stared down at the drawing for a moment, then back to Lovina. "I have to make it right with you first. All the things I said about you being the Western Wildflower were wrong. God gave you a talent with words. You should use it. I know the Amish are humble people, but you shouldn't be ashamed to put your name on it. You are writing to glorify God. I was holding on to my *dat*'s old teachings and not realizing how hurtful I was being. I'm sorry, Lovina."

Lovina was taken aback by his words.

He thought she was gifted? Before she could even digest what he said, she blurted out, "Do you mean that?"

"Of course I mean it. Lovina, if you could only see yourself the way God sees you—the way I see you . . ." He shifted his gaze from her down to his hands.

"I wanted to say the same to you. You have been so good with Emily. God clearly equipped you to take care of her. And while it's hard to break the influence your *dat* has had over you, you aren't him. You are compassionate. You know better than to repeat his mistakes." Lovina shocked herself with her bluntness.

Thomas's jaw hung open after Lovina finished her remarks.

They sat shrouded in silence for a few moments, the words they exchanged hanging in the air between them.

Lovina finally broke the silence. "I brewed a pot of Feel Better tea. Would you like some?"

Thomas shook his head. "I don't think we have time for tea. I have one more thing to say. A question, really. And your answer will dictate what happens next."

"That sounds ominous. Go ahead. I'm listening."

"I want to raise Emily. You have given me the confidence I needed to see that with God's help, I can do it. But I can't do it alone. Lovina, I need your help. Will you raise Emily with me?"

"Thomas, I've decided to go stay with my sister in Kentucky for a while. I've made such a mess of things here for myself, and for you too. It would be better for us all if I just disappeared for a while."

Thomas's eyes went from their usual sparkly lake greenish-blue to nearly black. His nostrils flared and fists balled at his side.

"You aren't hearing me, Lovina. And you aren't seeing yourself the way God sees you either. You tell me that God has equipped me to care for Emily. You're right. And part of what He did for me was put you in my life. I've never known someone as selfless and giving as you. You are smart, resourceful, kind. And yet you want to fade into the background of every situation. Stop trying to be anonymous! And don't you dare even think about disappearing."

Lovina blinked hard several times. Clearly, she was missing something. "I don't understand what you are trying to say. I'm not going away forever. Just until this whole Western Wildflower thing dies down. That should be plenty of time for you to find someone to help you with Emily."

"I don't want anyone else. And I don't just want your help. I want you." He stood up and rounded the table to where Lovina sat opposite him. He dropped down to eye level with her and clasped her hands in his. "I want you to be my wife, to be Emily's *mem*."

"I-I don't understand." Lovina's heart thudded so hard, she was sure Thomas could hear it. She searched his eyes for understanding and found compassion and love reflected back.

"I'm saying that I see you the way God sees you, Lovina. And I love you. Do you think you could come to love me, too, some day?"

Lovina pulled her hands from his to cover her gaping mouth. "Oh, Thomas. I see you the way God sees you too. You are strong and capable, and your heart is so good. I already love you. But what about my limp? I'll never be able to walk the way I should. And my face." She touched the puckered scar. "Don't you want a wife who isn't so damaged?"

Thomas gave Lovina a wry smile. "Didn't you hear me before? I see you the way your heavenly Father sees you—fearfully and wonderfully made. And I'm thankful for your limp and even for your scar. I'm thankful that one of these other bachelors didn't sweep you away before I got here. You are the strongest and most beautiful woman I know, Lovina."

She wrapped her arms around him. He pulled her to him, and she melted into his embrace, letting all the hurts of the past just fade away. She rested her head on his chest and rested in the knowledge that he loved her, just as she was. Knowing that a man as *gut* as Thomas could love her boosted her confidence that the two of them could face any odds.

Lovina tilted her face up, smiling at Thomas, as he lowered his lips to hers, kissing her tenderly at first, then with more passion. Warmth filled her from head to toe. She had never felt more whole.

Finally, Lovina pulled herself away. "I guess we've decided what to do next, then," she whispered breathlessly.

"Kiss some more?"

Lovina smiled. "Well, yes, but that will have to wait. If we're going to be a family, we will need to go get our girl."

"*Ach*! Yes! We'll need to go up to the store and call Ms.

Williams to see if we can stop her from taking Emily to a foster home. Her mind seemed made up about me, though."

The two headed out the door and up the road to the store, hand in hand. Butterflies swarmed in Lovina's belly. Not only was she excited about her future with Thomas, but she was impatient to get Emily back to West Kootenai, safe and sound. Suddenly, she recalled something that Thomas needed to know.

"Dorcas Martin has been feeding Ms. Williams lies about you. Dorcas has been giving her little updates but with her own special spin on the facts." Just thinking about it made Lovina's blood boil.

Thomas's face lit up with understanding. "That makes sense. Her *dat* basically threatened to do the same to me. I think he wanted to set me up with her. He didn't say that exactly, but he nagged me about finding a wife and offered to make a match." He scrunched his nose up in disgust.

"We can explain that to Ms. Williams. I think when she learns that you and I have mended fences and plan to give Emily a family, she will see our situation a bit differently." Lovina's words sounded more hopeful than she felt. Would Thomas still want to marry her if he lost Emily?

She shook the doubt from her mind. It was time for her to stop listening to lies.

They arrived at the store to find Annie behind the counter. She looked at their clasped hands then smiled at Lovina. "This is certainly a surprise," Annie said, beaming at the two of them.

Lovina returned her friend's smile. "Can we use your phone? We need to try to stop the social worker who has Emily." Lovina's words came out in one panicked breath.

"Sure, sure. Let me know if there's anything else you need." Annie stepped back to clear a path for Lovina and Thomas to use her office for the calls.

Ms. Williams's phone went to voicemail, though Thomas dialed it three different times. He left an elaborate message the first time, but after that, he just left his name and a terse, "Call me."

"What else can we do, Thomas? I feel so helpless."

"Do you think we could get Wyatt to drive us to Whitefish? We could try to meet Ms. Williams at her office there." Thomas flipped the social worker's business card over to find the street address to her office.

"That's an excellent idea. I'll call him and see what he can do."

Within minutes, Wyatt's SUV was waiting outside the store, ready to whisk Thomas and Lovina away to find their girl.

The *Englisch* driver chuckled when he noticed the two holding hands. "Well, well! Looks like you two have a story to tell. Climb in and let me hear it."

They were nearly an hour behind the social worker, so they encouraged Wyatt to drive fast, promising to fill him in as they traveled. They asked to use his cell phone and continued to try to reach Ms. Williams with no luck. She must have turned it off for the drive.

They whizzed past the wooded scenery as they left the dirt roads of West Kootenai and pulled onto the more civilized road to Whitefish.

"So, the two of you are going to raise this little girl together?" Wyatt asked after Lovina and Thomas took turns telling him an abbreviated version of events.

Grinning, the two of them looked at one another and nodded.

"The only piece left to solve this puzzle is to find Emily," Thomas confirmed. He held Lovina's hand tightly, jiggling his knee up and down.

When they neared a gas station on the side of the road just past Eureka, Thomas shouted. "Stop, Wyatt! That's the car we're looking for!"

Wyatt slammed on the breaks and did a U-turn in the road, sending waves of nausea rolling through Lovina. She gave silent thanks that no one else was traveling that afternoon.

"She hasn't made it to Whitefish yet!" Lovina exclaimed.

Thomas helped her climb out of Wyatt's SUV and offered his arm as they walked into the store together. There stood a panicked Virginia Williams, but there was no sign of Emily.

Chapter Thirty-Nine

FRIDAY, SEPTEMBER 29

"Ms. Williams! We've been trying to reach you!" Lovina's voice wavered when she saw the panicked look on the social worker's face.

"I've been on the line with my office and the police so everything else went to voicemail, I guess." Ms. Williams waved her phone in the air.

Lovina had never seen the elegant woman look so tousled and distressed. Instead of her usual regal posture and self-possessed smile, her shoulders slumped forward as she leaned on the counter where the cashier stood. Beads of sweat popped out across her forehead, and scraggly hairs that had escaped her neat bun framed her splotchy red face.

Between Ms. Williams's appearance, the noticeable absence of Emily, and the mention of the police, something was terribly wrong. Lovina exchanged a concerned look with Thomas.

"Where's my niece, Ms. Williams?" Thomas asked, his voice strained.

The usually unflappable Virginia Williams broke down. "I don't know, Mr. Smucker." She buried her face in her hands.

The color drained from Thomas's face. Lovina tightened her grip on his arm, suggesting to him that he let her take the lead on this conversation. He nodded and took a deep breath.

"What has happened, Ms. Williams? How can we help?" Lovina tried to project a calm, helpful appearance, but inside, she felt like screaming. If Emily wasn't with the social worker, where was she? This gas station was the only thing along this stretch of road for miles other than the mountains that jutted up around them.

Just as Ms. Williams started to reply, a car with its siren blaring came squealing into the parking lot. A Montana State Police car pulled in, and two broad-shouldered, uniformed officers climbed out. They entered the small store, filling the already tight space.

"Good afternoon, folks, I'm Sergeant Clay Matthews and this is Officer Jeremy Jennings. I hear we are looking for a lost little girl." He glanced around at the collection of people in the room as though he was trying to figure out just how everyone fit in this situation.

Ms. Williams straightened. "Yes, Sergeant. I'm Virginia Williams, the social worker who was transporting Emily Spencer to a foster home. She asked to stop for a bathroom break, so I brought her in and let her go first in the single stall. I told her to wait by the door while I took my turn, but when I came out, Emily was gone."

Lovina leaned into Thomas for support. Emily must be terrified—wherever she was right now.

The officer nodded as he jotted down notes. "And what was your next move?"

Ms. Williams's voice shook as she spoke. "I called for Emily and looked around the store, but she was nowhere. The lady working at the counter told me that Emily had walked out the front door of the station and back to my car."

"When I heard that, I went out and looked around the area and called her name, but she was nowhere to be seen." Ms.

Williams crossed her arms over her chest and rubbed her upper arms.

Sergeant Matthews paced back and forth in the tiny store, making notes and conferring with Officer Jennings. "Since we knew it was a missing juvenile case, we went ahead and called Big Sky Search and Rescue. They've got a few volunteers on the way to help us search the area for the girl. I'm sure we'll find her. In the meantime, we'll try to obtain security footage to determine where she might have gone." He lifted his gaze to Lovina and Thomas, conspicuously dressed in their Plain clothes. "And who are you two? How are you involved with this?"

"I'm Thomas Smucker and this is my," Thomas searched for the right word to convey just how certain he was of his feelings for Lovina, "intended, Lovina Graber. We were on our way to find Ms. Williams to stop her from putting Emily in foster care when we saw her car parked here."

His intended. Lovina's cheeks warmed at Thomas's choice of words.

Sergeant Matthews asked Officer Jennings to take statements from Ms. Williams, the cashier, and Thomas and Lovina. By that time, several more police cars and trucks with volunteers arrived. He went out to brief them and grab some essential supplies from his cruiser, like flashlights and ropes.

Thomas paced around the gas station, his impatience obvious. Lovina stood off to the side, silently praying. *Oh, Lord. Keep her safe until we find her. Help Thomas lean on You for strength.*

Sergeant Matthews came back inside and updated them on the plan the team had devised. "While this area has a fair amount of traffic, we're doubtful that she was abducted. Security footage doesn't show any cars exiting the parking lot, just Emily walking across the road. Right now, we are going to send some volunteers to search the immediate area. She's been gone just over an hour, giving us about a three-mile radius to search. We have plenty of daylight left and an experienced team looking for her. If she's in the surrounding area, we'll find her."

Lovina hugged her arms to her chest. She hated the way that sounded—*if* she's in the area. Where else would a five-year-old girl be? Her stomach turned when she considered the alternatives.

"I'm going with you to look for her," Thomas declared. "I can't just stand here and wait for someone to find my niece."

The officer looked confused. "Your niece? I thought she was a foster child." He checked back over his notes.

Ms. Williams regained some of her composure. "She has been staying with her uncle, Mr. Smucker here, but she was on her way to a foster home."

"That makes it even more likely that she ran away on her own," Sergeant Matthews said, easing some of the tension that gripped Lovina. "Any ideas where she might have headed?"

Thomas thought for a moment. "She's not from around here—grew up in Ohio. She might have been trying to get back to West Kootenai, but she wouldn't have any idea which way to go."

Lovina had been staring aimlessly out the window while they discussed different scenarios. She noticed a thick covering of evergreen trees on the hill across the road from the gas station. It looked very much like the Grabers' Christmas tree farm.

"Thomas, I think I might know where she went. Look over there at those pines and spruces. They look a lot like *Dat*'s Christmas trees, don't they?"

"*Ja, ja.* That's it! She probably saw them and thought she could get to your home that way. Let's start searching there."

Sergeant Matthews nodded at Thomas's words. "You'll join us to help search?"

"I will. Standing here waiting is likely to kill me." He squeezed Lovina's hands, then pressed his lips to her knuckles. The trooper handed him a walkie-talkie and explained how to use it as he led him out the door.

That left Lovina to sit with Ms. Williams, who had spent the last several minutes on her cell phone with someone back in the Department of Children and Families office. The social worker rubbed her temples, her face creased with worry about what had happened to Emily.

"Ms. Williams, can I grab you a drink or a snack?" Lovina offered, once again trying *Mem*'s tactic of catching flies with honey.

The social worker looked confused. "You aren't furious with me? I figured Mr. Smucker would demand that I be fired, maybe even press charges for child endangerment."

"That's not our way, Ms. Williams. Plain people are called to love and forgive. You weren't negligent with Emily. What happened was an accident, and it could have happened to anyone. Now, would you like a *kaffe* or a Coke?" Lovina smiled reassuringly.

"A Diet Coke would be lovely, thanks." Ms. Williams pulled her shoulders back as though a weight had been lifted from them.

Though Lovina was still quite worried about Emily, she had faith that Thomas would be able to find her. She just needed to do her part to ensure that Ms. Williams would let the two of them take Emily home once she was found.

She walked to the drink cooler, grabbed a Diet Coke and an orange soda, one of her favorite treats, paid the clerk, and returned to Ms. Williams.

"Here you go." Lovina handed her the drink then took a long swig of her own soda. "I didn't realize how thirsty I was. That's refreshing."

Virginia Williams smiled at Lovina and sipped her Diet Coke. "I thought that you and Mr. Smucker were not working together to care for Emily anymore. But then I heard him say you were his intended. What's changed?"

"We had a little misunderstanding but have worked that out. Once we forgave one another for the way we had behaved over the last few days, we realized that we had to come after you and find Emily. Thomas and I want to raise her. Together."

Ms. Williams's eyebrows shot up. "Well, that's definitely a game changer." At Lovina's confused look, she continued. "What

I mean is that if you and Mr. Smucker can give her a stable, two-parent home, I think that might be the best placement for Emily. The whole car ride, she just chatted endlessly about all the things the two of you do together. It is clear she adores you."

"And I adore her. She's changed my life." Lovina's lip quivered. "But what about your concerns and Dorcas Martin's reports?"

Ms. Williams pursed her lips as if considering her words carefully. "I have no evidence to substantiate any of her claims. It seems to me that Miss Martin may have had an ulterior motive to make those reports. Hearing Emily's glowing description of you told me everything I needed to hear."

Lovina took another sip of her soda and closed her eyes tightly, whispering a prayer of gratitude. Now, if Thomas could just find Emily, they could go home and get on with their lives.

Minutes ticked by slowly as they waited for word from the rescue team. One officer remained in the gas station with them and occasionally got radio reports from those searching for Emily. No one had seen any sign of her, and the sun would be setting in a couple of hours. When it grew dark and cold in the Montana forest, things could get dangerous for even a seasoned hiker.

For a little girl, it could be deadly.

Chapter Forty

Thomas's chest was tight with worry—would they be able to find Emily before anything happened to her? He asked God for guidance and strength and charged forward, confident that the Lord would protect his niece.

Emily had no wilderness knowledge, other than the hike they'd gone on a few weeks ago and discussed some of the dangers, like animals and poison berries. But otherwise, she'd never really been out there.

Thomas rolled his aching neck from side to side. He hoped he had given her enough warning to stay safe, but the Montana mountains contained more dangers than he could possibly have prepared her for.

He bit back a wave of nausea. *Protect her, Lord.*

Working with Sergeant Matthews, Thomas paid close attention to his surroundings for any sign of his niece. How he would love to see the flash of her light-up sneakers right now.

He continued climbing the rough, muddy pathway and calling her name but found no trace of Emily. How high could she climb alone on this hill? He thought back to their mini hike on Labor Day and her lack of endurance. Hopefully, she had the same energy level today.

His walkie-talkie beeped and he heard the voice of one of the other searchers. He gave his coordinates and said he'd found no sign of her.

Thomas's heart fell at the lack of news.

Sergeant Matthews responded, "No sign here either. Why don't you head east down the mountain and continue the search there. We will keep climbing this path."

As precious minutes slipped by, so did Thomas's hope of finding Emily. He opened his water bottle and took a long swig before continuing on. He called her name over and over until his voice began to grow hoarse.

The pathway grew steeper and more slippery with mud created by the morning rain. Thomas concentrated on keeping his footing steady. He looked down to check the path for obstacles when he noticed an imprint in the mud.

"Sergeant Matthews! Look at this! It looks like a small footprint. It could be Emily's!" Thomas couldn't contain his excitement.

The officer crouched down to inspect the print. "Indeed it could! It looks like the print was made by someone crossing this path and heading west, not just traveling straight up. Let's go that way." He gestured to a wooded area and Thomas followed his lead.

The two men pressed ahead through the heavy layer of needles covering ground made uneven by clusters of trees and gnarled roots. Struggling to stay upright, Thomas pulled his flashlight out of his pocket and shined it on the dark ground, looking for more prints that would point the way to Emily.

"Sergeant, here's another print!"

The trooper pulled his walkie-talkie out and radioed the good news back to the rest of the team. Thomas climbed farther ahead and shouted Emily's name. He raised his flashlight and looked all around.

A flash of light bounced back to him.

A neon pink light.

"Emily? Can you hear me? Yell really loud if you can." Thomas prayed it was the light from Emily's shoes he saw.

He waited for a reply, but heard none.

He called again, his voice cracking. "Emily? Please? If you are out there, say something."

The only sound he heard was the wind in the trees as he waited for a response.

Finally, very faintly, he heard a voice. "*Oncle!*"

"Emily, where are you?" Joy and adrenaline flooded his body.

"I'm under these tree branches, but my foot is hurt. I can't walk on it." Her voice wavered with fear and pain.

He scanned the area with his flashlight until her sneakers came into view. "I see you! I'm coming over to get you, okay?"

"No! Just leave me alone. I'm mad at you." Though she adamantly rejected his help, Emily's stubborn protests sounded weak to Thomas.

"How about I just help you out from under the tree and Sergeant Matthews can carry you back down the hill?"

"Sergeant who?"

"Matthews. He's the state policeman who is helping me find you."

Sergeant Matthews offered a kind smile. "Hello, Emily. Let's get you out of there and back to safety, okay?"

"The police were looking for me? Am I getting arrested?"

Thomas bit back a chuckle. "No, no. You aren't in any trouble. Let's just get you back down the mountain and then we'll figure everything out."

Thomas lowered himself to the ground and held the pine tree limbs back to get a better view of Emily. Her hair had escaped the ponytail he had sloppily given her this morning, leaving strands of sandy blonde falling in her tear-streaked face. Mud spattered the *Englisch* clothes she'd changed into when Ms. Williams took her away. Her jeans were ripped in several places, and her shoes were caked with dirt. Her lower lip stuck out in a pout, and she resisted making eye contact with Thomas.

He reached down to her and pulled her out from under the tree limbs, wrapping his arms around her. Stiff at first, she finally returned his embrace and clung tightly to him.

"I'm sorry I let you leave, Emily. Lovina and I came after you and saw Ms. Williams's car parked at the gas station. We've been so worried about you."

"Lovie is here?" Emily's voice perked up at the mention of her dear friend.

"Yes. She and I want to take you home with us, if Ms. Williams will let us and if you'll go." Thomas worried that the little girl felt too deeply betrayed to agree to leave with him.

"Did Gus come too?" As usual, Emily was more concerned with the little fluff ball than anything else.

Thomas laughed. "No, he's waiting on you at home. Now, let's get moving so you can get home to him."

"Oh, *Oncle* Thomas. I'm sorry I got so mad. I just missed my Lovie so much and you were being so grouchy. I won't do that again, I promise."

"A lot of things are going to change for us at home."

She eyed him curiously but didn't ask any more questions. Thomas put her down for a moment so that he could put his walkie-talkie and flashlight away. She winced when she put weight on her swollen and bruised ankle, so she rode piggyback on him to the gas station, where a paramedic was waiting to examine her.

By the time they reached the store, Emily had dozed off with her arms holding tight to Thomas. For him, it felt just perfect.

Lovina met them at the ambulance. "Oh, Emily. I'm so happy to see you!" She smothered Emily with hugs and kisses and stayed with her while the paramedics checked on her ankle and general well-being. Then she helped Emily change into one of the Plain dresses Emily had insisted on packing.

Thomas pulled Ms. Williams aside. "I made a horrible mistake agreeing to let you place her in foster care. I doubted my abilities to care for her, but I'm more committed than ever before to raising her right. With God's help—"

"And Lovina Graber's help too?" Ms. Williams grinned, looking from one of them to the other.

Thomas smiled. "Absolutely. I guess she spoke to you."

"Indeed. And I'd like to apologize to you, Mr. Smucker. I was hasty in my decision to remove Emily. I didn't even allow you the due process I'd promised. I listened to unreliable sources in making my decision. I treated you unfairly. I hope that, going forward, you will be able to trust me to do the right thing on behalf of Emily. Which, just to be clear, I believe is for her to be with you."

Thomas's heart swelled with joy. Ms. Williams believed in him. Lovina believed in him. Most importantly, Emily believed in him. "Certainly, Ms. Williams. I forgive you. I'm learning more and more how important it is to give and receive grace freely, and it is a privilege to get a second chance to apply grace when raising Emily."

The paramedic finished his exam and wrapped Emily's ankle in a bandage. It was sprained but not broken and she would be able to walk on it just fine in a day or two. Until then, she could rely on *Oncle* Thomas to be her personal chariot.

Lovina returned to the gas station and summoned Wyatt, who had been staying out of the way of the search team by sitting and praying in his SUV. The *Englisch* man pulled around to pick them up. Thomas gently lifted Emily into the back seat and buckled her in, then he offered Lovina his arm for support as she climbed in.

Once she was situated, Lovina looked up at him, wordlessly conveying to him her gratitude for finding Emily and making things right with her.

His heart skipped a beat. He lowered his lips to hers briefly.

"Ewww!" Emily exclaimed. "No kissing, please."

The adults erupted in laughter. Thomas pushed the back door closed and took the front passenger seat for himself. Wyatt put the SUV in gear and sped away. They would be back home in

West Kootenai in time to enjoy one of Rose Graber's delicious dinners.

Emily settled in the back seat with Lovina and was soon asleep. Her adventurous afternoon had exhausted her. Thomas chatted amiably with Wyatt, relaying the rescue efforts.

"If you don't mind me saying so, Mr. Smucker, I can't help but think about the night I picked you up at the train station in Whitefish. I couldn't get a word out of you and, boy, did I try. You sure are a different fellow now," Wyatt declared as they pulled into the outskirts of town.

Thomas considered the *Englischer*'s words.

He *was* different now.

He came to West Kootenai with the intention of becoming his own man, separate from his father, but he'd brought much of his father's baggage with him. Until he broke free from those old habits, the only thing about him that changed was his address. With the help of friends like Ike and the Grabers, he had been able to weed out those lies and begin to live in the truth of who God made him to be. Because of Emily and Lovina, he had a whole new purpose too.

"I am different, Wyatt. I'm glad you noticed." Thomas turned around and locked eyes with Lovina. She smiled broadly at him. Yes, a new purpose, indeed.

Wyatt dropped them off at the Graber home and Thomas tried to pay him, but the *Englisch* man wouldn't accept his money.

"I'm just doing the Lord's work," Wyatt mumbled and shook his head, a broad grin creeping out from his mountain man beard. He clapped Thomas on the back. "It was my pleasure to be part of this today." He backed out of the driveway and was gone.

Thomas carried a sleeping Emily into the Grabers' house and placed her on the sofa, covering her with one of Lovina's quilts.

Henry and Rose were waiting in the kitchen, anxious to hear about all of the events that had taken place that day. Dinner was being kept warm in the oven because the news Thomas and

Lovina had to share could not wait. They took turns sharing the details in hushed tones so as not to wake Emily.

"I should have come to you first, Henry, to ask your permission to marry Lovina. I got caught up in the moment," Thomas admitted.

"Son, you have my blessing. I think the two of you will make a perfect team. Just remember that's what marriage is—teamwork. Keep that in mind and everything will be just fine." Henry clapped Thomas on the back. Rose sniffled and wiped tears from her eyes.

Emily came limping into the kitchen. "What's wrong? Why is Mrs. Rose crying?"

"Happy tears, dear one, happy tears," the older woman assured her.

"Emily," Thomas began, "Mr. Henry just gave us his blessing, so if it's all right with you, Lovina and I would like to get married. What do you say to that?"

The little girl's greenish-blue eyes widened and sparkled with sheer joy. "She'll be my Lovie forever? Yes! But don't forget, I told you so!"

Henry Graber pulled Emily into his lap and hugged her tight. "You had faith, Emily. We could learn a lot from you. How about you promise to call me *Grossdaddi* Henry from now on?"

Emily gave him a perplexed look, "If that means 'Grandpa' then you've got it, dude," she responded, bringing delighted laughter from everyone at the table.

Thomas shared dinner together with Emily and the Grabers, just as he had done many nights before. The only difference this time was that all the walls Thomas had built around his heart had been torn down, and a true family sat where strangers had been only a short time before.

Chapter Forty-One

WEDNESDAY, NOVEMBER 22

L ovina's eyes fluttered open and a smile slowly spread across her face. The cacophony of voices and movements from downstairs drifted up to fill her ears and heart. All of her sisters, their husbands, and her nieces and nephews awaited her presence at breakfast this morning. Then they had a busy day of cooking and cleaning to do before tomorrow, Thanksgiving Day.

The day Lovina would wed Thomas Smucker.

Lovina hadn't slept past 7:00 in the morning in years, but she had been up late last night finishing her wedding dress and the matching one Emily would wear. The two had chosen an unseasonable cerulean-colored fabric, but it matched the color of a clear Montana sky so perfectly, she didn't mind if it wasn't a true autumn hue. It was Thomas's favorite color.

After stretching her arms and wiggling her toes, Lovina rolled out of the bed and quickly readied herself for the day. She entered the bustling kitchen to a round of applause from her family.

"Well, if it isn't Sleeping Beauty!" Geneva teased. Lovina was thrilled that Geneva had decided to stay in Montana after the wedding instead of returning to Indiana with Melanie. *Mem* and *Dat* would need her help in their busy season.

Josie, Lovina's fraternal twin sister, who had arrived from Kentucky on Monday and who was always quick to defend Lovina, shushed their baby sister. "Now, Geneva, you know Lovina was up late last night finishing the dresses. She deserved a little extra sleep this morning." She wrapped her arm around Lovina and gave her a quick squeeze before handing her a stack of plates. "But now that you're up, can you set the tables?"

Lovina rolled her eyes but obliged her sister's request.

Dat had added the leaf to the table earlier this week, making it big enough to fit twelve adults, but with the addition of Amanda's twins, Josie's little boy, Melanie's son, and of course Emily, *Mem* had to pull a card table out of the basement to seat everyone.

Lovina scanned the room for Thomas. When she saw him, he gave her a smile, and butterflies exploded in her belly. Never in her wildest dreams had she imagined that she, a "damaged" twenty-five-year-old Amish self-avowed spinster, would be marrying such a kind, handsome man.

No matter how many times he reassured her, she still struggled with that nagging feeling that she was not worthy of him or his love. Yet at this moment, with everyone she loved gathered near, she could believe it. She sighed in deep satisfaction and passed out plates for everyone.

"Lovie!" Emily's voice rang out, catching her attention just before the little girl plowed into her, wrapping her arms around Lovina's waist. "Guess what I got to do this morning?" Emily's natural curiosity and enthusiasm for new tasks never grew old for Lovina.

"Did you"—Lovina paused dramatically, scratching her chin in mock contemplation—"cook five platters of bacon?"

Emily giggled. "No, silly. I got to change baby Caleb's diaper and rock him while *Aenti* Josie helped cook all the bacon." She beamed with pride.

Lovina smiled broadly. "All those baby dolls have given you good practice. You are already a good big cousin. Why don't you see if *Aenti* Amanda needs help filling up plates for Simon and Solomon?" Lovina looked at her harried sister balancing two plates in one hand while the twin four-year-olds ran circles around the table.

Emily scampered over to help Amanda, who shot Lovina a grateful glance. Lovina intercepted her nephews and guided them toward the card table.

While Lovina usually preferred quiet, the hustle and bustle that her family created warmed her heart today. She had so many blessings to be thankful for this year, and she promised herself she wouldn't let even one slip by without offering a prayer of gratitude.

Thomas wove his way around the table to where Lovina stood. She muttered an almost inaudible, "Thank you, Lord."

"What was that?" Thomas asked, cocking his head toward her.

"Oh, nothing." She smiled to herself. "Are you ready for the test?"

"What test?" Thomas's eyes widened with panic.

"You know, where you have to name each sister, her husband, her children, and one fun fact about her. Think you can do it?" Lovina teased.

He scanned the room and then looked back at Lovina, shaking his head. "I can maybe tell you the sisters' names, and I know James . . ." He trailed off, pointing at Melanie's husband.

"Close." Lovina laughed. "That's Joshua. I guess you'll need to study before the wedding tomorrow."

"You are kidding, aren't you?" The color drained from Thomas's face.

Lovina pressed her lips together to conceal a giggle. "I'm kidding about the test. But I'm serious. That's Joshua." She waved in her brother-in-law's direction and he returned a friendly glance.

"Shew. It's a *gut* thing you were just teasing because I have no time to study for a test today. I've got one important task I need to finish up before the day is over." He raised his eyebrows, pecked her on the cheek, then walked to the breakfast table.

Lovina followed and took the seat next to him. "Aren't you just a mystery, Thomas Smucker?" She passed the plate of biscuits to him and watched him carefully pluck one before passing it on to the person at his left.

He tilted his head close to hers. "David, right? Married to Josie?" he whispered.

Lovina nodded and passed him a bowl of gravy. "Well done! And I was kidding earlier. Melanie's husband is, in fact, James."

"I knew it!" Thomas exclaimed. All eyes shifted to him, causing Lovina to burst into laughter. Her heart was so full.

They finished breakfast, and Thomas joined *Dat* and the rest of the men as they did some work to prepare for the Christmas Tree Farm's busy season. Lovina, *Mem*, and her sisters worked diligently to clean up the breakfast dishes and start on the wedding preparations.

Because Lovina and Thomas were marrying on Thanksgiving when other Amish families were gathering for celebratory meals, they weren't having a traditional wedding meal for everyone in West Kootenai. Still, they would have refreshments and a meal for their family and close friends. Ike and Annie had promised to eat with them as did Susanna and her husband. Cooking for the Graber family alone was a big job.

Lovina was grateful that the wedding would be a low-key affair. She and Thomas wanted to marry as quickly as possible so they could adopt Emily together. The elders had granted them permission and a wedding plan came together quickly. Nothing mattered more to her than forming a family with Thomas and Emily.

After making several casseroles for tomorrow and loading everything into the refrigerator, Lovina stood at the sink, washing the last of the mixing bowls. As she stared out the window, an arm wrapped around her shoulder, stirring her from her thoughts. "You are a million miles away, daughter. Are you nervous about the wedding?" *Mem* asked.

"*Ach*, no, *Mem*. I'm not a bit nervous, just amazed that my life has turned out this way. I don't deserve any of these blessings."

Mem nodded sympathetically. "None of us do. Aren't we glad that we don't get what we deserve? God gives us more and better gifts than we could ever earn. His plans are always good."

Lovina smiled at her mother's words, and her smile spread when she saw Thomas come through the backyard. She fixed him a cup of her new special blend tea and slipped on her jacket, then joined him on the back porch.

Chapter Forty-Two

Thomas accepted the steaming cup from his fiancée's hand. This time tomorrow, she would be his wife.

He took a sip of the silky brown liquid and warmth filled him from head to toe, but not just from the tea. He never imagined himself as a married man with a wife who loved him, who looked out for his needs, who made him feel so complete. Now he couldn't imagine himself without her.

"*Danke*, Lovina. I was cold to the bone. This blend is new. I like it. What are you calling it?"

"This is my Happily Ever After blend. It has dandelion root, milk thistle, and passionflower. I added some honey and a touch of milk. I'm glad you like it."

"I do believe it might snow tonight. The temperature has already dropped, and just look at those dark gray skies moving in from the north."

Her teeth chattered a bit as she nodded in agreement with his assessment. "Are you ready for a Montana winter?"

He pulled his coat a bit tighter around himself and shrugged.

"Ready or not, it's coming, *ja*? Besides, I'll have you to keep me warm."

A blush crept up Lovina's neck, but she smiled at him. "Indeed you will, Mr. Smucker." She leaned into him and he wrapped his arms around her, pulling her into a cozy embrace.

They stayed that way for a few minutes, just enjoying the silence and the comfort of one another. Finally, Thomas released Lovina and removed something wrapped in a blue bandana from his coat pocket.

"I have something for you. I mentioned it this morning, but it wasn't ready yet. Now it is." Thomas extended his hand to her, giving her the bandana.

She accepted it, then held it in her palm for a moment before unwrapping it. "You shouldn't have gotten me anything, Thomas."

"It's something I made. And it was something I needed you to have." He ducked his head, almost embarrassed.

Lovina unwound the bandana, revealing a wildflower carved out of wood. Thomas had whittled a piece of silver birch wood to have the same smooth, delicate petals as the bitterroot flower, her favorite of the many varieties that grew in Montana.

"A flower. Thomas, it is lovely." She beamed at him with admiration of his talent in woodwork.

"Not just any flower. This is a western wildflower for my Western Wildflower."

Again, a blush filled Lovina's cheeks. "Thomas, that is so sweet. I love this." She turned the carving over in her hand, inspecting it closely, before closing her fingers around it tenderly.

Thomas placed his hands on top of hers. "I know I've told you that I believe God gifted you with a special ability to write, but I want you to know that I support you. Don't stop writing."

"I don't think I could stop if I wanted to," Lovina responded with a sly grin.

"Good," Thomas agreed. "And I want you to reveal your

identity to everyone who reads *The Budget*. They need to know that these powerful, Spirit-filled words come from you."

Lovina's eyes clouded with confusion. "But, I thought you felt like writing as myself for *The Budget* might be too prideful."

Thomas shook his head. "I know I said that in the beginning, but those weren't my true feelings. Those were my *dat's* words. I've been praying about it, and the more I do, the more I know he was wrong. You aren't writing for your own glory, but for the Lord's."

"If you are sure, Thomas. Only if you are sure. I wouldn't want that to ever come between us again."

"I know we are humble people, but I can't help but be proud of you, for what you do with the gifts God gave you. I don't think that's wrong. I made this wildflower to remind you—never be ashamed of your gift."

Lovina threw her arms around Thomas's neck and nestled into his warm embrace. As he cradled her small form, he thanked God silently for changing his heart and his mind. How many blessings would he have missed if he had stuck to *Dat's* stubborn way of thinking?

The back door snapped open and a white streak crossed the yard, followed closely by Emily.

"Gus, come back here!" Emily called, her breath hanging like fog in the air.

"What has Gus done?" Lovina asked, slowly unfurling herself from Thomas's embrace. Reluctantly, he released her.

"I made him this bow tie for the wedding, and he won't let me put it on him." She produced a lopsided bow made of leftover material from Lovina's dress.

Thomas laughed. "Gus is an Amish dog and doesn't wear bow ties, Em. Maybe if you waited until he was napping you could slip it on him."

"That's what I did, *Oncle* Thomas. I was tying the knot when he yelped and ran off. I guess he just didn't like the way it fit."

Thomas could just imagine Gus feeling choked by Emily's

makeshift bow tie. He chuckled and exchanged a glance with Lovina.

"How about you give that to me, and I'll put it on his collar," Lovina said. "That way you won't have to hold him still to tie it on him. He's used to the leash, so he won't fight it."

As usual, Lovina provided a solution that worked for Emily and saved everyone a whole lot of trouble. Did her gifts ever end?

Emily nodded eagerly. "Now, can you make us some hot chocolate? The twins wanted some and I'm still not big enough to reach the stove."

"Absolutely," Lovina replied. She rose from her seat on the porch and turned to go back inside, glancing once more at Thomas over her shoulder, her eyes sparkling with joy.

Thomas sat on the porch for another moment, savoring his tea. He offered a prayer of thanks to God for leading him to West Kootenai and for bringing Emily and Lovina into his life.

He glanced up at the expanse of blue sky above him and whispered the words of a psalm. For once, it wasn't one of the verses that *Dat* had twisted to support one of his piercing judgments. No, this time it was a psalm of praise. *"The heavens declare the glory of God; and the firmament sheweth his handywork."*

He had so much to praise God for.

Before, he only found fault in the people and things around him, but now he was grateful that everywhere he looked, he saw a reminder of his Creator's goodness and grace. He saw it in the mountains that towered around them and when the wind rippled across the wildflowers. He saw it in Emily's twinkling greenish-blue eyes. He saw it when he read the words Lovina wrote or held her hand to pray.

He looked forward to a lifetime of experiencing God's glory here, under the blue skies.

Epilogue

DECEMBER 13
THE BUDGET
WEST KOOTENAI, MT

We have had much to celebrate and give thanks for here in northern Montana this fall. John and Susanna Baker welcomed a new addition, a girl named Audrey Elizabeth. The men of West Kootenai celebrated another successful hunting season with the annual Antler Dinner.

Additionally, your scribe is thrilled to announce that she married Thomas Smucker, originally of Belleville, PA, on Thanksgiving Day. The bride and groom celebrated their vows by announcing that their adoption of Mr. Smucker's niece, Emily Grace Spencer, will be final in January. The family is building a new log home adjacent to the bride's parents on the property of West Kootenai Christmas Tree Farm.

-Lovina Graber Smucker,
The Western Wildflower

Thank you for reading *Under the Blue Skies*! Have you read our other Big Sky Amish novels? Be sure to read these sweet and tender Amish romances now!

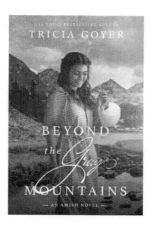

Available from your favorite retailer

He craves the stage. She wants a simple life. But when love sparks, what world will win?

She just wants to marry the man she loves...

Marianna Sommer always dreamed of a simple Amish wedding, but there's nothing simple about marrying rock star Ben Stone. She loves him—but what about her traditions?

Ben loves Marianna, but he has secrets that stand between him and his happy ending. His solution--go to the high mountains and search for answers.

Trouble lurks in the High Mountains...

When Ben finds himself in over his head, it'll take a miracle to make it back alive.

And suddenly, Marianna doesn't care what the wedding looks like...as long as Ben makes it home...

But if he does...and she discovers his secrets...what sacrifices will she make to save...and marry...the man she loves?

Secrets. Trouble. Sacrifice...Miracles..What will it take for love to survive?
Fall in love with the first book in the cherished Big Sky Amish Collection.

CONTINUE YOUR BIG SKY AMISH JOURNEY WITH
ANOTHER DELIGHTFUL STORY FROM TRICIA GOYER AND
CHRISTEN KRUMM

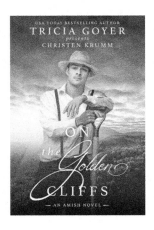

What happens with a social media influencer who has no secrets invades the life of a Amish Bachelor whose secret could destroy him?
Escaping to Montana is her only hope...
One wrong post sent influencer Lyla Taylor's social media empire crashing. Maybe six weeks in a high-end spa won't hurt... until she finds herself booked at a rustic Amish B&B. Thanks, but no thanks. Lyla is ready to hit delete and head back to civilization.
His secret could destroy his world...
For now, Amishman Reuben Milner has kept his life as a novelist hidden, focusing on caring for his mother and sisters. Then the wrong woman moves into the dawdi house rental. Nosy, outspoken, feisty—no way does she fit into their community.
But she might just be the one woman he needs...

When leaving isn't an option, Lyla decides to help Reuben spruce up their rental. But the more they work together, the more she wonders if returning to her former life is worth it. And the more he realizes what he truly longs for.

However, is it the simple life that Lyla's heart wants—or a particular guarded Amishman? And if his secrets are discovered, what will it cost them both?

Funny. Secrets, A found family...and a romance she's always longed for. But can it last?

Book two in the delightful and sweet Big Sky Amish Collection.

Buy now from your favorite retailer

LOOKING FOR MORE SWEET CONTEMPORARY ROMANCE? DISCOVER AWARD-WINNING BESTSELLING AUTHOR SUSAN MAY WARREN'S DEEP HAVEN COLLECTION

It's never too late to finish a love story...

Former Army Ranger Cole Barrett has a new mission objective—sell his grandfather's house in Deep Haven, and leave the town that contains his childhood hurts for good. Unfortunately, the tenant in the garage apartment refuses to move. Even worse? It's his childhood crush, Megan Carter, and her son.

Wedding planner and single mom Megan Carter loves Deep Haven. To her, it's the place where she makes dreams come true—at least, everyone else's. Hoping to purchase a local B & B and turn it into a premier event venue, she's oh, so close to her down payment...until Cole Barrett returns to Deep Haven. Even if he's not back to fulfill a silly childhood promise to marry her, she never expected him to evict her!

When a blizzard strikes Deep Haven, and Megan is overrun with wedding catastrophes, it takes a former Ranger to step in and help. Besides, the more he comes to her rescue, the sooner she'll be able to move out...and he can move on. And that's what they both want, right?

Return to Deep Haven with this magical tale about the one who got away...and came back.

Start this sweet contemporary romance today!

Acknowledgments

I owe endless thanks to my husband John, who has been my biggest supporter and encourager throughout my writing journey. Without his constant belief in me and his continuous words of encouragement, I would never have had the courage to give the Sunrise audition a chance.

My daughter Audrey has been an amazing craft partner, always ready to lend a helping hand, and offer a fresh perspective. I am truly grateful for her creative input, which has helped shape this book in so many ways.

My sons Jack and Sam have been two of my most enthusiastic cheerleaders, always reminding me to keep going, no matter how tough things got. Their steadfast support has meant the world to me.

My mom and dad deserve special thanks for raising me to be faithful and creative, and for instilling in me a love of books and storytelling from an early age.

Thank you to the real wonder dog, Gus, who provided endless cuddles and the inspiration for Lovie's dog, and his sweet sisters, Charli and the late Bella Boo.

I am also grateful to my mentor Tricia, my Big Sky sister Christen, and the entire team at Sunrise for their incredible support and guidance. They were always there to encourage me when writing seemed impossible, and their unfaltering belief in me has helped me push through even the toughest moments. Thank you all for pulling me through those times when I didn't think I could go on.

To my prayer huddle (Jeanne, Carrie, Penny, and Erin), thank you for supporting me with your prayers and for always being there to lift me up in times of doubt and uncertainty. Your love and encouragement mean the world to me and I love you dearly!

I would also like to thank my church family at First United Methodist Frankfort, my West Liberty friends and family, my cousin Kim, my Second Street Sisters (Johnna, Kela, Gala, and Susan), my fellow writing bestie Megan, my DERD teammates (Veda, Erin, Jocelyne, John, and Justin), and my Louisville ACFW friends. Your unwavering support, belief in me, and your prayers have sustained me.

Finally, thank you God for being faithful to complete a good work in me, over and over again.

Connect with Sunrise

Thank you so much for reading *Under the Blue Skies*. We hope you enjoyed the story. If you did, would you be willing to do us a favor and leave a review? It doesn't have to be long- just a few words to help other readers know what they're getting. (But no spoilers! We don't want to wreck the fun!) Thank you again for reading!

We'd love to hear from you- not only about this story, but about any characters or stories you'd like to read in the future. Contact us at www.sunrisepublishing.com/contact.

We also have a regular updates that contains sneak peeks, reviews, upcoming releases, and fun stuff for our reader friends. Sign up at www.sunrisepublishing.com.

As a treat for signing up, we'll send you a free novella written by Susan May Warren that kicks off Sunrise Publishing's Deep Haven Collection! Sign up at https://sunrisepublishing.com/free-sampler/.

About the Authors

Tricia Goyer writes out of her passion for God and her love for family and others. The author of more than 70 books, she writes both historical fiction and nonfiction related to family and parenting.

This USA Today best-selling author has won a two Carol Awards and a Retailer's Best Award. She was also an ECPA Gold-Medallion Nominee and a Christy Award Nominee and won Writer of the Year from the Mt. Hermon Christian Writers Conference.

Tricia's contemporary and historical novels feature strong women overcoming great challenges. She is a beloved author of Amish fiction, having written the Big Sky and Seven Brides for Seven Bachelors series.

Whether for fiction or nonfiction, Tricia's writing style is vivid and heartwarming, allowing readers to take home more than engaging stories, but also messages that inspire faith and hope. Her goal is to write stories that matter. Visit her at triciagoyer.com.

Elly Gilbert lives in central Kentucky with her husband, daughter, and twin sons. A lifelong bookworm, she finds joy in reading and writing inspirational fiction and devotions for adults and teens. When she's away from her desk, you can find her scoping out the nearest nacho joint with her family or snuggled up with her rescue dogs, Gus and Bella. She adores leopard print, never turns down dessert, and believes that when it comes to earrings, bigger is always better. Visit her at ellygilbert.com.

facebook.com/mrsellygilbert

instagram.com/MrsEllyGilbert

bookbub.com/authors/elly-gilbert

amazon.com/stores/Elly-Gilbert/author/B0BWVK2Y95

Big Sky Novels

Big Sky Amish Collection

Beyond the Gray Mountains

On the Golden Cliffs

Under the Blue Skies

Big Sky Series by Tricia Goyer

Beside Still Waters

Along Wooded Paths

Beyond Hope's Valley

Under the Blue Skies
Big Sky Amish Book 4
Published by Sunrise Media Group LLC
Copyright © 2023 Sunrise Media Group LLC
Ebook ISBN: 978-1-953783-42-4
Print ISBN: 978-1-953783-41-7

For more information about Tricia Goyer or Elly Gilbert please access the authors' websites at the following addresses:
Tricia Goyer: https://triciagoyer.com/
Elly Gilbert: https://linktr.ee/mrsellygilbert

Published in the United States of America.
Cover Design: Emilie Haney, eahcreative.com